CHILDREN OF TOMORROW

D0512717

CHILDREN
OF TOMORROW

A. E. van Vogt

NEW ENGLISH LIBRARY/TIMES MIRROR

First Published in Great Britain 1972
Copyright © 1970 by A. E. van Vogt
All rights reserved
Originally published in the USA by Ace Books

First NEL Paperback Edition May 1973
Reprinted July 1973
Reprinted April 1980

NEL Books are published by
New English Library Limited from
Barnard's Inn, Holborn,
London EC1N 2JR.
Made and printed in Great Britain by
Hunt Barnard Printing Ltd.,
Aylesbury, Bucks.

ISBN 45004598 6

I

SOMETHING was looking at a street in Spaceport, Earth. It watched through an invisible lens that saw everything clearly, even though it was night.

For several moments, the focus of the watcher's attention was a fine upper-middle-class home. Then the view swung slowly around, and there was the street. First, the observer paused briefly to notice several other houses of equal excellence to the first. Then it turned its attention to the far end of the street, where there was an intersection and a low metal structure at one corner.

The structure was square, and it was about the height of one and a half men. On a paling above it were the words in a luminescent material: SUBSURFACE.

The meaning of this seemed to interest the watcher; for it now utilised its mysterious system of observation to jump the distance at a speed that was as fast as the blink of an eye.

At this close range, it was possible to make out the shape of a sliding door in the structure, and beside the door a sign that read:

HIGH SPEED MONORAIL SERVICE

Downtown   8 minutes

New York   5 hours

Note

Intercity Lines Require Transfer

There was a faint rumble below, an even fainter hissing sound, and then the sliding doors slid back, away from each other. Each disappeared into a slot in the metal structure.

Inside the doors was an elevator with seven people in it; five men and two women. These emerged and quickly separated. All except two of the men moved briskly off along the intersecting street, out of the watcher's line of vision.

The two men came forward along the street of fine homes. As they did so, the viewer drew back in front of them at the exact speed of their walk. Its interest seemed to be in them.

The thing that was watching was not qualified to evaluate a human being in any complete way. But its information included an awareness that here were two men: one in his early forties; the other, older, with a touch of gray at his temples. The younger man was good-looking, and carried himself with an air of decision and confidence. There was a suggestion of overaggressiveness in his bearing, and something about him urged moment by moment that he didn't like people to oppose him. Except for that, he seemed very mature and capable.

The older man seemed of a milder disposition, but he was well-dressed and his manner showed success and conveyed that he had his own views and his own experience for coping with the world and the people in it. It was he who spoke, shaking his head a little, chidingly.

'It seems strange, John,' he said, 'that after nearly ten years your first act is to use me as a buffer between you and Estelle, just as it was your last act before you left.'

The man addressed as John, protested. 'I don't remember it that way, Dez. I thought we all went somewhere and celebrated before my departure. But I have to admit – I'm going to need your help tonight. I called Estelle this morning when we grounded and indicated I'd be home in an hour. That was a mistake, because I got held up. And Estelle's tone of voice this morning told me that she still doesn't understand things like that.'

'Oh, she's changed, too,' was the reply. 'In fact, there have been a lot of changes here in Spaceport, Mr Commander Lane. For example, your daughter, who was six, is now sixteen, and belongs to an outfit.'

'To a what?'

'You'll see.'

John Lane shrugged with, as always, impatience; but his manner remained friendly. 'My dear Mr Desmond Reid, my old friend, my supporter at key moments, you may continue to be mysterious, but it doesn't matter. As I understand it, I remain fleet commander but spend time at a desk. Thus I shall discover all these matters for myself, and' – his voice grew firm – 'in each and every instance, I shall do exactly what I think is indicated. My wife, my daughter, my job, certain things that I left unfinished out in space . . .'

Desmond Reid said in his mild fashion, 'I see you have some shocks coming, John. Since you went out there, your type has been psychologically categorised. The fullness of a new truth has moved into what was formerly an information vacuum.'

Lane was calm. 'I'm always open to good scientific thought.

Never rejected a new weapon in my life until it was fully investigated and tested.'

'Good!' said Desmond Reid, and because his tone had more force in it than would normally be required, the younger man gave him a quick, searching look. But he said nothing.

In silence the two men now turned into the yard of the house which the invisible watcher had first concentrated on. As they climbed onto the porch, a woman came out of the door, put her arms around John Lane and began immediately to sob. He held her tightly, and so it was difficult to see exactly what she looked like, other than that she had blonde hair and was slender of build.

Presently, Lane half carried, half led her into the house. Desmond Reid followed, closing the door.

The thing that was viewing the scene made no attempt to follow the trio inside. In fact it now drew back to the street, and waited.

Inside the house there continued to occur a number of the things that a husband and wife do and say when they have not seen each other for nearly ten years. But kissing and words of muffled happiness can only go on so long between the most joyous of couples. And truth was they were not that joyous.

Desmond Reid, watching from off to one side, saw that the moment of reality was approaching. He observed it first in the man. Lane seemed slightly bored, and accepted the woman's kisses with distinctly less enthusiasm. In fact, he must have realised that something had to be done, because gently but firmly he drew his wife over to a couch, and said, 'Where's Susan?'

The woman, drying her tears and still sniffling, murmured, 'Oh, she's with her outfit. They had late business tonight.'

Lane frowned, and glanced at his watch. 'It's after eleven,' he said. 'Maybe I've got this mixed up, but that's pretty late even for a sixteen-year-old.'

She made a dismissing gesture, and leaned against his chest, hugged him. 'Don't worry about Susan,' she said. 'She asked me to give you her love.'

From where he sat in a chair across from the couple Reid noticed a peculiar expression take form on Lane's face. He made a gesture, and caught Lane's eye. But it was too late. The thought was there, and a shake of the head from a wiser man could not stop it.

Lane said, 'I'm afraid I don't understand.' He unmistakably saw the warning expression in Reid's face, but his voice merely went up as he continued. 'I have been in distant parts of space for 3488 days and nights. And now you tell me that on the evening

7

of the day that I return, my only daughter is off somewhere. She could not cancel some minor meeting with other children in order to be here when I came.'

The woman visibly stiffened, and then she drew away from her husband's chest, and for the first time showed her full face. Thus seen, she was identifiable as being in her late thirties, rather good-looking despite the swollen eyes. Nonetheless, it was a sad face. It showed the effects of her years of separation from the man she had married: grief, sorrow, frustration . . . and resentment.

It was the resentment that now tightened her lips and narrowed her eyes slightly. 'Darling,' she said, 'all day long I've been making my peace with the false promises you made in your phone call this morning. And I decided eight times not to bring it up, but now I notice in the tone of your voice that same dominating quality that was there when you left. And I must tell you, dear, that in your absence you have been categorised as being an unsuitable type for a father. So just be calm. Mind your own business out there in the world, which you have always preferred to being at home. And leave Susan to me and her outfit.' She smiled at him through her tension. 'Okay?'

From across the room, Desmond Reid clapped his hands. 'Bravo, Estelle, that's well said, and presents exactly the point that should be put over to John before he gets himself all upset and off on the wrong track.'

Reid turned to Lane, and said, 'John, your wife is a wise woman, and has just given you good advice. Why don't you decide right now to heed it?'

Lane was silent. There was a faraway expression on his face. But presently his gaze flicked from his wife to Desmond Reid, and back again. At first he seemed in a mild state of shock, then his jaw tightened.

He said, 'Let me understand this. You are saying that I, specifically, have been named as an unsuitable father?'

It was Reid who replied. 'All space personnel residing here in Spaceport have been categorised on the basis of past records and tests, and you are in the category of —'

He stopped, and Estelle finished: ' — the category of what you said.'

'And Susan knows this?' asked Lane. A touch of color was in his cheeks.

'Of course.' It was the woman. 'That's necessary so she doesn't develop any fantasies about you.'

'Like admiring me, for example,' said Lane in a dangerous tone, 'as a dedicated officer.'

8

Estelle's color was suddenly higher. 'That dedicated part,' she said, 'we must discuss some time.' Her tone indicated that she would be glad, personally, to point out a few truths about it.

She must have realised from the expression on her husband's face that something was about to explode, for she caught his arm, and said, 'Now, look, Mr Lane, you are home, you are welcome. We are glad to have you back. Susan has missed her father. I've been taking my resentment pills regularly like a good little wife. So let's not get all carried away by unnecessary emotions.'

Across from them, Desmond Reid stood up. To Lane he said, 'Your wife is saying all this so well, I think I can safely leave you in her hands.'

As the older man climbed to his feet, Lane had automatically – with the courtesy of his military training – jumped to his feet. A faint, wry smile twisted his lips. 'Your timing, as usual, is perfect,' he said. 'And you may count on me to handle this entire matter objectively.'

Reid said doubtfully, 'I question if that's quite possible for you, John. Remember, this is not a fleet matter.'

Lane continued as if he had not heard, 'As for Susan, I shall have a conversation with her when she comes in later on, and we'll come to some agreement as to how late a young lady should be out at night.'

Reid shrugged, and glanced at Estelle. 'Well, my dear,' he said, 'we tried.'

She was also on her feet, and she spread her hands. 'It doesn't look like he got the picture,' she said in a baffled tone.

Once more, Lane glanced from his wife's face to that of his friend. There was a frustrated expression on his face. 'All right, if you two are so clever and I'm so stupid, tell me where Susan is right now and what she's doing.'

Estelle said, 'She's with her outfit.'

Reid said, 'That's all you'll ever need to know, John.'

He walked to the door that led to the hallway, turned, bowed to Estelle, said, 'Goodbye, John. I'm glad you're back.' Once more, turning, he went out into the hall, and then opened the outside door. As he walked onto the porch beyond, he reached back, and drew the door shut behind him. The automatic lock clicked.

II

A FEW minutes before Demond Reid emerged from the home of Commander and Mrs Lane, the invisible observer abruptly abandoned its vantage point across the street. It did its remarkable movement thing – and the next instant was three blocks away.

It seemed to know exactly where to go, for the invisible 'lens' was focused unerringly on a chase sequence that had, seemingly, just begun. A young teenage boy was running at uneven pace away from a group of slightly older boys and girls – running directly toward the observer. The very moment the watcher took note of this action, an older boy broke free of the group and raced in pursuit of the runaway.

The younger boy's method of running was almost unnecessarily awkward. He was scrawny of build, and evidently weak, for he staggered and even lost his balance a few times. His pursuer caught him easily, and brought him down with a tackling leap onto the grass beside a pretty white fence.

The captured boy continued to struggle, and actually managed to crawl three feet with the other one holding onto him. This brought him within the ten foot range of the watcher, who was thereby able to project a thought at him.

Do you need help, son?

No, my father.

Then all is well?

It seemed like a good moment to have someone touch me. Thus, during a confusion, I can test my ability to delude the senses of he who touches. His name is Mike Sutter, and he is one of the two leading members of this outfit. I think I have succeeded, because I am convincing his perceptive system that I have the shape of a human being.

Good. Are my various suggestions applicable?

Yes. In running away, I pretended that I was afraid of the human father, with whom you have lodged me. My pretense is that if I am home late, he will punish me. I am pretending that the Red Cat outfit, which is what this group is called, will not be able to protect me from him, and they say they can.

The observer was pleased, and telepathed:

Since touching and feeling are the decisive perceptions – after

10

vision – I'll watch until this episode completes.

Thank you, my father.

Even as the silent conversation proceeded, the older boy, Mike, stood up, and simultaneously pulled his captive to his feet, held him there while the group of teenage boys and girls walked toward them.

The alien being, who had so swiftly come to help – if needed – his child, surveyed the young people with a grim interest. As with the older men, Lane and Reid . . . earlier . . . he was not wholly competent to assess human beings of any age. Which, of course, was why it had been decided to infiltrate the human city of Spaceport.

They must find out exactly what the human race was – how helpless or capable it was, its defenses, and its weaponry.

The watcher looked, first, at Mike Sutter. It saw a slender, wiry, olive-complexioned youth, intense and handsome. Remembering what its own child had reported about Mike – that he was one of the leaders – the observer noted the bright, gray eyes of the boy, and a certain impatience – which reminded it of a similar emotion radiated by John Lane.

The alien knew that its own child bore the human name of Bud Jaeger, but it did not have any identification of the other teenagers, except what was visible. Since it was unlikely that everyone of the young people would be addressed by name, the watcher made do with the visual and the auditory, determined in future to know them anywhere.

The first boy to come up to Mike and Bud was thickset and strong-looking. Since he lacked the intensity of Mike, and seemed in fact to be stolidly unemotional, the alien decided that he was not too intelligent. Following the same line of reasoning by opposites and association, it noted that of the five other boys and four girls also stayed back out of the way. The remaining two girls moved briskly up to Mike. One was blonde and of medium height; the other brunette, and small.

At the exact moment that the girls walked up, Bud made an attempt to break away. But Mike hung on grimly. His effort having failed, Bud kicked at Mike's shins. It was a glancing blow at best, but it must have been painful. Mike winced, then drew one hand back and struck Bud in the chest.

Once again, it must have been painful for Mike, for he pulled his hand and shook it violently – as if he were striving hastily to vibrate the pain out of it.

The two girls seemed not to notice his sudden physical anguish. The blonde girl half turned back toward the good-looking blond boy, who had stopped a few feet away and was watching the interchange with a manner that had a firmness in it that yet suspended immediate judgement.

She said, 'Lee, I don't think Mike should be allowed to hit Bud.'

Before Lee could answer, Mike said in an outraged tone, 'Susan, before you jump to any conclusions, please notice: I'm the only one that's been hurt so far. Bud kicked *me* in the ankles – and he's got bones in all the wrong places. 'Cause when I hit him just now, I nearly broke *my* knuckles –'

The alien, who had been anxiously aware of the two actions, projected a thought at its child:

Aren't you making too many tests in a short space of time?

No, father. For a few moments there, and actually still, there was another period of confusion. Mike's attention was on the other members of the outfit. I want to establish in Mike's mind that it hurts to hit me. I analyse that he's the impulsive one, who may lash out at me without waiting for instructions from Lee David, the leader of this outfit.

Lee David. That is the husky blond youth who has just come up?

Yes.

And that girl, who was addressed as Susan – the blonde girl. Is that Susan Lane?

Yes. And the girl beside her is Marianne Baker. Although he doesn't seem interested, she's trying to be Mike's girl.

You've learned a great deal on your first evening.

This is my time for indoctrination.

All right, son.

The watcher was more at peace now. The minutes were passing; and the pseudo-human, Bud Jaeger, was handling the situation with a skill that would have been admirable in an older alien.

It was that Lee David was reading his watch. The blond youth, who seemed to be the oldest member of the outfit, looked up, and said in a voice that was surprisingly deep-toned, 'Well, jabbers, it's twenty-five to twelve. I think that's long enough to keep Bud out this evening. Sack, Mike?'

The wiry, dark-haired boy hesitated. 'Lee, why not until twelve?' he asked finally. 'Our usual time for stoppers.'

Lee smiled. 'Bud is scared enough. I think we've got the same result.' He glanced around at the others, seeking agreement. 'Sack?'

A chorus of 'sacks' greet his query – all except Mike, who was silent, but who finally said reluctantly, 'If that's the way you want it.'

The blue-eyed Lee gave the slightly younger boy a quick, challenging glance, as if questioning the other's tone. A moment later, he asked, 'What's the push, Mike?'

Once more, Mike hesitated, then: 'No push.'

Lee replied instantly, 'There's a doubt pushing out of you. Jack it out, so we can scan it.'

Mike's expression was clearing. He removed his hand from the grip it had on Bud's coat collar. 'All unpacked, Lee,' he said. A warm, friendly smile creased his face. 'All sack.'

Lee said, 'Sack.' He turned to the others, made a dispersal gesture. 'Sack,' he said once again. He turned and walked quickly over to Susan. 'Let's go, moocher,' he said.

Susan caught his arm. 'Sack, everybody,' she said.

All except Bud answered, 'Sack.'

The pert, little brunette took hold of Mike's arm, stood beside him and with him watched Lee and Susan walk hurriedly away. Mike, watching, shook his head, but he was tolerant now. 'Too bad,' he said.

Marrianne gave him a quick glance. 'What's the push, Mike?'

Mike shrugged. 'I'll tell you when I take you home,' he said. Without waiting for a further comment, he turned toward Bud. 'Sack, Bud.'

Bud asked anxiously, 'Does that mean I can go?'

Mike nodded.

'But who's going to go home with me, and face my old man? He said he'd beat the tar out of me if I went with an outfit.' His tone was one of rising fear.

Mike said, 'Bud, we've explained the choice. We can take you to the Hall, or take you home. Make up your mind.'

'Oh, I've got to go home,' Bud shrilled. 'I've got to. I wouldn't dare stay out all night.'

Mike pursed his lips, and turned to the heavyset boy. 'Albert, take Bud home.' He handed Albert a tiny instrument. 'If his father makes trouble, press this button. You'll have help in three minutes. Sack?'

Bud was not to be reassured. 'What kind of help?' he half yelled.

Mike gazed at him steadily. 'Sack, Bud,' he said, in a steady voice.

The tone arrested Bud's attention. His small face twisted up toward Mike. 'What does that mean?' he asked.

'It means that I want an answer that shows that you've heard what I said.'

'What kind of an answer?' Bud seemed transfixed.

'Say, "Sack, Mike".'

'And if I say "Sack"!' Bud persisted, 'that means I've heard

13

you, and that I believe you, and that ends our conversation, and I go home.'

'You're pretty sharp, Bud. That's what it means.'

'But I *don't* believe it,' said Bud.

Mike said placatingly, 'You'll soon have confidence in our word, Bud. Except very occasionally, we speak what we think.'

'How do I know this is not one of the occasions when you don't?'

'Because I tell you it isn't.' Abruptly impatient, Mike broke off. 'Sack, Bud.' He spoke in a deliberate tone.

There was a long pause, during which the watcher telepathed the alien child:

Say it, boy!

I'm still testing.

I know. But I analyse that, with Mike, the moment has come for agreement.

Nevertheless, my father, I really will have trouble when I get home. You selected Mr Jaeger because he was a man who would resist outfit control of children. He's already told me that so long as I stay with him, I'd better not get in with an outfit. I'm not sure I can handle a grown human being without giving myself away.

'I'll go over there with you, my son. So don't worry.

The alien child replied:

I'm not afraid for myself. But I don't want to be found out before my mission is completed. I should tell you, however, that I already believe that I, a mere boy of my race, overmatch these human beings completely, and I might even deduce that they have no defense against people like us. I already feel, my father, that we could capture this planet.

The watcher was disturbed by what seemed to it to be a too-rapid judgement.

Don't be hasty, my son. Things are not always what they seem. Take the allotted time. Complete your espionage mission.

The rapid interchange ended and Bud looked up at Mike, and said aloud, slowly, 'Sack – Mike.'

Mike Sutter and Marianne Baker stood side by side as Bud walked off beside Albert. When they were out of earshot, Mike said, half to himself, 'Funny kid. Look at the way he walks. Kind of shuffling.'

The watcher, who was still focused on them, waited grimly. Was it possible the boy suspected? That the close contact situation had not been properly handled?

Mike was shaking his head. 'Well, there's another problem. Looks like there's no end to them.'

Marianne caught his arm. Her pretty little egg of a face looked

14

up at him worshipfully. 'Mike, what's the push about Lee?'

The watcher was relieved to realise that her words distracted the human boy. Mike shrugged. 'He ended the evening before it was time for a private reason that he didn't jack out.'

'Then why didn't you push?'

Mike was thoughtful, the tolerant expression back on his face. 'It's not always easy to know when to push, and when not to. Susan's dad came home today after the longest hike in the history of Spaceport.'

'Oh! You think Lee – ?'

Mike nodded. 'I think Lee wanted Susan to get home early.'

'What's wrong with that? Why didn't we just let Susan off for the evening? We've done it before.'

The boy shook his head. His lips tightened. 'No. Her old man is a booter, if there ever was one – just like my dad. The outfits cannot compromise with people like that, because they don't compromise. And a concession merely looks like weakness.'

He had started walking as he spoke these words. Marianne hastily fell in beside him. Mike finished his thought: 'Looks like we've got lots of problems coming up just about when I figured there'd be some peace. So I could use a little mooching, moocher.'

'Sack, Mooch.'

They mooched.

III

APPROXIMATELY ten minutes had gone by. Inside the Lane house, during that time, Estelle nervously retreated into her bedroom, undressed, hesitated – half expecting that her husband would be anxious to join her – but when there was not a sound, her lips tightened. With determination, suddenly, she put on a pair of pajamas and then slipped into a lounging robe.

And, still, she half expected him to come to her; and so, once more, sitting there on the edge of the bed, a little uncertain as the seconds went by, she went from anticipation to wonder through the old, old resentment, and finally – again – an outraged anger.

But in her, such an emotion could not remain long. She thought abruptly: That man, that incredible man!

With that, the anger faded, and she got up and went out of

the bedroom and into the book-lined room with the bar. Her husband was silhoueted against the window behind the bar, and she saw that he was in the final stages of mixing himself a drink.

With his usual instant courtesy, he held his own glass out to her. When she shook her head, not trusting herself to speak — yet – he asked, 'May I pour you your favorite?'

For a moment the expression on her face toyed with the thought of testing whether he did, in fact, remember her favourite cocktail. She decided against that. It might weaken her resolve, might make her feel that he did care for her in his fashion — which was not good enough, thank you.

Whereupon, she shook her head, no. As she did so, she grew aware that the man was gazing at her, as if taking her in with his whole vision. In the past, she had thought of it as being eaten by his eyes; and from him, she had enjoyed the sensation. With it, always, there had been the implication that she was indeed a tasty dish. Unfortunately, after a moment, she was impatient with his stereotype. Truth was, after ten years she no longer felt herself to be delicious and delightful to the taste, and his long absence actually proved that that was his real opinion also.

Despite her rejection of his pattern, she could not quite bring herself to say rejecting words about it. She thought: After all, I've been making my peace with this villain all day . . . and, of course for a decade before that. The time to leave had been when he accepted the distant-space assignment six years before without coming home.

I've paid my debt to society, she thought humorously, standing there. I've served my time . . . It would be rather foolish to wipe it all out in a sudden peeve.

Lane suddenly put down his glass, and said, as if realising what her thoughts had been earlier: 'After all, dear' – his voice was gentle – 'we can't go to bed until Susan is in, and safely in her room.'

Normally, that wouldn't be true. But Estelle had to admit, now, that the awareness of Susan not being home had been there in the back of her mind, restraining her from being totally outraged by her husband's behaviour. Tonight – she had to admit it – Susan, failing to find them up, would undoubtedly come bursting into the bedroom; and it would be unfortunate if they were in some compromising man-woman relation. Fact was, these jabbers were a little bit – just a little – naive. Not in some things, but they were not really up to the adult male-female business.

'I suppose you're right,' she said. And her face showed that the concession, though grudgingly given, was real.

Lane gave her a quick glance; and he, now, was relieved. In

his eyes was an awareness that something of her ten-year anger had faded with that agreement. He said quickly, as if he felt the instant need to take advantage of what he must have decided was surrender: 'Dear, why don't you go to bed, and when I've had my little meeting with Susan, I'll join you?'

The woman hesitated. Then: 'Your little meeting?' she echoed. The prospect seemed to be wearying to her.

Lane said, anxious to please, 'I'll make it very gentle. First a nice reunion. The very light suggestion, next, that it's wrong for a young lady to be out so late. And then the intimation that now that I'm home, she can withdraw from this gang.' He spread his hands. 'After all, she's still only a teenager. It seems very simple to me.'

Estelle shook her head, and sighed. 'The same, going-to-have-his-own-way, John Lane. Never a doubt in your mind that you have the answer to a problem you've never even taken the trouble to understand.'

Slowly, Lane walked back to where his glass rested. He picked it up, and he was visibly fighting a return of irritation. He took a long sip of the brown liquid, and evidently had control of himself again. 'Now, see here, darling, I just have to tell you that you cannot protect Susan from having a talk with her father. So why don't you go to bed?'

Estelle's manner stiffened in a kind of surprised understanding. 'Oh,' she said, and her eyes lighted, 'so that's what you've missed in all that Mr Reid and I tried to say.'

'Missed?' Lane's tone was puzzled.

'Susan doesn't need any protection from me,' the woman said, simply.

Lane stared at her, puzzled. 'I guess I *don't* get it. What are you talking about?'

The wife said, 'The outfits will protect Susan.'

The husband's determined face took on a strange, blank expression. Her words must have been totally incomprehensible, for he just stood there, blinking a little.

The wife continued, and her voice had an arguing quality in it as if she was trying to penetrate his fog. She said, 'Don't you see, honey? The outfits are established. No single person can resist them. Not you . . . Not anyone.'

That reached the man. He was suddenly immensely astonished. He said, 'You've been arguing with me for *my* protection?' He spoke slowly.

A pause. Lane had put his glass down again, and on his face, now, was a look. It was as if the meaning of her words was tangling inside him with all of those steely, positive ideas by which he conducted his life. The conflict, whatever its form, was brief. The firm lips tightened decisively. He said, grimly, 'Now, I know the situation is serious. I'll . . . talk . . . to Susan.'

Estelle sighed. 'I must have said the wrong thing. Please . . . let me put it in simple words. Outfits are raising the children of Spaceport, and have been doing so for the past eight and a half years.'

Lane shook his head. He was impatient, but also smiling in a tolerant, superior fashion. 'I began to get the picture. Some idiots have started another fad and the kids are living it up.'

The woman was also impatient, suddenly. 'The idiots were those who went out into the universe, and left their children here to fend for themselves, and never gave them another thought.'

Lane said in an even tone, 'I thought I left my daughter in a beautiful home, to be cared for by her mother and a daily school schedule that would keep her out of trouble.'

The woman's color was high. 'What you *thought*, and the reality, are not related. The school and the mother were not enough – get it! In fact' –she was calmer – 'it is believed that the presence of some type fathers is probably as harmful to a child as his absence.'

'*My* type?' Lane asked.

There was that in his tone which made her give him a sharp, searching look. And then she was suddenly griefy, and she said, 'Don't you hurt Susan.'

The surprise of that brought a halt to whatever hardness was building up in the man. He was taken aback. 'Hurt my own daughter! Of course, I won't hurt her. I love her very dearly. Her picture and yours were always on my desk on every ship I commanded.'

Silence, As if they had arrived at an impasse. The woman looked resigned, even a little tired – as if the unaccustomed argument had been too much for her. But it was she who finally spoke. 'All right,' she said. She turned way, and moved toward the bedroom.

' 'Night,' Lane called after her.

She did not reply, did not turn. As the man watched, she disappeared into the hallway toward her bedroom. Lane now carried his drink to a table beside a chair. He had to adjust the light for his own way of sitting. But presently he was in the chair, and he picked up the newspaper that was there, and he began impatiently to read.

IV

TIME went by. One section of the paper was discarded, and fell to the right side of the chair. More time. Lane pushed the paper aside, climbed to his feet, and deliberately walked over to the bar and in the same deliberate fashion made himself another drink. Then back to the chair. Another section of the newspaper struck the floor and lay there.

A lot of anger had built up. He let the paper drop, reached to his collar with both hands, and loosened it with a jerk. Down came the hands, picked up the paper from his lap, but instead of reading, he glanced at his watch. His jaw automatically tightened as he saw that it was eleven fifty-eight.

Abruptly, he tossed the rest of the paper to the floor, and holding the liquor glass tightly, as if it were an extension of his fist, brought it up to his mouth and forced a sip through his clenched mouth. It was as he set the glass down that he heard a sound.

Footsteps were coming up the walk outside. Lane stood up and went to the window beside the bar. It was the kind of plastic that could be adjusted to admit light in either direction, separately or together, and at the moment it was adjusted so that what light there was outside could come in. As Lane peered out, he heard muffled voices. A female soprano with a lot of youthfulness in it, and a husky male voice that was harder to evaluate in terms of age.

Now, he could see them on the front porch. There was a light over the door. A tall – five foot six – slender, blonde girl of unmistakable teen-age appearance and a strongly built boy of perhaps eighteen, also a blond, were standing with their arms around each other. It was not a close embrace: more like a dancing closeness.

The girl kissed the boy on the left cheek, and said softly, ' 'Night, Lee.'

The boy kissed the girl on the right cheek, and said tenderly, 'Good-night, sweet moocher.'

Whereupon, he released her. He stepped closer to the house, out of Lane's line of sight. There was a sound of a key in the lock. The click of it came to him from inside the house. So, a moment later, did the noise of the door itself opening. Lane stayed at the window. The boy stepped into view again. He

19

handed the girl what must have been the key. Whatever it was, she slipped it into her purse. Now, she disappeared from Lane's view, and there was the sound of the front door closing. The boy turned, walked rapidly toward the street, let himself out of the gate, and went off to the right.

There were small sounds coming from the entrance hallway. Lane made his way across the den to the door that led to the hallway, which was broad here, almost as big as a small, longer-than-wide room. He stopped; and it was evident, then, that the carpet floor had muffled his approach. Because Susan was already in the hallway, and her back was to him.

A kitten lay asleep on the big chair, which stood just to the right of entrance hall doorway. She bent down, and gently picked it up, cuddling it in her arms. Still holding the kitten, she turned, saw Lane – and stopped, teetering. Then:

'Dad!' She came forward a little shyly, and, still holding the kitten, put one arm around his neck and shoulder, pressed against him, and kissed him on the cheek. 'Oh, dad, you are back. At last.'

Something of the previous hour's rigidity went out of Lane. Awkwardly, he put his arms around her, and was about to kiss her on the lips, when she turned her right cheek to him, and said, 'The right cheek, dad. Boyfriends and parents kiss a girl's right cheek. Other girls and younger kids kiss her left cheek. You might as well learn right now.'

Lane was taken by surprise. He completed his kiss, his lips involuntarily pressing her right cheek exactly on the spot that she held out for him. He would have stepped back and away, then, but she still had her arm around his neck, and her blue eyes were misty.

'Oh, dad,' she whispered, 'I'm so glad you're back. I missed you.'

Lane was recovering. A lot of the anger was gone, and there was a touch of mist in his eyes, also. He spoke gruffly, 'So am I, my dear. And this time it's for good, I hope you'll be glad to know. We'll all three of us have a normal family life for a change.'

Susan, who had been maneuvering the kitten, balancing it, preventing it from falling by nuzzling it against her chest, brought her other arm down, and picked up the kitten in both hands. She held it up to his face. 'Dad, meet Fuzzy.' She pressed the little animal against his cheek. 'She'll be up on your lap a lot if you're really going to be home, so you might as well get aquainted, and learn to love each other.'

In order to deal with the kitten, Lane released Susan from his embrace. With one palm he lifted the kitten out of her hands. With the other he caught Susan by the arm and drew her into the den.

'I want to talk to you for a minute, Susan.'

Susan suppressed a yawn. 'I want to talk to you for a thousand hours, dad. But not too much tonight. I can scarcely keep my scanners open.'

Lane's expression hardened a little. 'That's what I wanted to talk to you about. Here – sit down.'

He had brought her into a chair. She sank into it and accepted the kitten when he handed it to her. She stared up at him, face more serious, suddenly. Lane pulled a straight-backed chair over from the library table, and settled himself into it in front of her.

'How old are you, Susan?'

'Sixteen.' There was a faraway look in her eyes. She said without looking at him. 'It's bad when a girl has to have the thoughts which have suddenly come into my mind.'

'Eh?'

'You're not really going to be a booter, are you, dad?'

It was clear from the expression on Lane's face that the conversation had taken an unexpected turn. But his eyes also showed that he was not a man who allowed any evasiveness to detour him from his set purposes. 'Booter,' he said in an even tone. 'That sounds like one of those labels that somebody slips into another person's mind – particularly an unwary young person's – and as soon as it's been sneaked in, thereafter, that person judges life by the label.' He finished, 'I mean, don't judge me until I've said my say.'

Susan nodded. She looked relieved. 'That's fair,' she said. 'But I'd really rather wait until the dawn light. I can see I'm not up to thinking about what you're going to say, because I feel confused already.'

'I'll make it brief,' said Lane.

He thereupon explained to her what he had said earlier to his wife: his surprise and disappointment that on the evening of his return, his only daughter had gone out, and remained out until midnight.

'I was with my outfit,' said Susan. Her tone indicated that the explanation should take care of his concern. She went on, 'If you're a booter that won't mean anything, but if you'll wait a few days and find out what all this means then it won't bother you.'

'We've already discussed the word booter,' Lane replied. 'It has a special significance which you have accepted and which I don't accept. So why don't we remove it from the conversation, and go on from there.'

The faraway look was back in Susan's eyes, which were also a little misty again. She said. 'No matter what happens, dad, remember this jabber loves you as a father, and will never change that.'

'You're still thinking with the label, I see – ' Lane began. And then he stopped. He sat there, with the expression on his face of a person who suddenly feels his first helplessness. He said finally, 'Dear, we're just going to have to get past these rote answers you're giving me.'

Susan nodded. 'That's fair,' she said. 'No father rote, no outfit rote. Sack?'

There was a pause. Lane sat, tapping one knee with the fingers of his right hand. His face muscles had tightened considerably, but there was still restraint.

He temporised. 'I suppose,' he said, ' "sack" means is it all right, or is it okay. But what does jabber mean?'

'A kid over fourteenth birthday and under nineteenth.' Susan smiled suddenly, and her whole face showed an amazingly attractive personality shift. The smile had a magnetic brightness to it. Until she smiled, she was pretty. The smile made her a dazzling beauty. She said, still smiling, 'Jabbers still jabber, dad. Let's face it. A twenty-minute jab lasts two hours.'

Lane was not about to be diverted. 'What would father rote consist of?'

'What you just said,' she said instantly, 'about missing me when I wasn't here. That's an untruth, and you shouldn't do untruths – ever.'

'What's the lie in it?' Lane demanded in a dangerous tone.

'We're different generations, dad. We pass each other. We touch hands. You talk to me to find out if all is well, to make sure I'm not jumping the coop. Then I go somewhere and you go somewhere else. Togetherness would be boring to me and only a duty to you. You couldn't say your real truths in my presence, and you can see that when I say mine in *your* presence, it just makes you mad, doesn't it?'

There was a peculiar sound at that point from the hallway. Somebody stifling a cough, or something. Lane climbed stiffly to his feet as Estelle came in. 'I thought I heard voices,' she said in an oddly muffled voice of her own. She seemed to be having some physical difficulty, for she stood visibly shaking a little. Lane went over to her in alarm.

'What's the matter?' Her body coninued to shake. 'May I get you a glass of water?' She nodded mutely, and he hurried over to the bar. When he returned with the glass, Susan was disappearing through the den door into the corridor.

' 'Night,' she called over her shoulder.

Estelle had recovered remarkably during those few moments. But she accepted the glass, and took a sip, and then said, 'I sort've waved Susan to go to bed,' she announced. She drained the glass, and added, 'I heard the last part of that conversation, and I thought you'd had enough inter-action with a jabber for one night.'

A strange tenseness had come into her husband's face as he spoke. Abruptly, he clenched his hands and narrowed his eyes. 'You were laughing at me. That was what gave you that shuddery look. You were trying to hold it in.'

Amazingly, the woman had to fight again. She started to quiver. Her face broke into a smile, and then she fought that down by compressing her lips. Finally, she managed to murmur, 'Darling, forgive me, but I could see you were slightly overwhelmed.'

Lane was outraged. 'That is absolutely untrue. I was trying to be fair.'

'All right, all right.' His wife nodded vigorously. 'I agree. That's what you were doing, and I'm glad.' She gave him a long look. 'They're pretty pure, aren't they – these outfitters?'

There was a struggle visible in the man's strong, hard face after those words were spoken. He was obviously still furious, but another thought was gaining the upper hand. An I'd-better-bide-my-time thought. He actually took a step backwards, as if he were physically pulling away from a crisis. Nonetheless, when he spoke it was evident that there was no basic surrender.

He said in a level tone, 'I can see that it's not only the kids that have had ideas put into their heads. But, still, it is late. It's been going on for some time. It won't change tonight. So I'll just let it pass for now.'

His wife gave him a searching look. 'There's something about your tone of voice, and the set of your jaw that suggests you're having those old secret reservations. And I have a feeling I'm not going to like what you're scheming right now, when I finally find out what it is, but' – she shrugged – 'one of the things I came out to tell you is that I'm getting sleepy.' She shook her head and stared up at him, seductively. 'You wouldn't want to come in bed and find me sound asleep, would you?'

Abruptly, the hard muscles in the man's face relaxed. He smiled, and grabbed her. 'My same old darling,' he said, and hugged her.

From somewhere in the region of his neck his wife said in a muffled voice, 'Ten years older. And every minute of it hurts inside me in a way that you're going to have to make right. So,

23

don't waste any time starting in.[5]

Lane continued to hold her. 'Listen!' he said, 'you go back to bed. And I'll be there in about one minute and thirty-three seconds.'

'What are you going to do?' she asked, as she drew away from him.

'Clean up.' He indicated the newspaper on the floor, and the bottles on the bar.

'I'll clear that away in the morning,' Estelle said. But she was already heading for the door to the hallway.

'You know I don't like to leave a mess,' said her husband.

'Same old John Lane,' his wife said as she disappeared through the door and off into the darkness beyond.

Lane was brisk now. He picked up the sections of paper, folded them carefully but quickly, and laid them on the library table. Next, he put the bottles that were on the bar into the cabinet, out of sight. From somewhere a cloth appeared in his hand. He wiped off the bar top. The cloth vanished into a receptacle behind the bar.

The job done, he walked to the door, and stood there, finger on the light switch, taking a last survey of the room. His expression showed that he saw nothing that needed to be done. He pressed the switch, and then for a moment there were vague sounds of him walking down the hall. Pause. A door shut with a click.

Silence.

On another street in a poorer district, the invisible viewer waited before a single story white house: the Jaeger home. It had previously been the house of the couple with whom Bud lived. And so, when Bud and the large boy, Albert, arrived at the gate, the unseen watcher did not explore the environs of the place. It remained just outside the gate, and observed them enter and go up to the door.

Bud held back. Whereupon, Albert stepped past him, tried the knob, and found it locked. Without hesitation, he thereupon pressed the doorbell button. A faint buzzing sound came from inside the house.

A long pause. Finally, the door opened, and a thin woman in a nightdress with a pale blue robe loosely fastened over it, stood on the threshold. 'Oh,' she said. 'It's you, Bud.'

'Yes, uh, mom,' said Bud.

To the watcher at the gate, the woman's voice had implied that she expected someone else.

The woman had thin brown hair. Her face was middle thirties, but lined; and both it and her body expressed sadness and resignation. She spoke again. 'Your dad is still out on the town.

You'd better get in here, and into bed, before he discovers how late you've been out.'

For just a moment, Bud hesitated. During that moment, he communicated with the unseen watcher: *I have to admit I am greatly relieved, my father. But Mr Jaeger's absence tonight only postpones the time when he finds out that I am now a member of an outfit.*

To the father, the entire existence of such groups for teenagers was an unfortunate event. But he had a more urgent awareness at the moment. He telepathed: *Hurry! Get inside! I sense someone is coming.*

Bud scurried awkwardly past the woman. She retreated into the house, and closed the door. Albert turned and walked to the gate, opened it, stepped onto the sidewalk beyond, and then turned and closed the gate. Standing there, he must have become aware of the distant figure that had just rounded the corner. The big boy's whole manner spelled out his recognition that the approaching man was Bud Jaeger's father. He was noticably torn between two feelings: Leave, or wait and see what happened.

What he did, abruptly, was, he walked over and stood behind a tree.

At least a minute passed. At the end of that time, a hulking male of medium height, late thirty-ish in age, came weaving up to the gate. The man had an obvious difficulty in maintaining his balance even when he stopped moving. He fumbled the gate catch. Then he bent down and looked at it. Then he fumbled at it some more.

Seen close, the man's face showed a certain ruggedness. But there were purple veins in the nose and upper cheeks. And the small eyes were slightly too near each other. The man's lips were bulky, as if slightly swollen, and loosely held together.

Observing him, not for the first time, the viewer had the private awareness – again – that in espionage, one often had to deal with partially destroyed entities. When he was not drunk, Len Jaeger was a skilled toolmaker; and, as such, had successfully applied for a position in Spaceport – all this before he was ever selected for his role.

When he suddenly produced a son, the authorities were surprisingly unsuspicious. Of course, it was true that his real son had run away. What should have caused wonder, and didn't was that such a runaway would ever return to such a father.

This human entity finally solved the gate mechanism. It swung open, and he surged through on up to the door of the house. He stood, then, with his finger pressing the door-bell button until, once more, the door swung open, and there was Mrs Jaeger.

'*Sssshh!*' she said. 'You'll awaken Bud.'

If the admonition penetrated to the man there was no sign. He stepped past her, and staggered noisily on into the house out of sight of the watcher. The woman did not immediately follow him. She seemed undecided. It was a momentary delay only. Leaving the door ajar, she walked out onto the little porch, stepped down to the walk, and came along it to the gate, which she closed. Hurriedly, now, as if afraid of being seen, she turned about; and, holding her robe and nightdress way from her feet, she half ran back the way she had come. The door of the house closed behind her.

For nearly fifteen minutes after that, the boy, Albert, waited behind the tree. At last, he seemed satisfied. He emerged from his place of concealment, walked past the gate, and rapidly made his way along the street. He disappeared around the same corner from which Jaeger had first come into view.

The unseen watcher did not budge. His would be an all-night vigil.

V

NEXT morning came in its slow pace to the Lane household. In Susan's room, the morning light filtered vaguely through the plastic two-way window. The light adjustment was for almost pitch dark, but not quite.

In the dim light it was possible to make out what was unmistakably a nice room. There was a makeup table with a large, glinting mirror. A dresser stood against the wall by the window. Pictures on the walls built-into-the-wall drawers, a built-in television, and a cunningly concealed door that opened into a spacious wardrobe. And on the bed, covered by a thin sheet, Susan lay sound asleep.

Suddenly, movement. On the bedside table to Susan's right, a clocklike object produced a flag. The flag sprang into view with a click-clack. An instant later a chime sounded inside the clock, giving forth with a prolonged bell-like Middle C. As the musical note died away, a voice spoke from the clock. A familiar, girlish voice. It said, 'Good morning, Susan . . . it is 7.30. Time to get up.'

The girl in the bed did not stir.

In the breakfast room at the far side of the house, Lane was sitting at the table. He had a small notebook beside his plate, and his manner was preoccupied as he wrote into it at some length. Presently, he put the pen down, ate the rest of his breakfast – a few mouthfuls – and then, without looking directly at Estelle who was sitting across from him, he said. 'I notice that hasn't changed.'

The woman had been watching him, waiting for him to finish his notation. His sudden words caught her by surprise. 'What?' she asked.

'Outfit or no, it's still as hard to get a kid up as when I was young.'

His wife was recovering. She smiled, but her voice was calm as she said, 'Susan isn't perfect about getting up, but she's pretty good. She has so many duties, I wonder sometimes that she can stand it. It would drive me out of my mind.'

Lane looked up, frowning. 'Duties?' he echoed.

'For the outfit.'

'Oh.'

There was a tone to his voice that caused the blonde woman to look at him sharply. She said finally, 'Now, remember what you agreed.'

The expression on the man's face showed that his thoughts and her words were not entirely in accord. He looked exasperated, then briefly cynical, and then his lips twisted ever so slightly, indicating that he hadn't really agreed.

But he said aloud, 'I remember.'

His voice sounded false. Estelle sighed. 'Really, John' – wearily – 'do we have to go over all this again?'

Lane shrugged. 'You're trying to imply something that does not exist.'

'You agreed –'

'I agreed not to make a further issue of it with Susan,' said Lane. 'I didn't agree to like it.'

The woman's eyes were abruptly misty. She took out her handkerchief hastily from her sleeve, and wiped her eyes Lane watched the little byplay impatiently, and then said in an irritated tone, 'For heaven's sake, Estelle –'

'What I'm visualising,' she said in an unsteady voice, 'is you around here, sullen, going into silences – like you used to, whenever you didn't get your own way. It just seems too much to look forward to after all these years.'

Lane sat gazing at her. His shoulders sagged a little. It was the same body response of helplessness that had briefly come over him the night before with Susan. But in the end he shook his head rejectingly. 'You're hitting hard,' he said. 'I haven't done any of those things yet.'

She half sobbed, 'I spent half the night fighting for the small concession that you finally made, and now it looks like you didn't really concede anything.'

'I agreed to wait,' said Lane. 'And I'm waiting. I'll defer judgement until I hear the facts. But if Susan were to leave her outfit of her own free will, I can tell you it wouldn't hurt my feelings any – the way I feel right now.'

'What a strange remark!' She stared at him. The grief was gone out of her as suddenly as it had come. Her face tightened with suspicion. 'I can't imagine what could be going on in the mind of someone who would say a thing like that.'

'Estelle – let up!' her husband protested. 'I haven't done anything. I give up. Have mercy.'

The woman was still suspicious. 'Can I trust you?'

'To do what I said – yes.'

'All right.' Her tone was still grudging, but her face changed. A smile brightened her eyes, and crinkle of lines around her mouth showed satisfaction. She said swiftly in an undertone, 'I hear sounds. I do believe someone is coming.'

There were indeed sounds. They came from the hallway beyond a door behind Lane. Lane listened for a moment, and then he shook his head, puzzled. 'If I were to guess, it would be that a one-legged, hoofed animal is approaching.'

He had scarcely spoken when Susan came into view. She hopped into the room on one foot as she put her shoe onto the other foot. This complex operation required her to use only one hand. In the other hand she carried a booklet.

The shoeing task completed. She put the raised foot down on the floor, and became a two-legged human being, whose appearance indicated that a lot of work had been done in an incredibly short time. Her hair was combed, and done up in a peculiar sweep to one side of her head. Her face looked washed, and presumably her teeth were brushed, for they were brilliantly white. Her skirt and blouse were on straight, and tucked in, and her stockings gleamed in even lines.

'Good morning, mom,' said this youthful apparition. " 'Morning, back from-the-universe dad.'

'Good morning, dear,' said Estelle.

Lane was hesitating. His daughter's greeting was somehow not to his liking. That's what his expression seemed to indicate. Or else, despite his assurances to his wife, the earlier feelings in him were too strong to be overcome, now that the moment for action had arrived.

Estelle was abruptly tense. 'John, Susan spoke to you.'

Lane turned in his chair. 'Susan,' he said, 'do you always address people by their latest exploit? Suppose I said to you, "Hello, just-got-up Susan?" '

Susan was drinking her orange juice. She lowered the glass. 'Can we start over, dad? I'm willing. Good morning, dad. I'm sure glad you're back from the universe.'

'Good morning, Susan,' said Lane.

The words still came hard. His tone was slightly peevish, as if he was still one-down in a conversation that – his manner implied – should never have started in the first place. The man watched perhaps too grimly as his daughter finished her orange juice, gave him her delightful smile, and then glided over and put the booklet she had been holding onto the table beside his plate.

'What's this?' Lane asked. His gaze fastened onto the print on the cover, and he read slowly, aloud, *'Rules and Regulations for Outfits.'*

Susan drew back, and for the first time when she spoke, her voice seemed formal. 'Bringing you this,' she said, 'is part of the outfit program to communicate with parents.'

'You sound like you're quoting,' said Lane, quickly.

'Paraphrasing is more like it,' Susan said.

'What I don't understand,' said her father, 'is why should it be a program?' At that moment, he caught a glimpse of Estelle's face, with its disapproval, and he said hastily, 'All right, Susan, I'll consider myself communicated with.'

'It's only a communication if you read it,' said the girl. She seemed uncertain now, as if the unvarying intensity of his basic hostility was getting through to her finally. 'Well – ' she said, vaguely.

It was a bad moment, and Lane's expression recognised that the situation could only be saved by a gesture of goodwill from him. For the first time, he managed a smile. 'I think I've got something better for you than reading this book, my dear about-to-leave Susan.'

The words caught his daughter at the door. She came to a stop, and turned slowly. She was visibly halted in her flight plan, which was clearly the solution she had come to. To leave, to put Lane and the problem he was causing behind her – that was what his communication prevented, barely in time. The man was momentarily staggered by the disaster that was so narrowly averted. He glanced involuntarily at his wife; and saw in her stricken expression her awareness of the same dark truth. His body shrank a little as he obviously visualised what might have

29

happened if Susan had actually escaped; and there he would have been alone with Estelle.

Lane swallowed and said hastily, with a forced smile, 'Your mother has been making strong representations to me . . . so just forget our little conversation of last night. I intend to get some data before I – ' He stopped, grimacing.

Whatever it was he might have said, was lost to history. Susan came back from the door, and put her arms around him. 'Oh, dad, I knew you were a great guy.' She kissed him warmly on the left cheek. As he kissed her on her right, she said, 'Dad, is it true that when you were out in space, you ran into some dangerous aliens?'

Lane completed his kiss. He was smiling now, cynically. 'Now, dear, if I had classified information about that, I couldn't tell you. But the fact is, the whole story is in the papers. We spent a year in evasive flight, making sure they didn't trace us back to earth. The fight was very brief, three months – which in space is like three day's battle on earth. Then the long, tiresome getaway.'

'It sounds awful scary,' said Susan. 'But' – she glanced at the clock – 'look at the time.' She trotted to the door. 'See you.'

After she had disappeared down the hallway, there were a few additional noises. The sound of her footsteps. Then her voice from a distance, saying, 'Oh, my dear little Fuzzy pussycat, good-bye; I'll see you later.' Next, the front door opened softly and closed loudly. If there were other Susan noises after that, they were indistinguishable from ordinary street sounds.

In the breakfast room, no word was spoken by the parents as the girl made her exit. When she was finally gone, Lane pushed the booklet she had presented him away from his plate. Estelle, who had been watching, reached forward and pushed it toward him again. Lane looked down at it somberly and then up at her. 'I don't have to read it, do I?' he said.

'It says in there somewhere,' stated his wife, 'that a jabber is old enough to evaluate a parent, but what they're normally not able to evaluate is what they should do about it, if their judgement is negative. The outfits tell them what to do. I thought you might be interested to know what they say.'

'Why don't you give it to me in one sentence?'

The woman shook her head. She was not unfriendly, and her tone was not as critical as were her words. She said, 'If you can't give ten minutes to your daughter after ten years, then I also may find myself making a negative judgement of you. Only for me there's no book of rules that tells me what to do about it.'

The man sat shaking his head in a puzzled fashion. 'I guess I'm home again all right, because suddenly the world of logic has vanished. Suddenly, I can't count on an agreement being lived up to. We settled all this last night – remember? I agreed to suspend judgement. I *have*.'

'You haven't. Not really.'

Her husband gazed at her with steady gray eyes. 'Think, now, with me, to decide is to act. I haven't acted.' Pause. 'Have I?'

For a long moment, the woman sat gazing off into some undetectable spaces above his head. Abruptly, she shook her head, and bit her lip. A smile broke through, crinkling her nose. 'Oh, hell!' she said. The smile broadened. 'I keep forgetting, I'm married to a fleet commander. Every night from now on, Susan and I can look forward to you coming home and making exact statements with exact phraseology.'

Lane said, 'I never leave people in any doubt as to where I stand.'

She shook her head. 'That's not true,' she said. She broke off quickly, as the thunder clouds darkened his face, 'I've seen you do devious scheming to get your own way. And you can be extremely secretive.'

'Oh, that.' His sudden anger faded, and he smiled grimly. 'You're talking about the tactics and strategy of winning.'

The blonde woman sighed. 'Just don't bring your warfare rules into this house,' she said.

Her husband glanced at the wall clock beyond her, and stood up. 'Time I was on my way.' He bent over her. His lips came down to within inches of hers. 'Do I get a goodbye kiss?' he asked.

Her friendly eyes looked up into his questioning ones. 'I married you for better or worse,' she said. 'I guess a kiss comes somewhere on the better side of the spectrum.'

It was acceptance. His head came all the way down. Simultaneously, his fingers grasped the wrist of her arm that was partly on the table. Without ceasing to kiss her, he drew her to her feet and into his arms. His lips sought, and hers received, the caress. She did not return the pressure of his lips, but she did not reject him.

She went with him, presently, to the door, and watched him go down the walk and along the street out of sight. Then she returned to the breakfast room, and stood for a while staring down at the outfit booklet where it lay beside his plate. Finally, silently, she picked it up, carried it to a cabinet with dishes in the glassed-in top and drawers below. Slowly, she drew open the top drawer, put the booklet on the silverware that lay there in neat rows, and then slowly closed the drawer again.

Whereupon, with a faraway look in her eyes she began to clean up the breakfast dishes.

VI

WHEN Susan departed from her parents' home, she walked rapidly along the street that led to the monorail. In daytime, the entrance of that fabulous transport system was a metal housing of rugged design half-hidden in heavy shrubbery. The girl went past it, straight on to a second street. And again without pausing to a third street. Abruptly, she was in a different world. The quiet, expensive homes had become less expensive in appearance with each block that she traversed. And now she found herself approaching a business street.

Unknown to Susan, a little drama was developing on the street ahead. A sullen-faced, good-looking brunette girl was coming along the business street, briskly at first, and then more slowly as she became aware of a boy across the street.

As she watched him from the corners of her narrowed, calculating eyes, she saw that he had spotted her. The instant she had his attention, she made a peremptory gesture, pointing ahead. The boy nodded, and began a slanting crossing of the street which would intercept the dark-haired girl a dozen or so feet from the intersection of the business street and the street along which Susan was coming.

The boy was sandy-haired, slim of build and of medium height. He wore the brown trousers and yellow coat of the Yellow Deer outfit; and, as he came up onto the sidewalk, where the sullen brunette was waiting for him, he was unmistakably nervous.

There was a faint, devil-may-care smile on the girl's face. She motioned him with a toss of her head to follow her. And then she led the way into a shallow alcove. Guilt radiated from him as he walked after her. It was in the way he held his body, and in the dark, oozy sweatiness of his face.

It was about twenty seconds after they went into the alcove that Susan rounded the nearby corner. She was walking rapidly past the alcove when she grew aware of the couple. She stopped. She turned. What she saw was the sandy-haired boy and the dark-haired girl standing with arms around each other. They were lip-kissing.

Susan walked slowly into the alcove. Her face was troubled, but she clearly knew what she must do. As she came to a point about half a dozen feet from the two, she said, 'All right, jabbers.

That's enough.'

The dark-haired girl was amazing. She didn't react. Her body did not make the convulsive involuntary start of the surprised person. In fact, when the boy literally *jumped*, her arms tightened instantly around him. Held him. Kept his face against hers.

But it was a pretty sad-type kiss that was now in process between them. And, after a long moment, she must have realised that she could not contain as much masculine emotion as was shuddering in her taut, capable but after all, only feminine arms. And, so, reluctantly, she released the highly charged young male, stepped back, and stood watching him with a certain amount of contempt in her face. But there was triumph also. Her expression said that she, at least, had achieved from the interchange what she expected.

The boy was by this time a lost soul. All the color had drained from his cheeks. His heart must have been pounding for he was breathing heavily. His fear was so obvious that Susan was embarrassed. 'Joe,' she said, 'it isn't that bad. All you have to do is report this to your outfit. And you'll only get a third stage dashing.'

If Joe heard the reassurance, it did not show. He tried to speak, but it was only a noise and not a meaningful word that came from his lips. The dark-haired girl watched his dissolution, her lips curling. 'Typical outfit material,' she said with a sneer.

Nonetheless, she made her first attempt now to help him. 'Joe,' she said, and her voice dripped with cool assurance, 'It's only the word of a one-cheek-kisser against yours.' She shrugged. 'I don't count, of course.'

A pitying expression had come into Susan's face. 'Joe,' she said, 'why don't you just leave? And be sure to run. Running alters the adrenalin in your system when the pressure is this strong.'

This time he heard; for he started off, uncertainly at first. Then, as the two girls walked after him, he actually broke into a loping run. As they emerged from the alcove, Joe was twenty feet further along the street, running.

The dark girl called after him, 'And don't you ever come near me again, you coward.' Her tone was vicious.

'*Ssshhh,* Dolores,' said Susan. 'You know there is no such thing as a coward.'

Dolores was scathing. 'You outfitters have all kinds of weasel words for what people do. It didn't stop the Red Cats from kicking me out.'

Susan said, 'It's not the same thing. You wouldn't admit you were wrong. Joe will.'

Dolores stood there; the faint, angry smile that had been on her face faded. Only the anger remained. 'I wasn't wrong. I was Lee's moocher until your sweet phony little face got to him. Look at me now. Look what you did to me.'

Susan was suddenly uneasy. She had been in this conversation before, her expression said; and she didn't want a repeat. 'You know the rule,' she said, slowly, 'when such a shift happens. Join another outfit. They were willing. You weren't.'

'I couldn't be that two-faced,' Dolores snarled.

A change came into her expression. The words, the memory, seemed to break through to the turmoil underneath, to the jealousy and fury that was there, always close to the surface. Without warning, she struck at the blonde girl.

It was an awkward blow, and it landed on Susan's arm. Susan winced, but it was obviously not too painful. She backed away, said in her steadiest voice, 'Go to school, Dolores!'

But the dark-haired girl came forward, her face grim, her eyes narrowed. 'I hate your guts!' she said. Up came her arm. Once more she tried to strike. But Susan evaded the attempt, and said, 'You know the rule for me on this I won't fight. My job is to prevent you from doing something that will make it necessary for something to be done about you.'

The blonde girl was more relaxed, after an initial strong anxiety. A rescuer was coming. In the near distance on the street behind and beyond Dolores, a familiar boy's figure had come into view. She recognised Mike Sutter. He had been sauntering, but as he saw the tableau ahead of him, he began to walk faster. And as Dolores, in a second impulse to violence, again ran at Susan and tried to hit her, Mike broke into a run.

He was wearing soft-soled shoes; and, besides, Dolores was totally absorbed with her own anger. Her attention was so completely channeled, her purpose so violent, that it was not until Mike's strong lean arms caught her from behind, that she even became aware that anyone else was around.

Once more, as with her reaction when Susan interrupted her tryst with Joe, Dolores was instantly and fantastically able to meet a new situation. 'Oh, it's you, Mike, darling,' she crooned. She pressed back against him, and, twisting her head far back and around, tried to lip-kiss him. 'It's all right, sweetheart Mike, lip-kissing is fun.'

Mike managed to twist his head, and her mascaraed lips smeared a red path across his cheek. 'When I start to lip-kiss,' he said, 'it will be with lips of my own choice.'

'You mean, with little Miss Nothing Marianne?' said Dolores sweetly.

The words and her tone irritated Mike. He was a strong boy;

and he now spun the dark-haired gir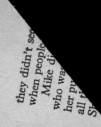
and power. Such strength and such
by Dolores. Something of her self-c
of her. She gasped, and struck at hi
her solidly held at arm's length, h
shoulders.

'There are no nothings in this wo

'Then,' snapped Dolores, 'how
her web in a little house by the rai
silkworm palace?'

'The outfits are going to change all that,' said Mike. As he
spoke, in his eyes was a strange idealistic look so common to
outfitters. It was obvious that his words seemed real to the youth.

But he was also a person with an exceedingly short span of
interest in unnecessary problems. 'Look, Miss Munroe, if I release
you will you go quietly off to school with our blessing, and with
another request that you behave yourself and rejoin an outfit?'

She was recovering from her rough handling. A faint smile
quirked her lips. It was an alienated smile, infinitely contemptuous. 'It's a little late, Mike dear. I've discovered how much fun a
jabber can have without the outfits and their holier-than-thou,
do-your-duty riding herd on my morals.' Her smile was infinitely
superior. 'Life is much more interesting now.'

Mike was not to be diverted. 'But if I let you go, you will go
quietly off to school?'

'I plan to get an education,' she said, loftily. 'And I'm looking
forward to college, with all those wonderful moonlit nights.'

'You'll never make it through college,' said Mike. He had
removed his left hand from her right shoulder. And now, with a
quick motion of his body, he caught her left arm and, putting the
other arm around her body, walked her a dozen feet before she
braced herself and stopped. 'Think you're smart, don't you?'
Dolores snapped.

Mike stepped away from her, but he remained standing between
her and Susan. It was evident that the situation was too much for
the brunette girl. With a dismissing twist of her body, she whirled
away and walked rapidly off in the same direction that Joe had
gone many minutes earlier.

Susan also moved forward. Mike took her arm, and the two of
them walked rapidly, though not as fast as Dolores, toward the
school, the grounds of which began slightly over a block away.
Mike was puzzled. 'What happened? How did all that start?'

'Oh!' It required an effort for Susan to put her thoughts back
to the event. Her attention had gone forward to something else.
'Oh,' she said, dismissingly, 'she was lip-kissing Joe in there, and

me coming.' She broke off. 'Mike, what happens
grow up?'

not immediately reply. He was watching a woman
coming toward them along the street. The woman had
rse hanging open on her arm, and she was applying lipstick,
e while gazing intently at her face in the small hand mirror.
e was not pretty, and so hers was essentially a wasted effort.

The woman passed them, with Mike half turning around to
observe her as she went by. Susan, who had been involved with
her own thoughts, became aware of Mike's wandering interest as
he dragged his feet a little, and so held her back also. She turned
her head and looked briefly, and then said chidingly, 'Mike, it
isn't polite to stare at people.'

Mike nodded; and they were quickly walking again at their
former pace. 'She reminded me,' he said. 'I see my mother every
day looking into her mirror. She's in her late thirties, but she
acts as if it's her late sixties. So' – he shrugged – 'part of the
answer to your question is, they get scared of growing old and
dying.'

Susan made a negating gesture with her body. 'Mike,' she
said. 'I'm not interested in what's wrong with people when they
grow up, but with what's right. What do they get out of it?'

Mike frowned. 'Growing up is inevitable, so what's your
problem?'

'I'm just asking' – with asperity – 'I thought you might have
some thoughts about, but if you don't – sack!'

Once more, she had lost Mike. His gaze was on a man and a
woman who were coming toward them along the street. The
couple was oblivious of their surroundings. The man held the
woman's arm tightly; too tightly, for she kept tugging in an effort
to pull away from him. But he was not about to let go. The
woman's expression, and her way of holding herself as she walked
was reminiscent of Dolores Munroe at her most rebellious. The
man's face was dark with anger; the woman's defiant.

As the two older people walked by the boy and the girl, the man
was saying. 'If I ever catch you talking to that fellow again – '
His manner, and a gesture he made, indicated that mayhem
would result. But the woman was not cowed. Her accusing words
came: 'And what about you . . . and that woman?'

They were past, and Mike, somewhat sobered, was facing about
and walking strongly forward beside Susan. He shook his head.
'I really don't know what's been good about growing up in the
past, except you're on you own. But' – his lips tightened – 'it's
going to have to be better in the future than it has been. The
outfits are going to have to see to that.'

36

'How can they do that? They don't exist anywhere but in Spaceport.' Susan's voice had a let's-be-practical note in it.

'Oh, we're going to have to expand,' said Mike. 'There's no question.'

His words had no audience. Susan's attenion, this time, had jumped elsewhere. 'Oh, there's Bud Jaeger,' she said. 'Did we decide what we were going to do with him?'

'No, but' – Mike's face indicated that the problem had diverted him from the future of the adult world – 'we might just as well go the routine. Give him some young kids to look after, and just make sure that we keep an eye on what he does.'

The unseen watcher, moved a few feet behind Bud – as he came out of the side street and crossed over to the school grounds – was the first to see Mike and Susan. *Two of your outfit's members are coming,* he telepathed to his child.

They're no problem during school hours, the boy replied. He changed the direction of his thought: *My father, do I really have to keep going to this school? Why can't you just look over this city of Spaceport the way you're doing?*

Because, was the patient answer, *it is not enough merely to have an external view of a culture. What we have to find out absolutely must include a careful, thorough infiltration, whereby one of our people discovers what is really going on. Now, remember, we had to pursue that fleet for an entire year. They used every trick they could think of to throw us off their track, and prevent us from tracing them to their planet. But here we are. Our fleet is waiting out in space; and there's no hurry, my son. If we attack these villains and fail, it will be because of your impatience, or something you missed because of indifference. That must not happen.*

All right, all right, said the boy: *But it sure is boring to have to learn things that you'll never have any use for.*

Warfare and conquest have their own knowledge requirements, and knowledge is always a relation-to. So it is important. We do have use for what you learn . . . The invisible father presented these admonishing thoughts to his son, throughout showing no slightest criticism or judgement in any emotional way.

The conversation between them ended as Mike and Susan joined the shuffling Bud. The three greeted each other, and walked into the school building near that street.

Again, the unseen watcher stationed himself near that door – waited.

VII

JOHN LANE emerged from Exit Eight of the monorail elevator. Directly in front of him, as he walked forth, was a sign which read:

WARNING
CLASSIFIED TERRITORY
Identification Required

After ten years' absence from ground rules, during which time he had moved up to top command of a fleet of space battleships, it was a little irksome to have to step into a cubbyhole and submit to a computer check. But he did it now with the faint, fixed smile of a superior officer who is prepared at all times to prove that, if a system is necessary, he is not above it.

Naturally, he was in the cubbyhole very briefly. After instants only, a green light flashed in the panel in front of him. Behind him, the door unlocked with a click. The same color of green was glowing from a source at the top of the check station outside. Which, of course, was to be expected, but it degraded him – slightly – to have to have it there.

In emerging, Lane faced a long, wide, gleaming corridor. There were many men, particularly men in officers' uniforms, visible as far as the eye could see. They emerged from one door, walked a distance, and disappeared into another. Always, evidently by chance alone, by the time one group had performed this operation, another group was in process of doing it.

It was out of this tangle of people that a familiar figure presently came forth. Lane recognised Desmond Reid, and walked briskly forward to meet him. The two men shook hands. Reid apologised: 'Hope you haven't been waiting long?'

'No, no, just got here!' Lane replied truthfully.

The older man took his arm and led the way to a side corridor. He was shaking his head. He was grave. 'Hard day ahead for you, John. It's another debriefing session, and it's going to be rough.'

'Same problem?'

Reid nodded. 'Everybody's in a state over that clash you had with the aliens. I sense fear, tension, the feeling that not enough precautions were taken.'

Lane was calm. 'When we began to run out of fuel, we had a simple choice. Either never return at all – just die out there – or bring the fleet here in the belief that it would be valuable in an emergency. It took a long time to build those ships, remember?'

'I remember,' said Reid, grimly. He pointed. 'This way.' It was another corridor. As they walked along it, now, Reid continued. 'Will you swear that only military consideration motivated your return?' He broke off. 'I'm sure you'll be asked that question. What I mean is, you didn't let consideration for Estelle and Susan influence you.'

Lane stopped. He was scowling, and angry. 'Are you out of your mind? Of course, I did. Not only my Estelle and my Susan but all the Estelles and Susans of forty-eight thousand men.' He laughed curtly. 'You don't think for one second that the officers could have retained control of those vessels if we had ever announced that we were not coming home.' As he spoke, his frown became positively ferocious. 'If that's the kind of thinking that's going on, I won't even talk to the bastards. I only mentioned the alternative to coming home. No one – not me or anyone – ever considered it seriously.'

'The fate of the entire planet may be in the balance,' said Reid, slowly. 'What about that?' He was abruptly apologetic again. 'I'm only asking, John, because in a few minutes this is what you're going to be facing.'

Absently, Lane patted his friend's arm. His eyes were still narrowed, but he was suddenly concerned and not in a rage. Finally, he said, 'I'm glad you're doing this, Dez. These kind of thoughts are a year behind me, all resolved, answered, and put away in their little cubbyholes. I appreciate what you've done for me just now. For the first time I understand why I didn't get home yesterday until Estelle was ready to jump out of her skin. The debriefing committee handled me with such respect, I didn't get the real direction of their thinking.'

His stern face relaxed. He stood there staring, initially thoughtfully, but presently with a faint humorless smile at the gleaming wall above Reid's head. At last, he nodded. His gaze came back to his friend. Reid, who had been watching him, parted his lips to speak again. But the younger man held up his hand, demanding silence. 'No more,' he said. 'I've remembered the whole discussion I had with my staff at the time. Listen! The key fact is, that there is a villainous – from our point of view – race out there. They attacked us without warning, refused all communication, and were obviously out to kill. Got that?'

Reid nodded.

Lane continued, 'They're not that far away, Dez, that we'll ever be safe. Only Twenty-one light-years. At such a relatively short distance, there's no escaping a confrontation sooner or later. On the other hand, suppose we had decided against coming home. Then, the enemy would know that earth existed, but earth wouldn't know that they were out there. Presumably, there would be anxiety and suspicion if we never returned. But people wouldn't actually *know*. Now, they do. And in addition we have the fleet that skillfully fought an engagement with a powerful force.' He spread his hands. 'That's it. That's the reasoning. I can see no flaw in it.'

Desmond Reid was nodding. 'Nor I, he said. His face was thoughtful. 'What should we be doing, John?'

'Building new vessels. Analysing what weapons they used against us from the damage we suffered.'

'Good man.' With abrupt warmth, the older man now patted Lane's arm. 'I knew my confidence in you when it comes to matters like this was not misplaced. But' – he smiled wryly – 'how did you make out last night with Susan?'

Lane did not reply immediately. His attenion had moved over to a young officer in full dress who was approaching along the hallway. The man wore an active flight badge, and he swaggered a little. When the youthful officer had passed by, Lane stared after him with a smile. He said in a significant tone, 'They're handsome, aren't they, these heroes of space?'

He turned, and saw that Reid was staring at him with a puzzled expression in his face. 'I presume,' said the older man finally, 'that that is your answer to my question about Susan.'

Lane laughed, caught his friend's arm, urged him into motion again, and, it was as they were walking, that he said, 'Don't worry about Susan. She'll never even know what happened to her; it will all be so smoothly done.' He broke off. 'When does the debriefing session begin?'

'It's already in session, but they're questioning your chief officer, Villiers.'

'Then I've got time to locate my new office, and sit in the chair behind the desk, and admire myself?'

'I'll take you there, myself,' answered Reid. 'But, now, about Susan.'

The younger man shook his head with a slow, wide, firm movement. 'Dez, I'd rather not discuss the matter.'

His friend accepted the second avoidance of the subject. They walked silently the rest of the way to a door that was marked: 'SPACE CONTROL HEADQUARTERS. John Lane, Senior Fleet Commander.'

Lane paused to read the lettering, and then shook his head good-naturedly, and said, 'I'm not yet quite clear what it means.'

Reid laughed. 'It's got to have its place somewhere on the upper part of the totem pole. You'll discover where when you pick up the intercom and find out who's calling you about what.' He held out his hand. As Lane took it questioningly, the other man continued, 'I've got to get back to the debriefing session. You'll be called soon.'

'How will I find my way through this labyrinth?' Lane waved vaguely, taking in all the corridors they had traversed and others that were visible in the distance ahead.

'Have one of your people bring you.'

With that perfectly sensible suggestion, he waved and, turning, walked back the way they had come. Lane stood for a moment watching the fine, firmly held body, the slightly graying hair on a distinguished-looking head. His eyes grew thoughtful, and he nodded gently to himself; and then abruptly, his gaze still on the receding figure, he made a gesture that was half-salute, half-wave of respect.

Whereupon, he brought his hand down upon the knob, spun it, and entered a large room that, at his first quick glance, looked very much like the control desk of a large spaceship. Slowly, Lane pushed the door shut behind him. Then, with wondering face, he walked toward the left wall, which was nothing more nor less than a huge viewplate. The shiny screen was at the moment showing a view of space: Blackness with a dusting of stars in the background. The man's eyes grew misty, as he gazed at that scene so familiar to him from so many years out there. He continued his investigatory tour, walking past the glass window and door leading to what looked like a conference room, and past the viewplate to the machine that covered almost the entire rear wall. The purpose of this second machanism was equally obvious to his experienced eyes. It was an advanced type computer. The lights that played over its transparent windows, and the coding that built up in those windows, made meaningful patterns to Lane. He nodded half to himself, and there was pride in his face now.

Still nodding, he said softly to himself, 'I guess it won't be such a bad job after all. I won't be as out of touch as I feared. I will, in effect, be out there, and yet live at home with my family.'

As he spoke the word 'family,' his eyes narrowed slightly. He had been walking slowly in the direction of the other side wall, which was lined with a series of small gadgetry. Now, he stopped, spun on his heel and walked to the large metal desk that stood in front of the huge computer. There was an intercom on the desk. Lane pressed a button on it; and when a man's voice presently answered, he said, 'This is Commander Lane. Who am I talking to?'

'Scott, sir. Andrew Scott. A sort of liaison secretary, sir, is my job.'

'Good,' said Lane. 'Mr Scott, I noticed that there were several junior officers aboard this building. Get me a list of the active flight men in port.'

'Very well, sir.'

'How long will it take to get such a list?'

'Well, sir,' was the reply. 'I'm in the room on the other side of the computer that is also in your private office. And – right now – I – am – programming – the – computer – and here is the list, sir. May I bring it in?'

Lane had to smile. 'You certainly may,' he said. He stepped back from the intercom, and looked around. He had noticed no doors, on entering, except the one to the corridor, and of course the beautiful glass entrance to the conference room. As he waited, there was a small sound at the far left of the rear wall, where the computer did seem to narrow down a bit. One of the metal panels swung open and a man of about his own age came in. He was a dark-haired, brown-eyed, thick-jowled, slightly plumpish individual, dressed in civilian clothes – as was Lane. The latter accepted the computer printout sheet that was handed to him, and said, 'Wait.'

It was not a long list. The active flight officer aboard consisted of aproximately thirty-four names by quick glance estimate. There were only four captains on the list. Lane indicated them, said, 'How old are they? Let me have pictures of the two youngest?'

Scott did not even leave the room. Moments later, he came back with the printout that the computer had unrolled for him in the small alcove directly behind Lane's desk. There were the four photos, and the ages of each man. One was twenty-seven, and one all of twenty-six and one half, and the other two were both twenty-eight. Three of the men were adequately good-looking, but on the photo the fourth man was sensationally handsome. He was unfortunately one of the two twenty-eight-year-olds. But Lane quickly decided that would have to be unimportant.

He looked up. 'Mr Scott.'

'Yes, Commander.'

'This man, Captain Peter Sennes – I want you to locate him for me. Have him here in my office – let me see.' He stroked his jaw, and mused out loud, 'Yesterday, the debriefing committee adjourned for lunch a 12:30 – so ask him to be here at one. Tell him that I intend to invite him to my home for dinner tonight or tomorrow, whichever is more suitable for him. Will you do that?'

'Of course, sir.'

'And Mr Scott.'

'Yes, sir.'

'Call my wife, and tell her that I may have a guest for dinner tonight or tomorrow. Will you do that?'

'Naturally, sir.'

As Scott turned away, the intercom buzzer sounded. The plump man walked over quickly, and pressed the button. 'Commander Lane's office,' he said.

A voice said, 'The President's Space Committee is ready to resume its debriefing of Commander Lane. Will you have him step over as soon as possible.'

'I'll need a guide,' said Lane to Scott. He spoke quickly.

'I'll show him the way, personally,' said Scott into the intercom. He glanced at Lane. 'When, sir?'

'Right now,' Lane replied.

'We'll be there in two minutes,' Scott said into the instrument.

He broke the connection, and motioned toward the hall door. 'After you, Commander.'

They went out into the hallway, Scott opening and then closing the door.

Silence settled over the room after they had gone, except for the faint, faint sound that energy makes in machinery that is always at 'on'.

On the giant viewplate, the stars continued to shift positions slightly, as the superbattleship that was out there (and from which the star scene was being broadcast) continued in its orbit around the earth.

From that screen, a voice said suddenly: 'Position now 116-27 angle 52, and all is well.'

VIII

MIDNIGHT came and passed. Then one a.m. . . . and later. On the king-sized bed in the master bedroom of the Lane residence, there was a movement in the darkness. The figure on the far right stirred. Another pause. Then the light over there turned on. It revealed Estelle Lane sitting up.

On his side of the bed, Lane turned over sleepily, opened his eyes, and looked at his wife questioningly. As he saw that she was staring at him accusingly, he also sat up, and said, 'What's the matter?'

'It's a quarter to two,' said the woman in an irritable voice. 'Captain Sennes should have brought Susan home by this time.'

Lane gave her a for-heaven's-sake-is-that-what-you-awakened-me-for glare. He started to slide back under the sheets, except that the expression in *her* face made him think better of it. He remained seated, and he said in a mild, reassuring tone, 'They're probably having a bite to eat after the show.'

It was obviously not a sufficient comment for the woman, that he changed his tactics. He sat all the way up, and said irritably, 'What's the worry about Captain Sennes when you're never concerned about her being out with that gang of young rascals she runs around with?'

'This is a man,' said Estelle.

Lane was scathing. 'You've got it all mixed up,' he said. 'When I was sixteen, about 20 per cent of high school boys got to about 80 per cent of the girls, starting at age fourteen. The other boys were mostly nice, decent kids. Some of them, I know, hoped vaguely that a girl would proposition them, but you and I know that isn't the way it works. Now, here's my point. You can't tell me those 20 per cent of aggressive boys aren't still around, and that 80 per cent girls aren't still vulnerable to them.'

'Men are different,' said Estelle, with determination.

'Men are more discriminating, you mean. The average half-way decent man has learned not to grab at every available woman. It's too hard to shake them loose, once you've got them. And most men discover that early in the romantic part of their life.'

'You seem to know a lot about it,' said Estelle; and for a moment it looked as if his reply had changed the direction of her thought.

'Look, honey' – her husband spoke patiently – 'you know the whole sad story of my experience with women. I told you every unhappy detail before we got married.'

'To hear you describe it, you were the biggest boob who ever came up from the deep,' she said with asperity.

'Where girls and women were concerned, yes,' said Lane. 'And please note: I never *did* get your story of *your* experiences. As I recall it, there was a long silence in that department, whenever the subject came up.'

'Don't try to get off the subject,' said the blonde woman.

The man sat there, and he was visibly in a state of mixed emotions. One emotion that struggled to find a way to be communicated was a desire to point out that it was she, not he, who had gotten off the subject. Another emotion seeking for life of its own was a kind of here-we-go-again anger. But it was the third emotion that won: a sense of helplessness in the face of superior mental footwork.

He said with a sigh, 'I'm sure the captain will look after the daughter of a fleet commander on his first time out with her. Now, go to sleep.'

But it was he who slid down under the sheets, not she. The woman remained in her erect position, and said, 'Just why did you invite Captain Sennes for dinner?' She added as an afterthought, 'So soon after your return.'

'Darling, my having been away doesn't change what goes on at the Space Control building. That place never stops.' He turned on his side facing away from her. His voice was slightly muffled, as he continued, 'All of a sudden – just like that, looking at the guy – I realised that here was a chance for Susan to size up a Real Man, instead of those vicious kids.' He finished, 'I thought, maybe that's the real problem here. The best men are away. Girls and women lose their perspective.'

'I can't quite believe,' said the woman, 'that the thought came to you "just like that".'

When he did not answer, she also was silent for a while. Then she reached over and turned out the light. But as she was starting to slide down under the sheets, she hesitated. Her voice came out of the darkness: 'How long is Captain Sennes grounded?'

Lane's answer was a sleepy mumble. 'Originally,' he said, 'eight to ten weeks. But in view of the uproar over the alien thing, the expedition he was leaving on has been postponed. My guess is it will be cancelled. But he'll be on flight duty in eight weeks, no matter what, I imagine.'

Another pause. The silence was, however, thoroughly alive with a thought. It was the thought that was in the woman's tone as she finally said, drawing out each syllable as if the meaning in the words was just too much, 'E-i-g-h-t – w-e-e-k-s!'

'Go to sleep,' Lane muttered irritably.

After still another pause, there was the sound and vaguely visible movement of the figure on the far right finally and reluctantly going down all the way under the sheets.

There was also a permeating impression that he was not about to be spending her time sleeping.

In the bedroom, approximately fifteen minutes took about an hour of subjective time to go by. The same amount of actual time expended itself outside. At the end of those minutes, a man and a girl were to be seen coming along the night street in front of the Lane residence. For a time they were in the shadowed area between two street lights. But as they emerged into the brightness opposite the Lane gate, the two became recognisable as Susan and the space officer whose photograph John Lane had held in his hands that morning, none other than the handsome Captain Peter Sennes.

As Susan and the captain went through the Lane gate, the Subsurface a block up the street discharged a number of passengers. Two of these, both male figures, started along the street that would presently take them past the Lane residence. At first, in the distance, they looked like men. By the time they were in the shadow region between the lights, something about the way they walked implied youthfulness. As they now emerged into the brightness opposite the gate, they became the familiar figures of Mike Sutter and Lee David.

The two boys were silent, and seemed to be in a thoughtful mood as they walked. It was Mike who casually glanced toward the Lane veranda. For a moment his face was merely receptive. In fact, he actually did the well-known stereotype: he started to look away.

It was the double-take phenomenon, then. He looked again, jerkily this time, and simultaneously caught at Lee's arm, stopping him. From that moment, and for the minute or so that followed, it was all automatic. First, their heads turned and became fixed. Then, more slowly, their bodies moved around until they were standing almost touching. Throughout, they stared at what was happening on the veranda.

Susan and Sennes had reached the point, after some verbal maneuvering by the man, where he was unlocking the door for her. He turned from the task in such a way that he blocked any intent she might have had to simply take the key and slip past him into the house. Truth was, the possibility that she might attempt such a disappearing act was a thought in the man's mind only. Truth was, the erotic implications of Senne's earlier holding remarks had passed completely over the girl's head. And now, she accepted the key from him and presented her right cheek for him to kiss, like the good little jabber that she was.

Without hesitation, Captain Sennes put his arms around her and kissed her on the mouth, firmly but briefly. Susan started to struggle, and then as he removed his lips from hers, she protested in a muffled voice, 'Not my lips . . . my cheek. It's all right on my cheek.' The reason her voice was muffled was because, as she started to resist, the man expertly drew her face against his chest. For him it was the moment he needed to shift his hold on her and obtain a firmer grip on his next maneuver.

'No,' he said, 'not your cheek.' Having spoken, he used the hand that held the back of her head to keep her head steady while, with a quick movement, he again placed his lips against hers. All she could do after that was squirm helplessly. She apparently soon realised that she was completely captured by his overwhelming strength, for she presently merely stood there, her lips passive against his, and waited.

During the almost-minute of that kiss, Mike and Lee at the gate watched with differing emotions. It was all happening too quickly for genuine emotions to break through. What both boys showed at first was shock. At no time during the actual event did Lee indicate jealousy. He simply remained in a physiologic reaction of something akin to dismay. On the other hand, Mike with his quicker responses came out of his freeze state, and lunged at the gate. He was fumbling at the catch when Lee's restraining hand stopped him. Lee made a peremptory gesture, and after a moment Mike nodded. The two boys backed slowly to the right until they were standing behind a tree.

As they did so, on the veranda Captain Sennes relaxed his hold on Susan. She began to fight again, and he thereupon allowed her to break free. As she did so, she gasped, 'Till I'm nineteen, I should only be kissed on my right cheek, and I want you to remember that in future.' She spoke in a severe, censuring tone.

'Lips are much sweeter,' said Sennes.

'Good night,' said Susan firmly.

'You liked it, didn't you?' Sennes persisted.

'It's against outfit rules.' Her voice implied that that was all that needed to be said about the matter.

The man was not to be put off. 'But you did like it?' he said.

There was a pause. 'Well,' said the girl finally in her honest fashion, 'I'm looking forward to when I'm nineteen.'

'You weren't wishing it was someone else kissing you?' Sennes asked.

It was too complicated a thought for Susan. Since she hadn't wanted *anyone* to lip-kiss her, the idea of wanting it to have been *someone else* that kissed her, was outside of her reality. And – just like that – she was confused. The confusion manifested in a sudden shyness. Her body twisted in a girlish gesture of modesty, a muscle effort hitherto unknown to her. Abruptly, she *didn't want to hurt his feelings*, which was also something she had not previously experienced. Thus, in the space of moments, her energy level fell from the height where one couldn't hurt other people with simple, unantagonistic honesty into that negative depth where one tried to withdraw from situations with false responses.

While she was in that abyss, she said, 'I didn't have time to wish.'

47

'Now, you're beginning to sound like a woman,' the man said in an accusing tone.

And *that* was a new thought. 'How do you mean?' Puzzled.

'I mean, playing a game, pretending you don't understand – avoiding a direct answer.'

That was too much twist even for a Susan in a confused state. Since she hadn't had the original feeling attributed to her, the concept that she was now being false about a falseness simply, and abruptly, snapped her back to a semblance of normalcy. Not quite, but almost. 'You want a direct answer?' she said.

The officer hesitated. His experience told him that she was somehow escaping him. He forced a smile. 'I don't like the gleam in your eye,' he said.

And that was false. There was no gleam, no ulterior motive; no concept of what he was talking about. All in a flash he realised that he was losing control of the situation. Because he wasn't quite clear as to what was going wrong, he made a hasty attempt to salvage her for the future. 'Remember,' he said, 'you promised to go with me on a flight Sunday.'

'Cap it,' said jabber Susan Lane. 'If mother says yes.'

Sennes turned away. 'I'll be here at eight.' He headed rapidly down the steps, before she could deny him. ' 'Night,' he flung over his shoulder.

On her part, Susan started to enter the house. In the doorway she seemed to run into an invisible barrier. She actually took a step backward in order to turn and look after the man. The action was as automatic as it was because, in truth, it had no clear thought behind it. The series of madnesses that had been projected at her during those final minutes were still spinning around in her head. And so, she was still shy as she watched Captain Sennes open the gate, step out to the street, and close the gate behind him. He looked up and saw Susan. He waved at her. She returned the wave uncertainly.

The young officer smiled with triumph. Once more he waved, and then in his best military walk paraded off down the street. Since he was magnificently strong, one of the physical marvels who had been selected and trained for the special hazardous work of active flight duty, he made a graceful movement out of every step. He disappeared from Susan's sight behind a high hedge. It was a good exit.

On the porch, Susan stood with a faraway look in her eyes, not really thinking, and not feeling. ' 'Night,' she murmured in such a low voice that only she heard it.

Whereupon, she went inside, and closed the door.

Slowly, Lee and Mike emerged from behind the tree. They stood, then, watching the distant figure of Captain Sennes as he entered the elevator of the monorail. On Lee's face there was finally a tiny suggestion of grief. Mike was grim, but he put his hand on his friend's shoulder. 'Now, you're going to leave this to me, aren't you, Lee?' The older boy did not reply, and Mike's expression and manner indicated that he took the silence as agreement.

At this point, Mike said, 'Here I was thinking that these late monthly district meetings are pretty hard to take; and then we run into an unsuspected situation with one of our members, and maybe they're not so bad after all.'

Again, there was no answer from Lee. 'Let's go,' said Mike. He grabbed the blond boy's arm and pulled at him. Lee went without a word.

Inside the Lane house, the figure on the far right side of the king-size bed slowly changed position. In the almost darkness, it was difficult to make out the difference, but the impression that came up from the alteration in shape was that, suddenly, the woman there had relaxed.

Moments after that – since Susan had already made it into bed in another part of the house in one minute and thirty-eight seconds – the entire Lane household was sound asleep.

IX

NEXT morning . . .

The invisible watcher moved at the pace that a human walks behind Bud Jaeger. The alien child, who maintained the shape of a human boy, did his shuffling walk and appeared to be carrying his books under one arm exactly like the other teenagers. The communication that passed between father and son was brief.

The father said: *We have the impression that the human-manned space fleet in orbit around Earth has been alerted against a possible attack.*

You mean, said the boy, *they know our fleet is out there in the near distance?*

No, was the reply. *Obviously, if they knew we were around or located us, they would attack. What this means is that John Lane has made his report, and the human space authorities are taking no chances.*

Why are you telling me this?

I want you to hear anything Susan Lane says about her father when you are with the outfit. His movements may be the key to our decision. If, for example, he is suddenly placed back aboard his command ship, that could be the signal that they have spotted us.

You have nearly always been present, my father, when I am with the outfit. So you are as aware as I.

Yes, and that will continue where possible. But I cannot enter buildings, and it is my intention to follow John Lane occasionally, and so you will be by yourself. I assure you I shall be absent no oftener that is absolutely necessary.

Very well, said the boy, *I will watch Susan.*

The had come to the school gate, and Bud now entered the campus. His unseen father remained hovering just off the sidewalk and away from the human traffic, but he also was up high enough to avoid any kind of energy conflict with passing vehicles. From this position he watched Bud walk along toward the school steps that would presently take him to that entrance. And he was starting along the road in that direction when he saw Mike Sutter. The alien came back to the gate. Moments later, Mik emerged from the gate and stationed himself outside. It was an unexpected development. The watcher stayed where he was, and waited.

Approximately one minute and a hundred teenagers passed by. At that time, one of the approaching boys suddenly had a familiar look to him. The familiar figure was first only a head among many heads, then a head and shoulders. Still almost hidden by a group of other young people, Lee David approached the gate. He was evidently in deep thought because he did not see Mike until the slender youth stepped out, took his arm, and drew him off to one side. To the invisible watcher there was no longer any doubt. Something different was about to happen.

The fact (of the difference) did not seem to occur to Lee. The blond leader of the Red Cats outfit nodded at Mike, and then said, 'About last night, Mike . . . I've decided to trust Susan. Sack?'

The dark-haired boy shook his head in a slow, grave way. 'It's too late,' he said.

Lee stared at him, blankly at first. In that state, he echoed, 'Too late?'

Mike nodded. He looked unhappy but determined.

For a moment longer, the blankness remained on the older boy's face. Then a rush of color darkened his cheeks and forehead. He said through clenched teeth, 'Damn you, you had no business – ' He broke off. 'I'm the leader of this outfit.'

'I'm sorry, Lee,' said Mike, 'but the outfit is in agreement that where Susan is concerned you can't be trusted completely.'

Lee began furiously, 'But that's – ' He stopped. His eyes narrowed with sudden thought. 'I remember, the other night. You wouldn't push.'

'You broke up that meeting early on account of Susan's dad,' Mike nodded.

'Oh!' The outfit leader gazed off into space, a slightly bitter expression on his face. But the color faded from his cheeks. He seemed to be more thoughtful. 'I'm sorry you didn't push,' he said. 'I let something happen there that we shouldn't have done.'

'You mean,' corrected Mike, 'you did something *you* shouldn't have done.'

'No' – firmly – 'because of my anxiety not to let concern for Susan influence me, I let you – particularly you – judge someone to be a booter before he did anything. And Mr Lane hasn't done anything, Mike.'

'You mean,' Mike flashed, 'he hasn't done anything yet.'

'Mike,' said Lee chidingly, 'that's all that we ever need to know.'

A change had come over the slender youth. His dark eyes misted. He stood there, and it was he, now, who was disturbed.

The blond boy said, 'Sack, Mike?'

A long pause. Finally, in a low voice, Mike said, 'Sack, Lee.'

The older youth seemed to have recovered completely. 'What's the chatter?' he asked.

It was a sober Mike who glanced at his watch. 'I spoke to the outfit,' he said, 'and Marianne is facing Susan' – once more he looked at the time, as if because of his inner turmoil he had already forgotten what he saw the first time – 'just about now!' he finished breathlessly.

The reality wasn't quite like that. Susan was late. She arrived bleary-eyed, and she was in an awful hurry. If she hadn't seen Marianne first, the facing might have been postponed by the inexorable fact that school bells would be ringing in a minute or so. But she did glimpse the smaller girl. Whereupon, she faltered – and waved. And that was the moment. Marianne, her blue eyes bright with urgency, came running.

'Outfit sent me to face you,' she blurted. Having spoken, she burst into tears. 'What kept you?' she sobbed. 'First time I ever faced anybody, and you spoil it by arriving late.'

Because of the tears, it was not exactly a clear communication. Susan stood for a long moment, her body all geared to go toward the near entrance of the school. The fact that she hadn't had

51

enough sleep added its confusion. And now, the mumbled words from Marianne. Yet, suddenly, the meaning came through, and she was startled. 'You're here to face me?' She spoke slowly. 'Whatever for?'

Marianne was in process of gulping back her self-control. But she still glopped her words, as she said. 'I'm to tell you: Stay away from the outfitters today. Just go to your classes. You'll be judged over at Lee's tonight at 7.30.'

The meaning was no longer in doubt, and the taller girl changed color. There was a distinct energy drop visible in the way her body suddenly seemed less alive. But is was like somebody who had been hit hard, and was now angry. Her voice went up half an octave. 'What kind of chatter is this?' she demanded.

'I'm sorry, Susan,' said Marianne in a subdued tone, 'but you were seen.'

Blankness – or at least what looked like blankness. If the first dim awareness of what this might be about was stirring in Susan, she was neverthless struggling against letting that fact through to her consciousness. But the possibility was in her voice as she now, also, said in a subdued voice, 'What do you mean?'

For Marianne, it was the high moment. 'Last night,' she said, and now her voice clear and even loud, 'lip-kissing.'

The incredible. The impossible. The long-after-midnight hidden act for which she was not responsible in the first place. The secret that she had intended to keep secret – because she was innocent . . . Susan swallowed her sense of disaster, yet there was grief in her voice finally as she said, 'B-but he grabbed me.'

Somewhere the bells were buzzing, calling jabbers good and not-so-good to their student duties. But the two girls were totally captured by the intensity of the moment. 'I'm just the one that's facing you,' said Marianne loftily. Yet it was more than that, for she looked up at Susan with wide, fascinated eyes, and said, 'What was it like?'

The blonde girl's attention had gone on to another thought. And so the question really blanked her. 'What?' she said, astonished.

'Lip-kissing,' said the dark-haired girl, her blue eyes wide open and absorbed with *that* thought.

It was not a question to which Susan could give her attention. 'I don't remember,' she said vaguely. Her misty eyes, as blue as Marianne's but shadowed now, fixed on the other girl's face. 'Who saw me?' she asked.

'Mike and Lee.' Because there was no reply, because Susan merely stood there with a kind of cringing look on her face as she considered that meaning, Marianne added, 'Mike says you may not be a jabber anymore.'

The words were like a blow struck at a spirited animal; even if it was sick, it would get up. Susan mentally stood up and defended herself. 'I am, too,' she said, fiercely. And just like that, in a flash, she was angry again. 'Oh, that Mike – wait till I see him. This is ridiculous.'

The rage in her tone alarmed Marianne. 'You leave Mike alone. He's only doing his outfit duty.'

'There's something too much about that jabber,' said Susan furiously. 'I'll bet he turns into a booter when he grows up – just like his father.'

'You have no right to say things like that,' the younger girl shrilled. 'You're just mad 'cause you were caught.'

'I was *not* caught!' yelled Susan.

The sound of her voice was a single, echoing noise on what had become a silent campus. A few late students were hurrying silently, and singly, here and there; but except for that they were alone. Both girls became aware of that reality at the same moment.

'Oh, my goodness!' gasped Marianne.

Susan grabbed her arm, and said, 'Come along!'

She began to run, half dragging Marianne. It quickly became apparent that her companion was as strongly motivated as she, and was fully capable of keeping up with her, and no assistance needed, and so she released the younger girl's arm.

At the top of the steps, the two girls separated. Marianne ran off to the right, and Susan to the left. They entered separate doors, were briefly visible through the transparent plastic. They disappeared simultaneously into a blur of light and shadow inside.

Late that afternoon – after school – while Mike stood by, Bud Jaeger performed his first outfit duty. The object of his ministrations was an eight-year-old boy named Martin Rilby whose mother described how he would go into a wild tantrum whenever he couldn't have his own way. Having graphically described his behavior, the mother left the room, and Bud delivered the outfit lecture on that specific, common behavior of many little boys and girls. Bud completed his indoctrination: 'And if you don't stop, do you know what will happen?'

The tense child, speechless, eyes wide and fascinated, could only shake his head.

'You'll be taken to a room, and locked in; and for a whole hour a recording will be played of you in your last tantrum. That's the first time. If you do it again, it will be an hour and a half.' He broke off. 'The outfit has checked into the way your mother treats you at home, and she's doing perfectly fine. So it's you that has to make the change. Sack?'

The boy was staring at him, round-eyed. Something about that expression alarmed Bud, and he telapathed to his father who was hovering just beyond the window a few feet away: *Could it be, my father, that young children can see me as I am?*

Very young children, probably, was the reply. *But this one is a little old.*

Perhaps the reason the outfits have to deal with him is because he has remained childlike in some way, said Bud.

There was no time for further communication on that level. The boy had crowded up close to him. 'Do you always look that strange?' he asked.

'Martin!' said Bud. 'You also must be courteous.'

The boy backed away. 'I beg your pardon,' he said.

Bud recognised victory, and he was relieved. He continued his indoctrination hastily, 'You're going to have to measure up, Martin. Usually, we don't start raising little boys and girls until they're ten, but in your case we're making a special situation. When you finally get into an outfit, the way you're treated will depend on how you behave now. Sack? . . . Say sack?'

It was the overwhelm. The need to belong to a group. The wanting to be accepted. Martin swallowed hard, and mumbled, 'Sack.'

'Pretty good,' said Mike judiciously, when Bud and he were finally out on the street again. 'But now – Marty is your responsibility. You call his mother. You keep an eye on him . . . And you refer back to me only if you have to carry through on that threat – sack?'

'Sack,' nodded Bud.

X

THE invisible watcher was searching. In the darkness of early evening, he floated up the side of the apartment building. The Red Cat outfit had gone into the elevator; that was all he knew. How far up had they gone? His view through the gleaming plate glass of the entrance doors had not shown the signal light over each elevator, for the reason that the elevators were at a 90° angle to the door. And so he had to trace them with only one bit of information to guide him: that they were not on the first floor, and were therefore on either the second, third or fourth stories.

His guess was . . . fourth floor. Because that – Bud had reported to him – was the view floor. By deduction, since Lee David's father was a fairly high-level space officer, it seemed obvious that the David's would have one of the better apartments. So up to the fourth floor he went, and then began the search. From window to window he darted, pausing only to make the test, the perception probe, that would apprize him that Bud was inside . . . and found him after an indeterminate time – on the fourth floor.

It was unfortunate, then, that the windows were adjusted so that no light emitted through them from inside. And irritating that Bud merely acknowledged his presence, and then ceased his communication. Finally the father could restrain his curiosity no longer.

It is true, my son that I am here primarily as your protector. But I am also interested in the strategy by which outfits operate. He demanded *What are they doing?*

He was aware, then, of those dimly perceived mental processes by which another person showed awareness that he had been derelict of his duty. It was a guilty but excited Bud that replied: *As a courtesy to the Yellow Deer outfit, we're dashing Joe Patton. The Yellow Deer leader, Tom Clanton, is here, to make sure we handle him right.*

But what does it mean – dashing? . . . Baffled.

He's got to convince us. But we keep pushing him away.

He's got to convince you that he won't do something again? What?

While the telepathic dialogue between father and son continued, inside the apartment Mike was saying to Joe. 'My feeling is, you'd sneak off with that slab again if you thought no one would find out.' Having spoken the negation, he gave Joe a hard push toward one of the other boys of the Red Cat outfit.

This time, Joe refused to accept the rejection. He recovered his balance, and, with lips tightening, attacked Mike. His arms flailed. He staggered forward. His movements were so awkward that Mike had no difficulty avoiding him. In fact, he caught at one of the arms as it passed by him, and using it as a lever, propelled Joe toward Albert. Joe flailed at Albert, who ducked under his arms, caught him around the body, and pushed him toward Lee.

All of a sudden, the repeated imbalance, and what was undoubtedly a cumulative dizziness was too much for Joe. He grew angrier, but had less and less control over his movements. He fell, tried twice to get up, and then lay there on the carpet, giggling. 'Honest,' he giggled, 'it won't happen again.'

Tom Clanton, a sandy-haired, husky boy of seventeen, who had been standing off to one side, came forward, and said softly, 'What's funny, Joe?'

And that, also, was too much for Joe. He began to laugh wildly, his body twisted on the floor. His eyes rolled. He roared with what was presently obvious hysteria – became silent from exhaustion; mumbled, 'I just saw myself here, getting dashed because of a slab. That's funny.'

The girl referred to as a slab – Dolores Munroe – made a face as those words were spoken. She was sitting on a chair near the big window. She leaned forward, and stared at Joe on the floor ten feet away. Her voice projected clear and venomous into the silence created by Joe's exhaustion: 'That's typical outfit courtesy. Blame the woman. The Yellow Deer outfit ought to be called the yellow dog outfit.'

'Honest,' said Joe thickly – he seemed to be recovering a little – 'I don't even like her, the way she is now. She used to be a pretty girl, but the sickness inside her shows on her face; and I shouldn't ever have become interested in a girl who had that look on her face; and I knew it. And here I am . . . in trouble with my friends for that. How crazy can you get?'

'Joe,' said Dolores, and her voice trembled with rage, 'you're a stinker.'

Tom Clanton stepped closer to Joe, half bent over him. His voice was steady, as he said, 'Joe, I advise you to pay no attenion to anything that this former jabber says in her present state of mind.'

Joe sat up. The flush was gone from his cheeks and forehead, and there was sincerity in his voice as he said earnestly, 'Honest, jabbers, it won't happen again. I mean it.'

Mike came forward in that quick way of his. Lean-bodied and lean-faced, he stood beside Tom Clanton, and glanced around at the circle of faces. 'What's real bad about this is that Joe fell for the come-on of this slab – ' He made a swift motion toward Dolores. 'Now, he's done her harm.'

Dolores's voice came piercingly from across the room 'The only person who's done me harm is that little phony Susan Lane.'

Susan, who was standing near the door with Marianne, made a face as those words were spoken. But she said nothing.

Mike turned and gazed somberly at Dolores. 'Susan will be judged in a few minutes for what she's done. Then you'll see how a real jabber handles an outfit facing – the same kind that knocked you for a loop.'

Dolores's eyes widened. It was evidently new information to her. She said avidly, 'Susan – judged here tonight. What'd she do?' Her whole body was changing, almost as if she were expanding. There was suddenly delight in the way she held herself: a genuine, vicious joy. 'Hey, this I want to see.'

'It's not a show,' said Lee from where he stood in the circle of Red Cat members. He did not glance at either Dolores or Susan. But he broke rank at this point, walked over to Joe, and helped him to his feet. To Joe, he said, 'You know this isn't personal. We're doing a job for your outfit. You just heard what Mike said. It's true . . . every word. But in my judgement you've proved you're still a jabber.' He glanced back and around. 'Anybody here who doesn't believe that?'

No one spoke. Even Dolores looked straight ahead of her, and could not be bothered to comment. Lee glanced at Tom Clanton. 'Sack, Tom?'

The Yellow Deer leader nodded. 'Sack,' he said. His right hand went out, and caught Joe's arm. 'Come along,' he said.

Except for the opening and closing of the hall door, there was dead silence as the two boys departed. Yet in those minutes the group had broken up. The circle of faces and bodies that had surrounded Joe was scattered. Marianne had been edging toward Mike. Albert had started to follow Lee, and was standing half-turned from what had been the circle. Three other boys had moved just enough so that what had been a pattern was without form. The other two girls, who had been standing on the farther side of Susan, stepped back and leaned against the wall there. Only Bud had remained where he was, near the window.

Lee seemed to be bracing himself. He pressed his lips together, and tightened his shoulders. Moments later, he walked over to Dolores. The girl looked up at him with sullen eyes, but she did not quite look into his eyes. Slightly avoiding his gaze, she said in a defiant tone, 'Don't you dare hit me.'

It was one of those wild, meaningless statements. Lee was visibly pained, and a kind of patient impatience showed in his manner. Mike came over, and said, 'How about recommending the camp for Dolores? You've been holding off on this slab too long.'

Dolores said in a pitying voice. 'You're such a child these days, Mike. You don't seem to realise that I'm practically a woman.'

'If you're a woman,' flashed Mike, 'what are you doing snipping around the edges of the outfits?'

Lee laid a restraining hand on Mike. 'Let me handle this.' He turned to Dolores, said, 'For months you've chosen to be an outsider instead of an outfitter. But, as Mike says, you keep hanging around jabbers. Dolores . . . you've got to accept a bid from an outfit and stop all this foolishness.'

'I'm not joining any outfit,' said Dolores. 'In fact' – she hesitated; even for her it must have been a wild thought, but after a mere moment she made a body gesture of I'll-show-you, and finished airily – 'I may be getting married soon.'

Lee was embarrassed for her. 'Sssshh,' he said He made a placating, dismissing gesture. 'Dolores for you – after Joe – we've finally got to make a deadline. You broke out of our outfit, and so long as you were merely a nuisance to us we could tolerate and hope. But we're responsible for the damage you do to other outfits. So, all right – one week. You've got a week to become a jabber again.'

'What if I don't?' Defiantly. 'And I won't.'

'We call for help. We turn you over. The camp – like Mike said.'

'Still under Mike's thumb, aren't you?' said Dolores sweetly. 'Still echoing his judgements.' She was totally calm again. 'I'll think it over. I'll see how you handle this companion slab of mine over here.' She pointed directly at Susan. 'A fair judgement against her may influence my decision.'

'The two situations are not related,' said Lee curtly. 'Everybody gets his own judgement.'

'I want to hear hers,' said Dolores. Her lips curled cynically.

She had lost her audience. Mike had walked over to Susan. Seeing him there, Lee turned away from Dolores and started across the room. As he came up, Mike was saying, 'Lee and I were returning home from the district meeting when we saw that sailor lip-kissing you.'

Susan said simply, 'He took me by surprise.' There was a tiny bit of emotion in her voice, the barest edge of shame that she could be in such a predicament, of actually being faced by her outfit. 'He was extremely strong. I couldn't move.'

'I kind've believe that,' said Mike, 'but the outfit – all except Lee – thinks you should be placed on probation for a week.'

Susan looked shocked. 'B-but I didn't do anything,' she protested. And then she was silent for a moment. 'What does Lee think?'

'He,' said Mike, 'thinks you didn't do anything.'

'I,' said Lee, who had come up beside his friend, 'would like to point out that Susan has been one of our hardest-working jabbers. This is the first time she's been accused of anything. It's been outfit policy on an actual first offense to have this short probation system. I have a feeling that Mike is arguing for probation because he has got something about me that he won't push out. I don't think Susan should have something against me, against her.'

58

There was silence. Then one of the usually quiet boys, a brown-haired sixteen-year-old, said, 'But what was she doing out with a sailor in the first place?'

'That,' said Lee, 'is an unacceptable question. Jabbers have their own world at their homes. Their relatives, the family friends who come there – none of our business, unless something happens.'

Susan volunteered, almost timidly for a girl of her forth-right nature, 'This sailor is my dad's friend. If mother lets me he wants to take me on a flight Sunday. Is that all right? I was really looking forward to it until he grabbed me. But I cued him on cheek-kissing. I think he heard me.'

Mike was not happy with the prospect of another rendezvous, but he accepted it. 'You're free,' he said curtly. 'Just follow the rules . . . Sack?'

For Susan it was a limited solution. 'Sack,' she said reluctantly. Mike gave her a hard look. 'You'll swallow the probation?'

Susan actually gulped before she answered. 'I think it's unfair,' she said, 'but I'll swallow it.'

'Sack,' said Mike with satisfaction. Whereupon, he twisted on his heel, and went over to Dolores. 'You see,' he said, 'how a real jabber swallows her pride and accepts the judgement of the outfit.'

The rebellious expression on Dolores's face remained unchanged. If anything she became even more contemptuous. 'I'd give a lot to be as simple and pure as you are, Mike,' she said. 'But I guess some of us are just smarter, and see the world as it is.' Her lips tightened. 'You poor victim, letting that phony Susan convince you she's innocent – '

'That's enough!' It was Lee, sharp and hard. He had been standing slightly behind Mike, his face grim. 'Dolores, you use the word phony once more in this group, and you'll be in camp in one hour. We've got our rules. They don't include meaningless words.'

There was a long pause. Many emotions darted briefly into Dolores's eyes and cheeks. Her color changed from olive dark, accentuated by makeup, to a bloodless paleness, and then to a rich, red flush of anger. And yet in the end, she did her overly sweet thing, and said, 'I'll swallow that . . . *from you.*'

Mike interjected quickly. 'Dolores with that much of a start, why don't you swallow all your pride and join an outfit?'

The dark-haired girl stood up. 'That's impossible,' she said, 'for a woman, Mike.' She bowed facetiously. 'Good-bye, Mike. Good-bye, Lee. Good-bye, Marianne . . . ' She went down the line of people, naming everybody but Susan whom she thus pointedly

59

ignored. Having managed another insult, she walked to the hall door, and opened it. In the doorway, she turned, glared at Susan, and said, 'I'll be seeing you on slab row, dear. Welcome to the sisterhood, and remember once a slab, always . . .'

She left the sentence unfinished, and facing about, walked out and closed the door behind her. The silence that remained in the room after she had gone, was broken by Lee. He stepped close to Susan. 'Let me take you home,' he said.

The tall, blonde girl was actually very glad to have the invitation. But for a little while, as she fought off a need to shed a few tears, her manner was aloof. During that time, most of the outfit departed. Mike and Marianne, except for Susan and Lee, the last two to go out, left the door to the corridor open. Susan walked over to the door, but Lee gestured to her to wait.

He thereupon trotted over to a door at the far rear of the big room, knocked on it, and called, 'Mother, we're leaving now.'

Silence.

'Did you hear me, mother?'

'Yes, Lee.' Muffled. 'I'm coming.'

Moments after that the door opened. Mrs David, a tall, attractive, blonde woman in her late thirties or early forties, emerged. She was reading a book, and she closed the door automatically behind her without looking up from the page in front of her. She paid no attention to Lee or Susan but, still reading, walked to a comfortable chair beside a bright light, sank into it and continued to read.

Lee and Susan glanced at each other significantly. Lee shrugged. 'Good night, mother,' he said, 'I'm taking Susan home.'

'Good night, Susan,' said Mrs David without looking up.

' 'Night, Mrs David,' said Susan from the door.

Out in the hall, after Lee had joined her there and closed the door, Susan continued. 'When is your father due home?'

'Another year or so,' was the reply.

'Oh,' said Susan. She was silent as they walked to the nearest elevator. The others had already gone, and so they were alone in the big cage as it went noiselessly down, and the girl asked, 'Are you going to be in the space force, Lee?'

Lee shrugged irritably. 'Now, you know it doesn't work that way,' he said. 'You know as well as I that each generation of officers has been a brand new group. They come volunteering into Spaceport not for a minute suspecting what they're coming to. On the way in, they meet the children of the last generation of officers. And do you know where those children are going, Susan?' His eyes were big and round and humorous as they gazed into hers.

'I can guess,' said Susan.

'They're on their way out, Susan. They don't say anything to the newcomers. They don't want to discourage anybody, and they keep their peace whenever they're outside. But, Susan, do you know that they don't even like to come back for a visit.'

'Isn't there some hope,' said Susan, 'that the outfits will change all that? In fact, haven't they already a little bit?' She added, 'I heard.'

'It's hard to tell,' said Lee, 'what the facts are and what the propaganda. A booter thinks nothing of twisting a truth into a half truth to fit his argument. And I hate to say it but I've heard outfit supporters among adults distort the picture when they're dealing with people who are hostile to outfits.'

'But why lie? What's the point? The outfits are, well, just the outfits – that's all. We exist principally because our fathers have gone off to other stars, and so we had to take care of ourselves; only now we do it in an orderly fashion. It shouldn't amount to anything more than that. But somebody has got it into his head that it will also solve other problems, and I guess they'll be disappointed if that doesn't happen.'

'I guess we'd better start to think about that,' said Lee. 'Or pretty soon there'll be an idea going around that the outfits have failed. This won't be concerning me much longer, because I've only got a year and a month to go before I'm nineteen. But it'll come up more and more if that's what people are expecting. What we've got to promote,' he analysed, 'is what you said. We are what we are: we bring ourselves up through the difficult years. Nothing else. Nothing more.'

The elevator had come to a stop on the ground floor. The door opened, and they emerged from it and walked out into the night beyond the big plate glass doors. Outside, Lee went on, 'All this is true, Susan, except once in a while a girl, a daughter of an officer, marries a particular attractive volunteer, who somehow made her forget which generation she belongs to.'

Susan made an impatient movement with her body. 'If that remark is for my benefit, Lee David,' she said, 'you're no friend of mine.'

'You were the one that brought up the subject,' he retorted. 'Am *I* going to be in the space corps?' He shook his head. 'No, Susan, I am not.'

They walked on into the darkness.

On the street ahead, the unseen watcher had joined Bud Jaeger, who presently turned off onto another street. The father tele-pathed: *As I understand it, it is forbidden for the facial orifice of a jabber to make contact with the same facial orifice of another jabber, or of an adult of the opposite sex – is that correct?*

Yes, was Bud's reply.

Can you explain this to me? Why is this such a serious offense?

Since Bud had as yet no real idea, he changed the subject: *It looks like I'm not going to have the problem with Mr Jaeger that I feared. He arrived home again last night long after midnight. So, if that continues –* He broke off, unhappily. *I'm afraid I pushed that boy, Joe Patton, too hard once when I refused to be convinced. I wonder if he noticed –*

The father ignored the interruption; remained intent, said: *I should tell you, my son, that we were accidentally spotted out in space today. You know how big space is, and how carefully we evaluated which directions their vessels would most likely go. But there, suddenly, was this patrol craft. Naturally, and with reluctance, we had to act. Nobody knows what the repercussions will be, but we may have to end our study of this race suddenly . . . So the sooner you find out why facial orifice contact is a matter of such paramount concern to, apparently, everybody, the better I'll like it. I feel that we have spotted an exceedingly significant behavior . . .*

And that was, substantially, the end of that conversation.

On the street behind them, Lee David had reached the stage with Susan where he could ask: 'What's this about a flight Sunday with Captain Sennes?'

'I still have to get permission,' parried Susan defensively.

XI

SATURDAY. Susan and Estelle sat at the breakfast table. The woman glanced several times at her silent daughter. Susan was nibbling this morning, an action which usually indicated that she wanted something. Her egg was a half-finished yellow curdle on her plate, and her toast sat on the edge leaning over wearily. Estelle drained the final drops of her second cup of coffee, and put the cup down with the pretended finality of a coffee lover who knows that she shouldn't have a third cup. But –

It must have been a recognisable signal from all the years that they had been alone together at mealtimes. For Susan stirred. 'Uh . . . mother,' she said.

The words were just about the only stimulus that the woman had needed. She recognised that the request, whatever it was, was about to be made; and for that she absolutely had to have another cup of coffee. 'One moment, dear,' she said firmly to Susan. Her hand reached from the table's edge to the cup and saucer – grasped it, and held it while her body made all those balancing and other efforts necessary for her to get to her feet, and walked over to the coffee pot, which she always deliberately placed beyond arm's length from the table. There was a passage, then, of a small amount of time as she poured exactly the right amount of the steaming delightful liquid into the cup. Still balancing the now almost brimming cup, she returned to the table, and, still holding it, sat down. Slowly, she lowered her hand, making a perfect all points landing on the table cloth without spilling a drop. She took a deep breath, and said, 'What is it, dear?'

Susan, who always held her breath whenever the coffee ritual took place, sighed with relief as she saw that mission had been accomplished. But the entire hazardous feat had distracted her. She hesitated, and then said. 'Where's dad?'

Estelle was outraged. 'That isn't what you were going to say,' she accused. But she was guilty, and there was a possibility that her addiction to coffee had decided Susan to change her mind. Her next words fought to reinvoke the antestatus quo. She said, 'You've been sitting there with a look of deep thought. Tell me, what's on your mind.'

'But where is he? Is he still in bed?'

Estelle said reluctantly, 'Yes.' She hesitated, then, 'He came in late last night.' Once more the hesitation. Finally, she must have decided that she might as well make a complete transfer of information. She said with a sigh, 'There was some kind of an emergency.'

'Oh!' Some of the color drained from Susan's face, and there was the distinct expression that she saw whatever it was that had happened as a barrier to her own purpose, for she said reluctantly, 'Anyone hurt?'

The woman shrugged. 'I have no idea. I used to be so disturbed by these things that . . . well, your father just stopped telling me.' A pause. 'I doubt if it would bother me now. After ten years I feel very remote from all such details.'

Susan gulped, saw that her moment had come *that* unexpectedly, and said with a rush, 'Then it wouldn't bother you if I went with Captain Sennes tomorrow on a routine flight he has to make outside the atmosphere.'

The request flabbergasted Estelle. The effect was actually as if she had been struck suddenly from behind by an unknown assailant. The result: instant emotion of a highly disturbed kind. She mumbled, 'I don't think I – ' She stopped, and now she was outraged. 'So that's what you've been fidgeting about.' A key word in Susan's announcement belatedly reached her awareness, and she finished her first reaction on a note of helplessness by simply echoing it. 'Routine?' she said.

Susan was experienced in recognising negative signals when she heard them, and she had just heard them. It was clearly a situation that already, in these first seconds, called for the fight of her life. Her voice went up from its normal sweetness to a tone that was distinctly thinner and sharper. 'Look, mother,' she challenged, 'I'm the daughter of one of the heads of Space Control, and it's kind of ridiculous that I've never been up.'

'And I,' said Estelle with color high and voice spirited, 'am the wife of one of the heads of Space Control, and I don't feel at all ridiculous that I've never been up.'

'That's different,' the girl began with equal spirit. But that was as far as her energy could carry her. The hopelessness of defeat was already upon her. Never in the past had a counter-attack from her mother been so quick, so hard hitting, and so uncompromising. Down she went into the darkness of the sadder emotions. 'Aw, gee, mother,' she pleaded. 'Please don't say no. It really is a routine flight. Captain Sennes, being an active flight officer, has to put in so many hours a month even when he's grounded keeping newly built craft in flying condition.'

What does it take for a daughter to shoot down her mother? It happened right there. For ten years Susan had been Estelle's deep love, her darling sweetheart child, substitute for all her emotional needs. It was the begging note in the girl's voice that penetrated as far as sound and feeling can go. The woman sagged onto the table, her chin cupped in her hand. Sitting like that, she made a final attempt to salvage Susan – for that was how she thought of it. She did it by shifting responsibility to what she hoped would be a sturdier shoulder.

'All right, dear – ' she began.

Susan leaped to her feet. 'Oh, mother, thank you.'

'Let me finish!' Estelle spoke stridently. 'You can go if your father gives his permission.'

The final words caught Susan as she was putting one arm around Estelle, and with her head bent to plant a kiss. She still completed the caress squarely on one cheek, but she was slightly disturbed as she straightened. 'Mother,' she said finally, 'I've got outfit duties. So will you be a darling and ask dad?'

'Absolutely not,' the woman said in an adamant tone. Yet a minute later she had wearily yielded to more pleading. And an hour after that there she was presenting Susan's case to a John Lane eating a late breakfast. The way she put it was, 'Susan's argument is that you have no business sending other people into dangerous situations if you're not prepared to send your own daughter.' She finished swiftly. 'I'm just being an honest reporter. I don't agree with a single word of what I have just said.'

'Susan is absolutely right,' said John Lane, after a pause – after he had completed chewing a bite of toast and swallowed it and after his silence had aroused the hope in his wife that the request had evoked in him an outraged resistance.

'Now, don't be so easily persuaded,' yelled Estelle in alarm.

Lane was actually having a hard time to conceal his triumph. For just a moment there flashed into his face and eyes the look of a man whose scheme was working perfectly, and the realisation was elating to him. He said finally in a dismissing tone, 'I'm proud of Susan. Her interest in such a flight tells me she hasn't been totally destroyed by the outfits.' He broke off. 'In case you're wondering, I made a small inquiry yesterday and discovered that outfit members do not become space volunteers. So much for that gang of bums.'

The woman was outraged. 'So much for your informant. An F in statistics for that villain,' she snapped.

'What do you mean?'

'Remember,' she said, 'the kids of space officers *never* volunteered . . . Now, you remember that perfectly well . . . don't you?'

'For heaven's sake, Estelle,' said the man. 'Calm down. Look, all I said was – '

'I heard what you said.' She was almost in tears. 'You talked to another booter, and the two of you went into agreement on a lie. I certainly hope that isn't the kind of reasoning you do, and the kind of facts on which you base your decisions as a commander. I shudder for the fate of the world if that's the kind of logic we're depending on.'

The man froze. The words and their meaning hit too close to reality for comfort. His whole mental universe depended on decisions made about things, and by systematic thoughts, that had no certainties – ever – about them. Military 'science' consisted of a half dozen basic thoughts – no more. The rest was the general's on-the-spot fantasies . . . There was a possibility that he had fantasied wrong in bringing the fleet home as he had done.

Since the wrongness was not yet established, he was able to recover from her deadly onslaught. He managed a shrug, and showed the weary thought that women were dangerous. But also experience told him it was unwise to tell them that. So, now, with these awarenesses firmly fixed again, he said soothingly, 'Honey, relax. This is the space age. Susan really belongs to it, and for a few hours she's accepting that she does. So I'm delighted. Evidently, you don't belong to the space age. I urge you, don't try to slow the march of progress.'

'Look who's talking,' said his wife, scathingly.

'Please,' said John Lane in a pained voice, 'don't compare my opposition to the outfits to – ' He broke off, wearily, 'All right, you don't want Susan to go. If you wish I'll tell her that I was willing but that you said no. And that for the sake of peace in the family I shall have to back you up. Is that what you want?'

The blonde woman was abruptly confronted with the ultimate dilemma of the buck-passer, who had finally got the buck passed back with no other place for it to go. The prospect of having Susan hear those words from her husband was too much. Estelle sighed, and accepted defeat. And said. 'No, I don't want you to tell her that. I counted on you to have the courage to look Susan straight in the eye and say no. I can't do it. So, all right, all right – you win.'

It was the man's turn to sigh. 'I don't know how this got to be my victory,' he said. 'But let me say one more thing only. Tell Susan there'll be a flight warrant waiting for her when she gets to the field tomorrow morning. Will you do that?'

'I will just *love* doing that,' his wife agreed.

XII

AT first it was like getting into any transcontinental passenger jet. Only, in this one, Susan walked from the door a few short steps into the cockpit. There was a single seat in front of a view window – at least it looked like a window. The view was approximately 210°, actually curving back and around the seat on either side. There were safety belts for four persons; and they sat side by side on the single seat. A faint, faint humming sound came from somewhere in the rear. In that sound was a *feel* of power. The awareness of *how much* power did something deep inside Susan. Her eyes widened a little, and she tightened her mouth and pressed her lips together to conceal a lurch of excitement. As she fastened her belt with slightly trembling fingers, she glanced at Captain Sennes who was busy doing the same thing.

And at that moment she was inwardly on the verge of doing something that she didn't notice. Her impulse was to assign to the man the force of the machine. Admiration of the spacecraft kept threatening to transform into worship of the man who could fly it. As if he and the *power* of the ship were in some way an interacting unity.

Silently, he turned toward her; checked her three belts: the one around her waist, the one around her chest, and the one that attached to her helmet. He spoke his first words since they had come aboard. 'Move around. See how flexible everything is. Notice the limits.'

Susan pushed forward, sideways, and raised her head. All three belts had nearly a foot of give in them. She nodded her awareness; and that also was easy. Sennes had leaned back, and was pulling a cushioned microphone down to his mouth from a cradle above. He spoke into it; and she heard not a word but presumed he was talking to Control Tower. It gave her more time to look around. She now saw there was actually two glass sections separated by a foot-wide panel. One was the window with its view vista. The other had the shiny look of a TV tube. But it was a tube as big as the window, except that is curved down under her feet.

Beside her, Sennes was reaching up. This time he drew down a steering wheel, and adjusted it until it was about opposite his stomach. He glanced at Susan with a smile, and pointed at the lower glass. A picture was forming in front of him. It showed their craft from somewhere outside, a profile view. There was the long, wolflike nose, and the streamlined body with its wing and tail built for air flight. As Susan stared at it, the machine she was looking at lifted from the hangar floor, and floated through a roof opening and up into the sky beyond.

Since she felt no movement, she had a momentary sense of disappointment, and she said, 'But I don't feel anything. It is a simulation?' Her gaze came up at that point, and now she saw through the view window that they were above the ground, and still going up. Her view was still of a portion of Spaceport, but also she could already see beyond the river to the farmland beyond. The converging highways, the forests, and, farther away, the mountains. Susan ventured, 'We're nicely airborne.' In one of her jet flights to visit her mother's parents, somebody had said that.

The beautiful man beside her shook his head. 'Spaceborne' smiled. '*Omnivulture* doesn't need air to fly.'

'But it has a wing . . . and a tail.'

'True,' he nodded. 'We do use that for flight steadiness in the atmosphere.'

But Susan was not listening. *'Omivulture!'* she shuddered, belatedly picking up that word.

'It's battle class,' said Sennes.

'What an awful name!'

'But a beautiful machine.'

'It seems awfully easy to fly,' the girl said.

'Well-l-l-ll – ' said the man, doubtfully. For just a few moments, then, his mind's eye looked into the inner workings of the spacecraft. Beginning with the Boarder computer. The Boarder was at the moment 'feeding' off of the Father computer in an underground vault almost directly below. The two computers exchanged a steady stream of information bits, but it was electronically understood between them that the 'Father' provided the sustenance: the Boarder merely ate what was offered. It could fly the ship without an outside source of 'food,' but it never did unless it had to. But there was feedback. What the Boarder fed back was a sort of menu with a rapidly pointing finger, which said in effect: I'll have some of this . . . and this . . . and this. . . .

During the brief period that Captain Sennes mentally reviewed just that one operation, *Omivulture* rose ten thousand feet. Here were fleecy clouds. Through them and above them it soared, as his thought momentarily dwelt on the power that was being monitored so adroitly by the computers. A tiny light of green color flicked on-off rapidly on the panel in front of him, told him that an engineer in the buried vault in the ground had done his duty, looked in at the computer down there, and checked that power was 'norm.' Sennes could almost visualise the engineer glancing at another expert, and saying. 'Jupiter level.' He even fantasied the presence below of an ignorant VIP who in his innocence asked, 'Jupiter level? What does that mean?' And of course the engineer would lazily reply, 'Well, sir, the nuclear power plants on *Omivulture* class are built to lift off Jupiter or Saturn, and could even make a good try at escaping from the sun. It could accelerate to escape velocity but it actually has hovercraft capability and so can just lift away at any speed and simply fly by continuous nuclear thrust from any planet almost as if gravity does not exist.'

'Hey!' said the visitor, impressed – that was the way Sennes pictured it.

Above the clouds it had been blue for many miles. But those miles were soon behind and below. The sky became dark, and then black. On the panel another light flickered. Sennes said to Susan, 'Boarder just switched over to Mother.'

The girl stared at him. 'What does that mean?' she asked.

'Well-l-l-ll – ' said Sennes. And stopped as the letters 'Ac' glowed for a second from the panel. In his mind's eye, he now visualised the engineer in the space station which maintained a continuous orbit at 17,500-odd miles above Spaceport. It was common in these stations to have students under practical instruction. So what the man pictured was the engineer who had just acknowledged acceptance of Boarder by the Mother computer of the station, turning to the class, and saying, 'Mother has picked up an *Omnivulture* Boarder. Who can explain what that means?'

'Well, sir,' – after a pause, from one student – 'as I understand it, these Boarder computers always board near or equivalent. They're not loyal to any particular parent, and in fact are willing to eat at any table in their code frame. As I decode those figures on that panel, this Boarder was feeding off a Father below, but after it came up through the atmosphere it switched to Mother up here for its food. And though Mother is thousands of miles farther away in terms of distance, the thick atmosphere creates interference that in terms of reception puts Father farther away. The vacuum of space, in effect, constitutes the equivalent of less distance.'

'And why do we call the computer on the ground a Father, and the one up here a Mother?'

'The analogy' – another student – 'sees the woman as a satellite revolving around the male planet.'

The little mental drama ran its course through Sennes's mind. He said to Susan, 'Well, I suppose it is fairly simple. Right now Mother is guiding us. If we get out of her range, Boarder can take over. If something happens to Boarder, then I'm called in. Meanwhile, I supervise the galaxy.'

'What does *that* mean?'

'Means' – he grinned – 'I can talk to a potential girl friend.'

She was sixteen years old. A little bit of child was still in her body, a lot in her mind. She had never been motivated to want to be older than she was. She sat there in the front of a battle monster within feet of the vacuum of space. The view was of infinity, a black heaven that was bright with points of life everywhere. It was a fabulous moment in her life; and she was grateful to this masterful man for being willing to take the time to bring her. But she was nobody's girl friend. Very precisely, she began to explain these things to him; finished, 'I can be a moocher,' she said. 'But I've already got someone I'm moocher to. That's something Dolores never understood. She thought she was Lee's girl friend. Marianne is a little bit like that, too, with Mike. Stopping being a moocher is no shock. Losing a boy friend is like being divorced. So' – she looked at Sennes with an appealing smile – 'there you have it. Is it all right?'

He was twenty-eight years old, and he had simple answers for jabbers, designed to jar them out of their outfit brainwashing. 'Will you marry me, Susan?' he said in his most earnest voice. During the minutes that followed, he told a very silent girl about himself. Flight training at nineteen. Selection for special duty. Then after two years, disgust with space service. So for a year, asteroid mining, Boredom. As a result back to the service with no further regrets. 'But I need exactly and precisely you for my nest,' he said.

Whereupon, he moved over in the seat the full foot that the safety belt allowed him. And he put out his arm, slipped it neatly between her waist and the seat, and with irresistible strength drew her up against him. 'You see,' he said, 'this is really a love seat.'

It was quite uncomfortable. The pressure that the belts exerted pulled at their heads and bodies. In fact, even if Susan had wanted to be held, it was no fun. A strain, a struggle, a feeling of being twisted, and a sense of excessive muscle pull. Susan said with difficulty, 'I think you ought to let me snap back into my proper position.'

'In a moment,' said the man good-humoredly. During that moment he brought his other arm around, and with his hand caught her head. As he pulled it just a little closer, he leaned over and put his cheek against hers. 'You see,' he said 'jabber level affection is possible.'

'Mooching,' said Susan. 'Cheek to cheek. But I'm not your moocher, Captain Sennes. So let me go, please.'

Throughout, the young officer had been watching the panel. Now, a light was flashing on it. And so he was actually in something of a hurry to release her. But he was careful. First, he warned her: 'I am going to let you go, so be prepared. Brace yourself.' Her body stiffened. She pushed against the belts. But he kept his arm around her as he eased her back to her proper place. Next, he eased himself to his position. Then he said, 'We're approaching Tombaugh, and will be landing in two minutes. Tombaugh, as you know, is a third of a mile thick, big enough to have a Father computer. So a capable Father is now guiding *Omnivulture*.'

'I'm beginning to love *Omnivulture*,' said Susan. 'But I still think her name is horrible.'

'You'll have a different thought,' was the man's reply, 'if he ever tangles with the enemy. *Omnivulture*, you see, has a real low-grade mission in the event of armed hostilities. She goes right down to where the garbage is, and eats it up.'

70

The graphic description seemed to reach the girl. Her expression changed. She looked at him and shook her head, and it was the action of somebody who had suddenly become disturbed. As if she were visualising what he was describing, the deadly fighting tactic that his words implied. 'You mean,' Susan said slowly, 'you have to go in close and attack?'

Sennes gave her a swift glance with his almost jet black eyes. Then turned away rapidly to hide his momentary unconcealed triumph. Her expression seemed to imply that he had made the real kill and achieved the real purpose of this journey. A jabber's heart had been captured, or at least gently stabbed. The man said lightly, 'Well, Boarder and I go in close, and *Omnivulture* does the rest.'

'B-But you could get killed?' she protested faintly.

The officer's face remained serene. But it was not a moment when he could give further attention to the girl. The moonlet, Tombaugh, was visible by its man-built domes in the near darkness ahead. The plastic domes reflected earthlight, not brilliantly but sufficiently well for visual recognition. 'Since you've never been up,' he said to Susan, 'I want you to notice how difficult it is to see Tombaugh itself. Its surface is virtually nonreflective. It looks like the darkness of space. Notice?'

Susan leaned forward to peer into the darkness through the view window. *Omnivulture* had evidently slowed for a landing; and so the size of what they were coming to was a sudden awareness for her. Abruptly, *something* between the dome lights suggested its presence. A massive something. She gasped, cringed, shrank. But the seconds went by, and all that happened was – a door opened. At first it looked like a toy door. It grew larger. Then it also took on hugeness. It became the entrance to a vast airlock into which *Omnivulture* floated on spaceborne engines, and lightly settled to a concrete floor. The opening through which they had come was visible on the lower 'glass'. The picture showed the doors closing. Sennes made a cautioning gesture at the girl, but he did not look at her. He was watching the panel. A flight flickered on it, and he nodded. In front of them a door began to open. It was the entrance into the main part of the hollowed-out interior, and *Omnivulture* rolled forward into the hangar that was revealed to their gazes.

'Here we are,' Sennes said. His fingers grasped the wheel he had drawn down in front of his stomach just before take-off, and which he had not touched again until this instant. Now he grasped it and pushed it up above his head. 'Forty-three thousand miles in thirty-eight minutes,' he said with satisfaction. 'Not bad. Our top speed was slightly over fifteen hundred miles a minute.'

'But I scarcely felt *anything*,' said Susan.

'Thank Boarder for that,' he said. He was working on his safety belts with practiced fingers, and had all of his off as she removed the one around her waist. 'Let me help you with the other two,' he said. He undid them, and then leaned toward her face and kissed her lightly on the cheek within half an inch of her mouth. The girl started to pull away, but he had her arm, and said, 'Just a minute, that's on your cheek, not on your lips.'

'Are you saying good night or good-bye?' she asked in a severe tone.

'No, of course not. Neither.'

'Outfitters get to kiss only when they're separating. It's a good-bye thing.'

'This is a special type of good-bye,' said Sennes lightly. 'We're saying good-bye for a few hours to *Omnivulture*. We'll now have lunch, see some shows, then have dinner, and then maybe an evening show. After that we fly home, but by then we'll be on the other side of earth and it will take nearly an hour to return to Spaceport.' He paused 'Sack?'

She nodded. Her cheeks puffed a little from the emotion she was holding in. It prevented her from speaking. Finally, she managed to gulp, 'I'm not really dressed for all those things.'

'Nobody is, here,' said the young officer, reassuringly. He smiled. 'Better prepare for a little acclamation when they hear who you're the daughter of.'

Susan tightened her lips. 'Jabbers are not allowed,' she said in her severest tone, 'to bulge on the strength of what their parents have done.'

The man grinned. 'C'mon, now, admit it. You're a little proud, aren' you, of the old booter?'

Susan gave him a searching look. 'How come you're so sack on jabber chatter. I thought that was after your time.'

Sennes stiffened slightly. They were out of the long, sinister-looking machine now, and standing on the concrete. To divert attention from himself, he pointed off to his left. 'This way,' he said. As they walked, he said, 'You know the story of this moonlet, don't you?'

Susan shrugged apathetically. 'It's hard to avoid. The schools cram us with space stuff. It's such a waste. Nobody's going. Space is for outsiders from the real world. You know that. That's where you came from, isn't it – the real world?'

She could evidently let the subject go with little more than a dismissing shrug. But Sennes's mind did not work that way. His memory came by pictures, and he now carefully explained this to the girl. He finished, 'I've brought the subject up, and so according to my training I must now let the entire picture that's in my mind run its course. Is that all right?'

'What picture?' Susan asked, astonished.

'Tombaugh.' He was disgusted. 'You mean, you've already forgotten?'

'Oh, that!' said Susan. She made a gesture of indifference. 'Go ahead. Do what you have to. Don't mind me.'

It was not an ideal environment. But at least she stood silent . . . His visualised scene on Tombaugh accordingly went dutifully back to the pages of a book he had read in his student days. Mentally, he reread the paragraphs involved, of how a Professor Clyde Tombaugh, an astronomer (discoverer of the planet, Pluto), became convinced that earth had in its long history captured a train of meteorites ranging perhaps as large as half a mile in diameter. He called these predicted earth-orbiting bodies, moonlets. And he spent years vainly searching the heavens trying to locate the elusive satellites. Naturally, after Man moved out into space and discovered a number of moonlets, the largest was named . . . Tombaugh!

XIII

THE phone rang shortly before nine, and a jittery Estelle grabbed it off the hook.

'Mother,' said Susan's voice into her ear. 'We're just leaving Tombaugh. Peter says he'll have me home by ten.'

The woman formed the name, Peter, with her lips, but did not speak it. She raised her eyebrows, and obviously regarded the use of the first name of Captain Seenes as a significant development. However, all she said was, 'I'll be waiting?'

'Is dad home?'

'Not yet.'

'Has anyone called?'

'A girl. But she didn't give her name.'

'Sack. I'll see you, mom.'

There was the click of disconnection. The blonde woman replaced the receiver, and sat there with the look of someone whose stress-filled day was not yet over. Abruptly, she moaned aloud, 'Just *leaving!*' With that, she slumped down on the settee, and sagged there, eyes closed. Presently, a thought seemed to strike her. Eyes flicked open. Hand grabbed at phone, button-pressed a number. Waited as the ringing sound came out of the receiver. At last, the reply: her husband's voice.

She told him what Susan had said, and then asked, 'Where is Tombaugh right now?'

'On the other side of the planet. But don't worry. *Omnivulture* can bring them home in the time named.'

'Omni – who?'

'Darling,' he said in a tense voice, 'I can't talk to you right now. I'm terribly tied up.'

After she had hung up, John Lane put the receiver down; then he turned to face once again the members of the commission with whom he had been in continuous session for nearly eight hours. 'That was my wife,' he told the silent group. 'She is worried about our daughter, who went to the moonlet for the day with an active flight officer. Gentlemen, in listening to the disturbance in her voice over *just that*, I have decided that I shall vote against any publicity on this mysterious destruction of one of our scouting vessels. *My* feeling is that some time this week after we have verified what happened out there, if it is indeed the enemy, then I shall quietly take the fleet and attack. But absolutely no advance warning to anybody. I think a good portion of the population of this planet would go insane if they thought even once that an alien fleet may be out there on the other side of the Pluto-Neptune orbit. As you gentlemen may know, Pluto in its oval orbit will for some decades be closer to earth than Neptune.'

At the Lane home, Estelle had barely replaced her receiver when the phone rang. It was a familiar girl's voice at the other end. 'Have you heard from Susan yet?'

'She'll be home at ten,' the woman replied. 'Was it you that phoned earlier?'

'Yes. I'll try again right after ten.' Hastily: 'Good-bye.' The hang-up sound was clear and loud. Estelle shrugged, and spoke in the general direction of the ceiling. 'That's all we need, a mystery.'

Three blocks away, having replaced the receiver, Dolores Munroe emerged from the phone booth, with an expression on her face of a cat that has just caught and gobbled the mouse. Her eyes were cynical, her lips curled with anticipatory triumph even greater than the victory provided her by the information she had achieved from Susan's mother. She walked across the street into a coffee shop, and there was an insolent confidence in the way she held her body.

By 9:20, she was too jittery to stay in the coffee shop any longer. At that time she left the shop and walked rapidly along a side street that in less than ten minutes brought her to the Lane home. Four times during the next twenty-three minutes she changed her hiding place opposite the gate, in the end retreating behind a tree across the street which was lined up with the tree where Mike and Lee had gone to avoid Captain Sennes . . . a few days before.

It was exactly seven minutes to ten when the figure of Peter Sennes and Susan emerged from the Subsurface and walked along to the gate of the Lane home. Or at least, from where Dolores watched, they disappeared behind the tree that concealed the gate from her view. And she *guessed* that they were in the act of going through the gate. Swiftly, she came out from behind her own tree, and hurried to the other one. Moments after that she was peering around the hole, and was able to see the man and the girl on the veranda.

Up there Sennes was unlocking the front door. He turned and handed the key to Susan, and said, 'You've made it clear enough all day. So this is good-bye.'

Susan offered him her cheek. He pecked at it gently. As he did so, her face changed. She drew back, startled. 'Good-bye? You mean good night?' she said.

The man smiled faintly, shook his head. 'I'm a man, Susan,' he said. 'And a man wants a woman. Today, I've discovered that you're a jabber to the bitter end.'

'But,' Susan protested, 'I've enjoyed being with you. It's so – different. Why, that's another world out there when you go along with somebody like you.'

She was not looking directly at him; and so he flicked his gaze over her face to make sure that she was indeed reacting correctly. And then he said gently, 'Thanks, Susan. I appreciate the compliment. But I've only got a few weeks left of my leave. Best thing is for me to forget you as quickly as I can. Perhaps if I come back safely . . . you'll be older. Then it can mean something.'

Having spoken, he again glanced at her quickly. And there was no question. This girl was now disturbed. She touched his arm with a fluttering motion, as if to reassure him. The action was involuntary, which Sennes noticed. It was the signal he had been awaiting. Without further hesitation, he took her firmly in his arms. 'Now, do I get a good-bye kiss?' he asked. Without pausing for her to say to him yes or no, he kissed her on the lips.

And *that* was Dolores's moment. She walked from behind the tree with a loud clicking of her heels and, pausing at the gate, called out, 'Phony!'

On the veranda, the man released the girl. As they both looked

75

toward the gate, Dolores waved derisively, and walked, head high, off down the street. Sennes glanced back at Susan, puzzled. Saw on her face, shock. 'What was all that?' he asked.

'That's Dolores. She hates me. She'll report to my outfit that she saw me being lip-kissed.'

'Oh!' It was an unexpected development. The man was briefly nonplussed. But after a moment he saw how what had happened could work in his favor. He caught the stunned girl's arm, urged her toward the open door. 'You go inside,' he said. 'I'll catch Dolores. I'll speak to her.'

Without waiting for Susan to reply, he went down the steps at one leap. He did not pause to open the gate – simply hurtled the fence with the total ease of perfect physical condition. Dolores, hearing the rapid footsteps behind her, glanced back. Seeing who was coming, and at what speed, she became frightened, and began to run. Sennes called softly from the near distance behind her, 'I'm not going to hurt you. I just want to talk to you.' His tone was reassuring, and besides the girl was already having second thoughts. Her expression changed to a more seductive shaping of eyes and lips. She stopped, and as he came up, she said in her worldliest voice, 'So you're Susan's sailor?'

During the brief silence that followed, the two sophisticates sized each other up. Sennes said finally, 'I didn't realise I was running after such a prize package.' He now shrugged aside what she had said. 'Susan? That's over. I said good-bye to her tonight for good.'

Dolores had her cool back completely. She gave him her Utter Disbelief look together with faint cynical smile. 'It seemed more like an affectionate good night,' she said, significantly.

'It never was anything. Which is why I made it good-bye. So I hope you'll forget what you saw.'

He sounded the faintest bit anxious, and the sullen little brunette showed by the tilt of her shoulder that she considered that negotiation time had arrived. She said airily, 'I remember or forget things, depending on the way I feel.'

Sennes persisted. 'I would like you to feel like forgetting it,' he said.

Dolores's immediate answer was to turn away from him and start walking along the street. When she had gone only a few steps, she looked back in simulated surprise and said, 'Aren't you coming?'

It was an unnecessary question. The man had made up his mind – which is all that it ever took with him. In a moment he was beside her. Tentatively, he took her arm. When she did not pull away, he tightened this grip. 'You're a very beautiful girl,' he said.

'How do I rate beside Susan?' she asked.

'It all depends. Are you the unapproachable type of beauty, too?'

It was an attemp to down-rate the value of what she had seen, and Dolores wasn't having any. 'Oh, come now,' she said. 'Susan didn't look unapproachable.'

'I surprised her,' said the experienced male beside her. He himself did not literally regard the statement as true. He had his own understanding of why girls could be surprised. He finished, now, honestly, in a sincere tone, 'From Susan's point of view, it was surprise.'

The girl beside him had a short attention span when it came to Susan Lane. And suddenly the moment of disinterest was upon her. Once more, she was her seductive best. 'You don't look like the type that surprises girls. You look steady . . . and honest and aboveboard.'

'I think,' said Sennes softly, 'we're beginning to understand each other.' Having spoken, he swung around in front of her, and in a continuation of the move drew Dolores into his arms and lip-kissed her. He drew back presently, and gazing down into the sultry eyes of the girl, said lightly, 'See how surprising it can be.'

Dolores, who had not resisted for a single instant, but being after all only a few kilominutes away from having been a good little jabber, herself, was breathless. In her brief months of total abandon, she had never had a man of this age and particularly one so handsome. She gasped, 'I guess we do understand each other.' It was a remark that merited another and longer kiss, and the officer was the man who could recognise that. This time when he drew away, Dolores said, 'If I don't tell on Susan, you'll scrap her for me?'

'The quieter you are,' was the reply, 'the higher we'll fly. After all, she's my boss's daughter. I don't want him mad.'

The dark-haired girl was not looking at him. Her expression was thoughtful, and when she spoke it was partly to him and partly to herself. 'If I were to report her, she'd probably talk herself out of it anyway, and then if anyone saw me with you, they'd think Susan and I were playing games. So, then, maybe they wouldn't believe me.'

Sennes shook his head wonderingly. 'Are you always this complicated?'

Dolores was slightly defensive. 'You gotta figure things,' she said. 'The outfits just go by what they see.'

Her eyes were still slightly narrowed, and she was clearly still

77

in process of figuring, and when he kissed her once more. And, now, when they drew apart, they were both breathless. Sennes said, 'Look, honey . . . all I want to know is, have we just made a bargain?'

The beautiful, sullen face was flushed. For the moment, all memory of Susan was wiped away from it. She was caught in the passion of man-woman stuff. Even the sophistication was gone from her. 'Yes,' she whispered, and it was a strangely pure sound. Suddenly, her whole body trusted him, and even begged him a little to treat it tenderly. Which, of course, he would do in his fashion.

Arms around each other they walked rapidly to the monorail, and presently disappeared into it.

In the Lane house, Susan was fidgety all the time that she described the day to her mother. Presently, Estelle – who was genuinely weary from her long anxious day – stood up, kissed Susan good night. 'Your father won't be home till late again,' she said. 'So it's bedtime.'

'I'll be along in a minute,' said the girl. 'I want a drink.' She thereupon made a thing out of the drink, and when she returned to the living room discovered that her mother had indeed gone off. Susan headed for the phone, and pushed the buttons that, moments later, produced the buzzing sound in the receiver, of a distant phone ringing. Apruptly there was a click, and Mike's voice said, 'Hello.'

'Mike . . . Susan. Since you have your own phone, I thought I'd take the chance you were still up.'

Mike said, 'Glad you called. We've got an emergency. Nothing for you to do, but you should be alerted. The fellows are going over to help Bud Jaeger against his father.'

'Right now?'

'Now. Now, what was it you wanted to say?'

It was no longer an ideal moment, but the unhappy girl braced herself, and said it anyway. 'I have to tell you something, Mike,' she confessed. 'Tonight, when I came home, Captain Sennes lip-kissed me good-bye. It really was good-bye.'

There was a long pause at the other end. Then: 'Sack,' said Mike.

A click, as he hung up.

XIV

IN an elegant house not too far from where the Lanes lived, a man and a woman had gone to bed early and were sound asleep – as their phone rang. The man was evidently in the fourth (deep) stage of sleep, for it was the woman who finally groped for the receiver on the bedside table between the twin beds. She murmured an acknowledgement of the call, then listened for a long moment, and finally turned on the light. Which revealed her as being a rather pleasant-looking woman in her mid-thirties. It was impossible at this stage to make out the appearance of the man, because he was lying with his back to the light and his head was half-nestled in the sheet and the blanket.

By the time these facts became apparent, the woman had crawled out of her bed and was over at the other one shaking the man. It required several firm shoves, but finally he blinked and sat up. She watched him closely, and when she saw the light of reason begin to manifest in his face – which was that of a fairly good-looking man about forty – she said, 'Arthur, you're wanted as a witness for the outfit you sponsor.'

The man rubbed his eyes. Then he picked up his watch and looked at it. What he saw seemed to astonish him, for he said, 'At this hour! Who's on the phone?'

'Lee David.'

'Oh – Lee.' He was instantly more alert. His legs swung out from under the covers. He reached for and lifted the receiver with sudden purposefulness. Spoke into it in a firm voice: 'What is it?' Pause. 'And what is the address?' His wife had pen and paper for him at this point. He accepted the pen from her, and wrote on the paper while she held it. Finally: 'Listen, Lee, I've got to get my clothes on. But I should be over in ten minutes. Meanwhile, do what's necessary to protect the boy . . . Bud, what did you say his name was? . . . Sack, too.' He replaced the receiver, climbed to his feet, and headed for the bathroom door.

As it developed, it took him longer to get dressed than he had estimated. It was actually almost ten minutes before he finally got out of the house.

The invisible watcher made his jump over to the Jaeger house after his longest absence of the day, and found the male members of the Red Cat outfit were milling around in front of the gate.

Bud was there with them.

The observer noted that the door of the Jaeger house was closed, but the veranda and inside lights were on. However, it was difficult to determine what was going on inside.

What happened, son? asked the father anxiously.

Before answering, Bud shuffled casually closer – away from the gate. Then: *Mr Jaeger stayed home tonight, and he seemed to be sober for a change. So he noticed my outfit badge for the first time. He got mad, and started to beat me up. That alarmed his wife – who, as I've told you, knows what I've been doing – and she called the outfit. So the confrontation now has to take place. Which is too bad, because it really wasn't a difficult situation. However, he's gone off to the corner bar, and we're going over there to face him.*

I'm sorry I wasn't here to help you, apologised his father.

It really wasn't serious, said the son. *He hit me three times, and each time struck the hard – you know. It nearly broke his knuckles, so he stopped. Where were you?*

I've been jumping between the Lane home and the Desmond Reid home, with an occasional glance at the various takeoff hangars. We have a feeling important decisions are being made, and we should know where Lane, particularly, is every minute of the next few days. I thought you were safe in your room at home.

The telepathic communication ended as the observer saw that Lee David was coming along the street toward the little group of boys. He realised that the identity of the approaching figure was not as apparent to the others as to him, with his almost perfect night vision. They heard the rapid footsteps, and they peered into the shadows of the street in that direction. Suddenly, they also recognised who it was, for there was relief. Moments later, Lee joined them, and said, 'Bud, you stay here. And when Mr Arthur Laurieux our witness, arrives, tell him where we've gone. Sack, Bud?'

'You mean, I can't go along?' The boy sounded disgruntled. 'I wanna see what you do.'

'Where possible,' said Lee, obviously quoting, for his voice changed, 'outfit members refrain from facing a parent in front of his children. Sack?'

'Sack.' Bud spoke reluctantly.

The blond leader of the Red Cats turned to the youthful outfitters. 'Come on, jabbers.' Without any additional comment, he started forward past Bud. Moments later, the other boys were also in motion. The group made a long, thin line on the sidewalk. The sound of their footsteps faded rapidly.

When they had gone, Bud telepathed to his father: *Why don't you follow them, and tell me afterwards what they did?*

The invisible being there a few feet above the ground, in effect, shook his head . . . *Not yet,* he replied. *Please be aware:* the crisis is here. *My only purpose with you is to protect you until a decision is made about your espionage mission on this planet. Except for protecting you, my principal task is to keep a watch on Lane. He is deemed to be a key figure, and his movements significant. So, wait here while I go to the Lane home and watch who comes on the next subsurface – they run every fifteen minutes – but sometimes it takes two and even three elevator loads to bring up all the passengers. I have to make sure that Lane is or is not on one of those loads. That takes about three minutes. And I usually allow a minute before and one after to take account of possible variations or emergency situations in the monorail schedule. It will therefore be five minutes before I can be over at the bar, and observe the developments there.*

Be sure to go as soon as you can, said his son. *Because I'm going to have to live with that man these next few days of the crisis period. Is that not so?*

It is so. And I shall do my best, replied the father.

Since in his invisible state he was only a projected image, he made the leap (as always) at the speed of thought. He remained his intended five minutes . . . still no Lane . . . and then he switched himself over to the street corner, near which was located the cocktail lounge that was a Len Jaeger hangout.

Though the time had seemed long to the unseen alien, he found that the boys had arrived at the bar only a minute before. And that Mike Sutter, with big Albert trailing him, had just gone into the building to ask Jaeger to step outside and talk to the outfit. He saw that all the boys were tense, but they were also determined. It was one of the quieter boys who must have voiced what was in everybody's mind. He said, 'I hope Mr Jaeger isn't giving Mike a hard time.' Unfortunately, that was exactly what was happening.

Mike, on entering, had found himself in a vestibule which, as he walked slowly forward trying to accustom his eyes to the dim light, opened into a typical bar situation with an electronic synthesiser and its craftsman at the far end. The music from the synthesiser was loud, and had everybody's attention. Mike was thus able to walk the fifteen or so feet to the table where Jaeger was sitting with another bar habitué.

Stationing himself about five feet from the table, Mike waited until the music stopped. Then he called out, 'Mr Jaeger.' His was a youth's voice but with a man's courage in it. More impor-

6   81

tant, the words were spoken in a peremptory tone. What happened, then, was in a way too bad. Jaeger was taken by surprise, and he did a degrading thing. Somehow, the tone must have regressed him. He clearly took it for granted that he was in the presence of a superior, for he jerked in his chair, tried to get up, was in too awkward a position to do so, slumped back. But his body was at a kind of attention, as he uttered the words that ruined him, 'Yes, sir. What is it, sir?'

At that moment . . . his eyes focused on Mike. And now, when it was too late, he realised that this was the person who had addressed him. Confusion. Understanding. Rage! Such a great rage that his hulking body stiffened again, and froze there while Mike said, 'Mr Jaeger, the Red Cat outfit is outside, and respectfully requests that you come out and let us talk to you about your son, Bud.'

The words were visibly received as a new thought. Jaeger's bloodshot blue eyes narrowed – and shifted – a little. An anxiety reaction. But there was too much anger in the man, too much mortification, for fear to make much headway. Yet the two emotions produced a temporary stability. Like a transuranic element with a half-life of a few seconds, this rough-mannered male human at last made his effort to deal with what had begun as a disgracing startled reaction.

And so, he leaned back in his chair like someone who had got his cool in hand. And he said above the music, which had started again: 'Are you talking to me – kid?' The question was in its entirety meant to lull. Because, having uttered it, he launched himself out of the chair at Mike.

Perhaps, if it had been brighter in the dim lit room, and faces thereby more clearly visible, Jaeger would have noticed that Mike was no ordinary boy. Would have noticed that he was being watched from narrowed, alert eyes – and noticed that strong, wiry body. But it was not light enough. Or very possibly Len Jaeger was not, and never would be, able to appreciate the hopelessness of such an attack. Whatever the reason, he now experienced his second disaster.

When he got to where Mike had been, Mike wasn't there. Worse, the man's awkward body was so geared to make the seizure that when there was nothing in that space to hold onto – he lost his balance. Fell. Fell with such force that if he had been liquid, he would have splashed all over the room. As it was, he sort of – splattered. And it was not funny. It was a badly hurt Jaeger who fumbled dazedly to his feet, and in a condition of total berserkness charged after Mike. The youth had retreated to the vestibule entrance. Now, seeing the insane creature that was lumbering toward him, he gestured at Albert to open the door to the outside. Albert, who had been waiting right there, promptly did so.

It was not Jaeger's day, evening, or night. For him it was already a quarter to midnight, in fact. And at this late, late moment, he had a memory lapse. There was a sign beside the door, which read, STEP UP. Undoubtedly, he had seen, and obeyed, that admonition on his previous visits to this cocktail lounge. Yet, now, he neither saw the sign, nor remembered that it was there. O why?

Disaster . . . He tripped. He landed on his hands and knees on the concrete of the sidewalk beyond. It was a crash landing of a kind that can shake a man for days. Coming on top of what had already happened, it was too much. Twice, he tried to get up. He couldn't. He sank down on the sidewalk, and lay there in a condition of partial unconsciousness.

A small crowd was gathering. The outfitters who had waited outside, were bewildered. Mike hastened to Lee, explained quickly what had happened, and said, 'We'd better call an ambulance.'

At this point, Mr Laurieux and Bud arrived; and it was the man who phoned for the ambulance. In such a specialised city as Spaceport, with its great concentration of mechanical and energy assists to an enormous space program, the rescue services were tensely alert. The ambulance was there in four minutes.

Jaeger was beginning to stir, but not enough. He was expertly put onto a stretcher, loaded into the ambulance, and carried off into that temporary oblivion know as an emergency hospital. As these events progressed, Arthur Laurieux questioned people in the bar; and since no one had as yet considered the implications of the event, those who had witnessed the debacle sort of grinned as individuals tend to when someone slips on ice and nearly spills out his brains, and they told what had happened – and laughed at the moments of greatest calamity.

When he had the facts, the man took Lee and Mike with him; and the three went to one of the authorised substations of Outfit Central, and filed a report. In the report, Laurieux recommended that a charge of intent to harm be prepared against Jaeger – since his flying attack at Mike was clearly intended to capture with the obvious purpose of striking and hurting.

Such details required time. So it was not until after one a.m. that Mr Arthur Laurieux arrived back in the bedroom, undressed, and crawled back into his bed. His wife stirred as he turned out the light. 'What happened?' she asked, from the darkness across from him.

'You wouldn't believe me if I told you,' answered her husband.

'But I can sum the consequences up in one word: nothing.'

'Two hours of nothing?' she said incredulously.

'Nothing,' he said. But the word had a slight snore in it. Which sound increased until it was very definitely something.

At about the same time, elsewhere in the city, Captain Peter Sennes entered his underground apartment. As he came in, he saw that the lights were still on. And that the lieutenant with whom he shared the accommodation was in bed but still awake and reading. Sennes relaxed down on his own twin bed, and began to undress. His companion finally looked up and said, 'As you probably observed, after I got your phone call. I charged out of here at top speed.'

'Thanks,' said Sennes.

'I gather,' said the other, 'you made it with your little jabber, and brought her here for the crashing finale.'

The older man stretched, yawned contentedly, and then said with a faint smile, 'I made it with *one* of my little jabbers.'

The friend considered that for a long moment. Finally, he shook his head admiringly, and commented, 'I really don't know how you do it. These female jabbers have mechanical hearts and a rule book in their hands, and besides if the outfit ever catch you jabber hunting – that's the end, sir.'

Sennes was unconcerned. 'I hit the jackpot tonight. Beautiful Dolores. As full of hate as a panther, and as soft as a kitten. As for Susan – '

'I was wondering what happened to her.'

Sennes was calm. 'I gave her the good-bye routine tonight. I think she'll come through for me, too.' He disappeared into the bathroom with his clothes, and came out again in his pajamas.

The younger officer greeted him: 'Why don't you marry Susan?'

'Don't be an idiot,' said Sennes rudely, without turning.

His friend urged, 'You could do worse that be married to the daughter of the great man.'

The captain climbed lazily into bed before answering. He said then, 'I'm an active flight officer, Harry. I'm hoping to go along on some of the great expeditions. It's too hard on a woman to be left behind. They either go on the town – which I wouldn't care about – or they endure being in the nest. Thank you, no.'

'Susan is a cute kid,' said Harry.

Sennes reached over and turned out the light beside his own bed. 'They all are,' he said casually.

XV

THE long, streamlined, tanklike structure was waiting for John Lane and Desmond Reid as they stepped out at Level One of the Space Control building. The two men entered silently through a steel vestibule. The interior was somewhat reminiscent of the inside of a submarine: space was cramped, machinery jammed in everywhere. Lane evidently knew where to go, however. He led Reid through a tiny door near the entrance. The two men found themselves in a somewhat more spacious chamber, where a keen-eyed man sat in a chair before what looked like a control panel. Opposite the panel, there were built-in seats. And into one of these, wide enough for two persons, Lane and Reid settled themselves.

Behind them, from nearby, came the sound of the outer door wheezing shut. The impression was of powerful pressure valves now holding the door closed. As this noise subsided, the big truck began to move. It was soon rolling briskly along – somewhere. The direction was not obvious to people inside a machine that had no windows.

The man in front of the panel spoke first. 'Gentlemen,' he said, 'permit me to introduce myself. I am Dr Yanlo, physicist in charge, this evening – I should say a.m., for it is now about 1.35 a.m. – of this complex equipment that you see here. There are several assistants hidden back there somewhere' – he waved vaguely toward the rear – 'and two drivers up front. Though we shall, of course, take Mr Reid to his home first, our real job is to escort Commander Lane to his residence, and to maintain a continuous watch over him and his house until the present crisis is past.'

The man continued, 'You are seated in what we call the observation room. And if you will look at your left you will see there, not a viewplate as such, but a screen that shows energy symbols.'

For Lane, it was familiar equipment. On the screen was the faint blue sheen of what seemed to be a large plate of opaque glass. The glass was inset in a black metal frame. The whole instrument seemed to go back toward the rear of the heavily armored vehicle. What they could see was apparently merely an outjut of that large machine.

As it was, it spread generously across half the width and height of the interior . . . Across the screen there rippled tiny particles of light. They came in patterns and waves, but these did not move in a single direction – this was no modified TV screen with a one-way scanning system. Up, down, sideways, diagonally, simultaneously left and right – that was the movement . . . But they were patterns, nonetheless.

The scientist's voice went on, 'The screen *could* show a picture. However, at the moment we are reflecting random energy forms from the region of space beyond Pluto's orbit approximately 4,000 million miles, or six light-hours, away. It is the area where our scouting vessel was destroyed the other day. And, of course, normally that distance is too great for us to detect radio waves, or TV, or other organised energies, unless they have been modified specifically for, and aimed at, our receivers. Which,' he concluded briskly, 'we may speculate would not be part of the intent of an alien group, if such a group is, in fact, maneuvering out there.'

Lane's face had a thoughtful expression on it, as he listened to the explanation. Desmond Reid nodded a few times. Both men remained seated – and it was Reid who now spoke. He indicated the room, and his gesture also seemed to include the entire machine, and he said, 'When did all this get organised, and why? I must admit I was surprised when we came out, and you guided me in here.'

Lane was apologetic. 'I couldn't explain in front of the others.'

'It's all right,' Reid reassured him. 'I'm not complaining. But I can't see it being a real protection. If Spaceport is vulnerable from' – he glanced up at the ceiling – 'from out there somewhere, it's hard to imagine that some truck standing outside your vulnerable house would be any protection in an emergency.'

The younger man's stern face relaxed into a faint smile. 'I see you've got the same wrong idea of what protection consists of, as all these other people. To someone who joins the fleet, there comes a gradual, horrified realisation that one can spend an entire lifetime doing routine maintenance and routine cruising. Meanwhile, our existence makes people *feel* safer. Even those of us who are aboard units of the fleet *feel* more secure because they exist. Yet, what happened when we met the enemy out there. They attacked. Three of our units, which were unfortunately closest to the point of contact, were destroyed in those first few seconds. The rest of us, on my orders, withdrew. This meant that the fleet as a whole remained out of their range. Since we didn't wish to fight, we tried communication. There was no reply. Next we sent units forward to discharge their atomic torpedoes at the enemy – only they were not loaded. We merely wanted to see if we could penetrate their defenses. The torpedoes could not get near their big ships, but several of the smaller ones were hit. Our conclusions were that the large enemy ships carried equipment that could put out energy that would confuse the target-locating devices on the torpedoes, but that the smaller vessels did not carry such defensive equipment. It gave us a picture of their limitations, and so we felt better. Tonight, when I sleep with the knowledge that this armored tank is sitting outside my house with its antennae pointed up in the direction of the enemy, I shall feel better, also.'

'Yes, but – ' protested Reid, 'if the enemy is really watching, it will warn him that you are suspicious. And it will certainly cause talk in the neighborhood.'

'Wel-l-ll,' acknowledged Lane, and his smile was suddenly grimmer, 'I should tell you that I have kept the real information to the last. You may recall that you accompanied me home on my first night back?'

The older man sighed. 'I remember it only too well. You were in a very determined mood in connection with Susan. I've been intending to ask you how that came out.'

Lane said curtly, 'We'll discuss Susan some other time. What was interesting was what happened in connection with you *and* me the next morning.'

Reid blinked in his astonishment. 'Me?' he said.

'Both of us came to the Space Control, and both of us stepped in to the Identification booth – you did, didn't you?'

'Yes, of course,' the other man acknowledged. 'After more than twenty years, I've often though it was unnecessary. But I did it each day just as if nobody had ever seen me before.'

'Good,' said Lane. 'You will be fascinated to know that on that first morning after my return the computer of course accepted our identity, but reported your and my face, neck and hands – our visible skin – emitted energy of a wavelength hitherto not associated with a human being. Nobody really thought too much about that, but the next morning only I emitted that energy and not you. Again, this morning, my skin – but not yours – gave off this energy. Today, accordingly, these facts were brought to my attention, and – '

The older man was staring at him, shocked. 'John, are you serious? Are you implying that somebody is watching your house?'

Lane shrugged. 'That's what it seems to add up to, doesn't it. Because the only time that you came over was that first night. Apparently, the intensity fades in about twenty hours, Now, there's one thing – '

He was interrupted. *'Gentlemen, look!'* It was the scientist, in a hushed voice. *'A picture!'*

Lane was fast in his response. His head twisted leftward. And so, he actually saw the picture for the few seconds that it showed. His impression was of an unhuman face visible against a background of the interior of a highly mechanised room. Tall, gleaming panels of metal. Dials, knobs, plates, screens –

Then it was gone.

Lane spoke quickly, 'Can the computer reconstruct that as a still picture?'

The scientist did not reply – verbally. His hand slapped a lever up above his head. There was a grating sound, then a lurch. The heavy machine came to a grinding stop. A long pause. And it began to back up. Once more it came to a stop. The man busied himself anxiously with dials and switches on the panel in front of him.

While this was progressing, Lane turned to his companion. 'Did you see that?'

It developed that Reid had been too slow. He had observed a brightness out of the corner of one eye. He was willing to take Lane's word for what it had been. When he had listened silently to the description, he was very disturbed. 'You may have had your first look, then, at the enemy?' he said.

Before Lane could reply, the physicist spoke. 'I thought,' he said, 'we'd better not get too far away from where that came through, since we lost it so quickly – which is a puzzle. Losing it, I mean.'

'What's puzzling about it?' Lane asked swiftly.

Before the man at the panel could more than give them another glance from those sharp, probing gray eyes of his, two younger men emerged from a corridor behind him. Presumably, they had responded to some signal, for they silently sat down in little chairs that folded out from the same control panel. Their superior made a hand gesture at Lane, which seemed to say, 'Wait!' Whereupon, he and his assistants concentrated their attention on the instrument board in front of them.

Lane and Reid watched them briefly. Then Reid said, 'You indicated there was one other thing in connection with the energy emitted by your skin and mine.'

Lane nodded. 'Naturally,' he said, 'we immediately checked with all the computers in Spaceport – that is, those that monitor the identifying of personnel in the offices, the maintenance, manufacturing, crew, and other facilities involving approximately one million employees and staff officers.' A grim smile tightened his lips. 'It seems that one other person has *every morning* emitted this same energy. He is a mechanic in a minor maintenance plant. His name is Len Jaeger.'

The expression on Reid's face was one of bafflement. 'It seems an unrelated phenomenon. I presume you checked up on this man, Jaeger.'

'Naturally,' was the reply. The commander's firm lips tightened. The look on his face and in his eyes was suddenly sardonic. 'You asked about Susan a few minutes ago. Believe it or not, there's a connection between Susan and Jaeger.'

The older man gave his friend a quick, searching look. And then he shook his head sadly. 'There's satisfaction in your voice, John, which I deplore. In a deadly situation like this, you should not be getting personal pleasure out of a coincidence.'

'You call it a coincidence if you will,' said the younger man, and there was an edge of anger in his tone, 'but just listen to this: Jaeger and his family moved recently into Spaceport. Because his occupation is relatively innocuous and unclassified, we don't have a big dossier on him and on his family. There's a wife and a teenage son. But – now get this – the son has since his arrival become a member of the Red Cat outfit, of which Susan – as you well know – is still a member.'

'Well, then,' said Reid, and he sounded relieved, 'then everything is explained. If we reason backwards from you – ' He left the sentence hanging, made a dismissing gesture as if no more need be said.

John Lane bit his lip. He was visibly irritated. 'Not so fast,' he admonished. 'I don't follow your reasoning.'

Reid was calm. 'The only time I associate with you, I emit the energy. You emit it all the time. Ergo, as a result of Susan being – what was the word you used? – *still* in the Red Cat outfit, Jaeger has been close to you each day without you knowing it . . . Naturally, you wouldn't recognise a – ' He broke off. 'What is his occupation?'

'He's a machinist,' said Lane with a scowl. But his eyes showed thoughtfulness, and he was clearly trying to evaluate his companion's analysis. 'It's hard to imagine,' he said slowly. 'He lives half a mile from me. What would he be doing near me early morning or late evening, which is the only time I'm either home or en route from or to?'

'Well,' said the older man. 'what does the record show about when he emitted the energy? Did it begin the same time as you and me?'

The younger man's face had a disgusted look on it, abruptly. 'If I had built Spaceport – ' he began, impatiently.

'What's the problem?' asked his companion, quickly.

'Jaeger works in nonclassified shops,' was the reply. 'The computers in such shops are simpler. They *could* be connected with more sophisticated systems, but they weren't until the day after you and I showed a positive reaction. At that point, Security automatically put a watch on the whole city. Naturally, they had no idea what the problem was, and they still don't. But,' he spread his hands, and grimaced unhappily, 'that's when they spotted him.' His eyes narrowed. He nodded decisively, 'I shall have Jaeger brought to my office tomorrow morning.'

Desmond Reid had a faraway look in his eyes. 'Let's consider that settled, then,' he said. 'Now, about Susan. John, your use of the words "still a member" bothers me. So, I'm assuming that though the surface appearance is clear enough, you're working against her at some depth.'

Lane was calm. 'I don't care for your language,' he said, 'but it's true. I've set currents in motion.' He brought his teeth together with a click. ' A person like myself,' he continued, 'doesn't have to deal directly with the simple minds of teenagers. Knowledge of human nature is the key to sucess, where reason cannot prevail.'

'I think I get the picture,' said the older man sadly. He became grave. 'I gather you're not concerned about damage to Susan.

'Susan,' was the cool reply, 'has already been damaged by the outfits. All I can do is conduct a salvage operation, and hope for the best.' He shook his head, and made an effort at a comradely smile. 'Listen, Dez, Estelle and you and the others who stayed home here have been too close to this problem. First of all, there *is no problem*. But you've been whittled away at by the weaklings, and you've sold truth and propriety without even noticing it –'

He was interrupted. 'There is no problem?' his friend echoed. 'You can't be serious. The absence for ten years of a husband and father creates a problem, and when it is multiplied in that the absence involves tens of thousands of men, it becomes a very severe problem indeed.'

Lane's smile was cynical again. 'Dez, I also faced the no-sex situation, just as Estelle did here. Ten years, Dez. But I didn't groan or weaken. I saw the reality. I didn't blame the Space Authority, because – fact is – I chose this life. Perhaps I chose it before I thought clearly. Young people tend to be like that. But the government spent fifty thousand dollars on my basic education, and then an equal amount on the advanced stuff. So, now I'm one of the people they count on. And they *can* count on me. I shall do my best, regardless of the self-denial involved. So what do I find when I get back here? People have gotten soft about the kids. Instead of looking for a solution that would toughen their spirits, they catered to their alienation. Accordingly, it's taken for granted that these youngsters will scurry back to the outside world, and in their place will come unsuspecting suckers who will then go through the same cycle with their kids. That's wrong. I will not be a party to a faulty solution.'

'What has this got to do with the difficulties that you are causing Susan?'

The commander's patience began to show wear. 'For God's sake,' he snapped, 'you've got that backwards. On my return, *I* found Susan in difficulties. My judgement, based on my experience and observation in my own teens, tells me she's been conned. I am now in process of putting a stop to that.'

'I see.' The older man was smiling also, but in a disturbed way. 'I'm afraid the outfits are smarter than you think, and they're going to catch on to what you're up to. At which time you may discover what happens to booters when they run afoul of outfits –'

Lane stopped the next words before they were spoken by laying a hand on Reid's arm. Throughout their discussion, he had repeatedly sent quick, darting looks at what the three scientists were doing at the big instrument panel. Now, finally, the lead scientist gestured at his helpers, sighed deeply, shook his head, and turned toward his passengers. It was evident to both men that they were about to be given further information.

The physicist said, and he was clearly unhappy about it, 'What was puzzling, gentlemen – to answer Commander Lane's earlier question – was that it is difficult to know why we should have lost the picture so quickly. It would almost seem as if they became aware of us, and disconnected. And, of course, that's impossible, because their distance from earth is too great. You follow the reasoning?' He glanced from Lane to Reid and back again. 'Where they are beyond Pluto's orbit, is six light-hours away. That also means radio or TV hours. If they were to signal to us that they wanted to negotiate, it would require six hours for our reply to reach them by normal, direct transmission. And then six more hours for them to answer back. On the other hand, if they – like we do – have the ability to use ordinary waves as carriers multi-times faster than light-speed, then it would still take a few minutes at the enormous distance to the Neptune-Pluto orbit. But that reaction you saw took seconds only. As if something here in Spaceport tuned us out.'

'You can't tune in again?'

'I haven't been able to, so far. And' – the keen eyes were narrowed – 'that suggests we were cut off. Which means they have a feedback system which can detect when another receiver tunes in on them.'

'And you suggest,' said Lane, 'that they have such sensitive equipment here on earth?' His tone was strained. He was suddenly a very disturbed man. He turned to his companion. 'Dez, I'm dead tired, and so I've got to have some sleep. But this information should be communicated to Elliotson at Space Control.'

'I'm sure it should, and will,' the older man soothed. 'But don't get yourself all upset. After all, the fleet is deployed for defense. Our space radar network goes all the way out to Pluto – that's why they haven't crossed Pluto's orbit. It's difficult to imagine anything as large as an atomic bomb penetrating within millions of miles of earth without setting off an alarm somewhere.'

He stopped, because the man in the seat beside him had leaned forward, and was speaking again to the scientist. 'What about that picture we saw? Can the computer reproduce that?'

The physicist shook his head unhappily. 'I'm sorry, sir. Equipment aboard this armored vehicle is self-contained and therefore limited. I've already put through a requisition for an aerial laboratory, and when you talk to Commander Elliotson please ask him to authorise that at once.'

'By aerial laboratory,' asked Lane, 'you mean a ship that will float above my house?'

'Above this area, Commander. We need to patrol all the way from the Jaeger cottage, which is half a mile west of your home, past your residence and to the street where we saw the picture – that is, right here. But, now, if it's all right, I think we should get you two gentlement home and to bed.'

It was all right. Yet they were reluctant to give up hope. And during the rest of the drive sat watching the screen expectantly. Unfortunately, both before Reid got off, and afterwards, the energy patterns remained neutral. And they were still blank and uniformative when Lane stood up wearily, said good-bye, and got out of the machine, and so, as those aboard monitored his movements, walked through the gate, up to the veranda, and into his house.

The invisible observer first became aware of the armored truck when it felt an automatic response within the energy complex by which it operated on earth. It was by that reaction that it shut off the picture Lane and Dr Yanlo saw so fleetingly.

A few minutes later, it watched as the armored truck approached the Lane residence. Sensing energy probes, it drew back behind the Subsurface shrubbery . . . as Lane walked from the truck to the gate, and so into his house.

After Lane disappeared, the unseen energy duplicate of a remote Real Being emerged from its concealment, and boldy came closer to the truck. At first, it circled warily – from across the street. Then from the side. And then from above.

That was the mistake.

XVI

ESTELLE was reading in the chair beside the bar, when she heard the heavy throbbing sound of the truck. She obviously did not connect the noise with her husband, for she continued to stare at the book in front of her. But she was tired, and her face showed lines of fatigue. As she came to the end of that page, she leaned back and squeezed her eyelids in an unmistakable effort to fend off sleep. Presently, she opened her eyes again, glanced at her watch, and sighed.

'All right,' she said suddenly, aloud, 'all right, Commander Lane, I'm sure you're tired, also. But does life *have* to be this difficult?'

Only instants after she finished her complaint there was the sound of a key in the nearby front door. The door opened, and shut. As his footsteps approached, the blonde woman put the book onto the table beside the chair, and waited expectantly. Moments later, there was her husband. He stepped through the doorway, and stopped, stared at her in surprise. 'Still awake? My dear, you should have more sense.'

He came all the way into the room. 'I must make a phone call,' he said. As he picked up the receiver and button-pressed the number, his face was visible in the light from the floor lamp. His eyes had tiny blood lines in them. His face was not as fatigued as hers, but the skin was unnaturally dark. As soon as he had the phone connected, and had identified himself to a man called Elliotson, he said, 'Jim, we'll need one of the aerial labs type L-20 to support ground unit 67-A. A Dr Yanlo is in charge. Looks like a very able man. Fine. Good-bye.' He hung up, and reaching down took the woman's hand. 'Bedtime, darling, don't you think?'

There was muscle resistance in his wife, as he drew her out of the chair. Her body protested his assumption that he could walk into his house at two o'clock in the morning and find all signals at 'Go!' She waited while he gave her a kiss, and then said in an unaccepting tone, 'Aren't you interested in what happened to your daughter today?'

The man made a wry face. 'I see the unwelcome sign is out again,' he said.

There was a long pause after those words were spoken. Estelle closed her eyes, and sort of slumped in his arms. Finally, she sighed, and looked up at him, her cheeks wet. 'Ever since your return,' she said, 'we seem to have operated slightly out of phase. You have *never* been unwelcome. Even that first night I held my peace until you started to take charge like a full admiral without waiting to discover that there was no war. Since then there's been a kind of truce, with both sides stiffly standing at attention during moments of stress. When you said what you did just now, for the first time – for the very first time – there went fleetingly through my mind the thought: Is this marriage going to last, really?' She broke off, wearily, 'John, I don't think I could stand you not caring what happens to Susan. I just couldn't live with that.'

The wry smile had faded from her husband's face, as she spoke. By the time she was finished, he was shaking his head sorrowfully. 'It looks,' he said. 'like I'm going to have to make the fight to keep this marriage going. But if what you just said is all it takes, then there's no problem. Naturally, I knew Susan was in the care of one of our supermen – which is what the active flight officers are, if anyone is. And since the transport vehicle was the magnificent *Omnivulture* class, all I had to do was have the Father computer that deals with such, report to me periodically. So Father got it from Mother, and Mother got it from Boarder, that they spent the day on Tombaugh, and checked in at O-Base shortly before ten p.m. Now, what else would you like to know about my interest in Susan – aside from the fact that I don't care for her to be in an outfit?'

'Why don't you just forget about the outfits?' his wife said fretfully. 'You arrived so late into that situation – on her nineteenth birthday, she's out – automatically graduated. So it's just a little over two years.' Her tone was slightly pleading.

'I'll make up my mind about the oufits,' said the man, 'after I get a little time to study them.' He had released himself from her, as he spoke. Now, he stepped back. 'Estelle, you've got to let me form my own opinion on that. Don't try to get some kind of a blanket withdrawal out of me in connection with Susan. I won't do it.'

'It bothers me,' persisted the woman, 'that you were willing to let her go out with a man, where they would be alone in a plane, and then in a known pleasure resort.'

Lane sighed. 'I guess I need a drink,' he said. He walked to the

bar, and put out two glasses. He glanced over at her. 'Like one?'
She shook her head, an impatient movement. So her husband
poured himself a jigger of something, put in ice and water, and
then stood sipping. Finally, he seemed to relax, for he said, 'I took
that drink as a method of refraining from a hasty response. One
of the things, my dear, that bothers men about some women is
that they never let up. You can see the thought in the woman's
face, and in the configuration of her body muscles.'

He continued after another sip, 'What I'm saying is that, just
looking at you I could see that you were going to say more. I
had the thought: She's not going to let well enough alone, now
that I've established my innocence. I refer to your accusation
that I never thought of Susan all day. I did. So I'm cleared on
that. But what I observed in your face was: She will not be able
to restrain herself from continuing a fruitless argument. Whatever the new thought is, it will not be witheld, but will come
bursting forth, presumably in view of the subject, in the form of
an attack. And so now you've done it. My answer is: I deny
that you have spoken a rational statement.'

The woman was defensive. 'I don't see how you can say a
thing like that. It is well-known in Spaceport that grounded
officers prey on the wives of absent personnel and on female
jabbers. And so the rule of parents here, that is, of parents *who
care* – '

The man winced. Closed his eyes. Pressed his teeth together.
Clenched the hand that was not holding the glass, and tightened
the one that was. All were melodramatic acts of restraint.

His wife had paused to watch while he went through his
reaction. His response deterred her, made it harder to speak
again. But she braced herself, and finished in a determined voice:
'The rule is, keep teen-age girls away from the grown men.'

Lane set his glass down on the gleaming bar top. 'I gather, then,
that it is your considered belief,' he spoke in a deliberate tone,
'that Susan on her first outing to the theater with Captain Sennes,
and now on her second one to the moonlet, Tombaugh, allowed
herself to become involved in a sexual episode each time?'

Again, one of the long pauses. When his wife finally answered,
her words were defensive. 'I didn't say that. I said – '

'In your opinion,' her husband asked flatly, 'has this girl had
sex with any male, young or old?'

'No!' Explosively. Having spoken, the woman must have realised that her reply was too swift to be convincing, for she
added, kind of angrily, 'Now, you've got me on the defensive
on a subject that is not an issue. For God's sake, Commander
Lane, until your arrival home we didn't have problems like this.

Suddenly, we've got them. Suddenly, a Captain Sennes is invited to our home and is brought into close contact with our sixteen-year-old daughter. Suddenly, Susan is a confused girl – and she wasn't. That's what disturbs me.'

'Maybe I should have remained out in space!' her husband snapped.

The blonde woman was silent. But her expression said that in part at least she was agreeing with that. Lane was angry now, also. 'Well, let me tell you my belief,' he said. 'I believe that you exposed Susan to sex in these outfit situations, and that if she was vulnerable to Captain Sennes, it would be because she had already had her morals attenuated by these young gangsters.'

'That is absolutely ridiculous!' Estelle yelled. 'If you would ever take a minute away from whatever you're doing down there at Space Control, and –'

The phone rang, and her voice suspended its sound in mid-rage. She gave her husband a quick, startled, questioning glance. 'Are things *that* urgent?' She half whispered the question. 'A call at *this* hour!'

Lane did not answer her with words. He jumped forward and grabbed at the receiver. 'Lane?' He acknowledged. 'Yanlo, you've actually got hold of something?' His voice and manner showed bemusement. 'Yes, I've spoken to Elliotson. You should have an L-20 in minutes. Unfortunately, they are based across the river, but – All right. Do your best. Above all, get data.'

He hung up. And stood there for a moment all the fatigue, apparently – briefly – gone from him. Excitement transfigured his face. Hope was in his eyes. An *intense* yearning . . . He half turned away from the woman toward the door; and his impulse to leave and go where the action was, was plainly written in the way he stood. Like a leashed dog – or perhaps, rather, a caged animal – his head was up, his ears, so to say, cocked, and his nose sniffed the air. Like an animal, he had unmistakably sensed nearby prey, and every muscle was tensed to charge forth and do battle. But of course it would have been foolish to rush out into the night. And that thought was the equivalent for a human being of a leash or cage for an animal.

As the man stood there, thus poised and intent, his wife's expression transformed into concern. Presently, she moved toward him, and put her arms tentatively around him. 'Is it something you can tell me?' she whispered.

Her husband shook his head. However, her near presence seemed to recall him to his immediate situation. His arms and hands, which had been vaguely maneuvering at his side, reached out and grasped her. Held her. There was no resistance in her body now. So when presently he said. 'We'd better go to bed. It's not my duty shift; so I ought to let go and get some rest!' his words were evidently sufficient motivation. For he removed one arm from around her, and, keeping the other one in an embracing hold around Estelle, he thereupon led her out of the room and down the corridor into their bedroom. Arrived there, he took approximately one minute and twenty-seven seconds to undress and tumble into bed.

XVII

OUTSIDE –

One instant . . . the Invisible Observer was 'floating' 200 feet above the big truck. The view included a good portion of Spaceport at night. In every direction, long lines of lighted streets marched off into a remote, merging brightness. There were no really high buildings in the space city, so the appearance was of a peaceful metropolis where nothing untoward was, or could, happen.

The next second . . . the entire scene blurred. Then the whole city, with its square miles and miles of lights, began to turn like something being viewed from a cartwheel that was not only spinning slowly, but falling.

In the armored vehicle below, the first indication had been a needle surge in the panel in front of the first assistant. He grabbed at the controls of those particular dials, and then he turned to the chief physicist, and said in an unsteady voice, 'Sir, I think we've just tangled with an energy field of considerable power.'

'*Grab it!*'

The young man gulped, and said, 'I've got the magnets of Unit A holding it. Better start another motor, and take over on your master control.'

The older man's singularly keen eyes were wide and bright and excited. Up with a jerk came his hand. With a strong, levering motion, he drew a relay switch into closure position. The big truck body shuddered, as the second motor took hold.

'Look!' said the assistant, who had previously spoken. He spoke in a hushed voice. '*The screen!*'

The satinlike bluish surface was a mass of coruscating patterns. The chief physicist leaned forward, and his eyes were speculative,

Z <center>97</center>

alive with information responses. Presently, his whole face was participating in a remarkable byplay of comprehension. His gaze flashed from one meter reading to another, back to the screen, and then again to one of the dials.

Periodically, his voice came soft and confident, and it also telegraphed that a knowing brain was watching the action. 'More on A – quick! Give B a half dial more . . . Gentlemen, do you realise that the readings we're getting show that whoever is battling us, can just about match the power available on this truck? Leon, phone Commander Elliotson. Get that aerial lab. And, Phillip, get me Commander Lane . . . ' Pause, then: 'Look at that. If that's operating from 4,000 million miles, they're using a system that's faster than light *by many times*. Those are instantaneous responses . : . still, why haven't they reinforced it? It's still the same total energy output. Big, but not enough to everwhelm our magnets – '

He was interrupted. 'Doctor Yanlo.' It was Philip. 'I've dialed Lane. And the phone is ringing, so why don't you – '

The young man did not have to complete his sentence. Because the chief physicist grabbed at the phone, and it was he who answered Lane's 'Hello,' and conducted the subsequent conversation. When it was ended, and he had replaced the receiver, he went on as if there had been no break in the sequence of his thought: 'There's a mystery here, of remote control . . . This is the greatest day of my life. And yours. Notice everything. This is learning on the dynamic level of instant to instant change of data.'

One of the young men – Leon, the first assistant – had a haunted look on his face. He was cringing. 'Right now, doctor, I'm thinking of my wife and two children. This feels more like a to-the-death engagement in a war. And we're in the stage where we don't know what the outcome will be . . . Your analysis of faster-than-light energies is not reassuring.'

The other man interrupted at that point. 'Aerial lab has lifted from dock. They say, one minute.'

'Good, good,' said his chief tensely.

The second young man pointed at the screen. 'The patterns are changing. What do you make of those new shapes?'

The older man had already seen them, and he was suddenly pale as he watched the formation of squares and circles on the smooth surface. He glanced at the meter readings, and his eyes grew sad, as of he had already suffered a loss. All the needles were pressing hard against the front barriers. He said unhappily, 'They've quadrupled their power in the past few seconds. Get ready for an energy surge, as he breaks away. Let's try to save our

98

machinery – '

His unblinking eyes were alertly watching the patterns on the screen. As one of the patterns threatened to enlarge to a square the full size of the screen Dr Yanlo abruptly yelled, 'Now!'

Having escaped from the magnets, the invisible observer darted over to the Jaeger house, and to a location outside Bud's bedroom. His was a race that did not sleep. So the 'boy' was merely lying in bed, doing his usual good job of pretending to be in slumber. He responded to his father's telepathic call by slipping out of bed, and coming closer to the window.

Anything wrong? Bud asked.

Very much so. I was caught in a tractor beam, and had to ask for help. Now, pay careful attention. I may have to leave suddenly, because I have a feeling somebody else will be coming with more power.

The boy was anxious. . . . *Is this dangerous for us?* he asked.

I'm afraid so, was the reluctant reply. *By the time help came for me, I'm sure that whoever it was that hooked onto me, had learned a great deal. And of course he undoubtedly noticed how long it was before the new force arrived. So, these humans will probably reason correctly that we Dren use light-speed energies as carriers for faster-than-light transmission of both power and communication. They only have it for communication. Even worse, now that I was spotted once, I won't be able to remain. They'll saturate Spaceport.*

B-but – his son protested, *what will become of me?*

My present plan, said his father reassuringly, *is to try to probe in briefly sometime tomorrow, and see if your human father, Len Jaeger, is out of the hospital. If I can get at him, I'll install a command for him to resign his job and leave at once.*

He seems to be hurt worse than was at first thought, the boy replied uneasily. *It looks like he'll be in the hospital several days.*

Then you must take the Subsurface tomorrow after school. Go across the river to the east. Get off at the second stop outside – and I shall contact you there. Otherwise, be as human as you can. No experiments. No testing . . . The father's thought paused, then: *Oh, it's time. Here come a ship. I've got to break all contact with this planet. Goodbye –*

In the lab ship, L-20 Unit number B32, one of the scientists said, 'Got a sudden surge there from the vicinity of the Jaeger house. But it's gone now.'

'Keep cruising!' came the command from the bridge. 'That family will be investigated tomorrow . . . is my information.'

The great ship continued its protective cruise over the space city all that night, while the stars looked down from a blue-dark moonless sky.

It was dark when Lane awakened sufficiently to remember where he had signed off the night before. The sobering recollection brought him awake in moments, and he was relieved to notice that he had already benefited from what sleep he had had ... He felt distinctly better.

There was a sound of regular breathing from Estelle's side of the king-size bed. So he edged over. Got silently out from under the sheets. Put on his robe. Tiptoed out of the room and down the hall to the den. From there he phoned and presently had the account of the battle in the night between two fields of energy.

Having secured the available data, he had his call switched to Elliotson. The two commanders thereupon grimly discussed the implications of what had happened. And there was quick agreement between them that it would do no harm to have more L-20's in the air over the city. But they also agreed that the big *Watcher* vessels should not be easily visible during the daytime.

As Lane put it, 'This is a scaredy-cat planet. And, since the chances of a nuclear strike from way out there, are practically zero – the aiming mechanism would be spotted by our defense equipment – we'd better just wait it out.' He concluded, 'My own belief is that the aliens fought us out there to prevent us from discovering where *their* planet was. Then they followed us determined to find out where *our* planet is. And they found out. That puts them one up. Accordingly, we must achieve communication – or fight. Those are our alternatives. I'm going to suggest that we try to capture – not destroy – one of their small craft, and have a conversation with those aboard. I'm convinced that's our only chance to avoid a fleet battle to the death with the whole earth and solar system at their mercy if we lose.'

Elliotson, at the other end of the line, a narrow-eyed, red-faced man, said laconically, 'I have a feeling that the Commission wishes they would just go away. Failing that, I am in full agreement with your limited objective.'

Lane replaced the receiver, and returned to bed, This time he slept until the soft brrrring of the alarm awakened him.

At breakfast, Estelle watched him eat his breakfast, nursed her own cup of coffee like the treasure it was to her, and kept glancing at the time. She finally disappeared – came back, disturbed. 'Susan is not well,' she said nervously. 'She's going to stay in bed today.'

Lane kept his peace. He stared in a studied fashion past her, nodded his head judiciously, murmuring finally a non-committal '*Mmmmm.*'

Estelle poured herself another cup of the dark, liquid delight, and said uneasily, 'It's her first illness since childhood.'

'If you call a doctor,' Lane ventured, 'have him give her a general physical. We might as well know the truth.'

The woman was instantly outraged. 'What kind of remark is that?' she bridled.

Lane avoided even harder looking at her, as he said, 'I thought you were concerned. But,' he shrugged, 'use your own judgement. Personally, however, I've always found it simpler to work from facts. So if my requests have any influence on you at all, well, I'd still like to know.'

His wife took five sips, and now it was she who was not looking at him as she said, 'I really don't see any reason for calling a doctor.'

A small, sad smile came into her husband's face. He leaned back in his chair, and he shook his head at the woman. 'I wish you could see yourself and me at this moment,' he said, 'as I visualise us. Here I am, one of the three top fleet commanders, judged capable of dealing with a hundred thousand or more personnel. And yet I sense so much emotion in you that I cannot discuss my sixteen-year-old daughter with you in a rational fashion. I feel that if I make a frank remark you'll hold it against me.'

The woman was pale. 'You attacked her the first night.' She spoke in a low voice. 'You brought Captain Sennes into the house, and I sense that was a deliberate act designed to confuse the girl. And now, this morning, she's sick for the first time in ten years.'

As she spoke those final words, the color drained from the man's face. 'Good God, you're blaming *me* for her illness.'

She was silent, frozen there across the table from him. But her drawn cheeks and her tense body said that she did blame him. The man showed shock. He climbed to his feet unsteadily. The chair he had been sitting in fell over backwards. The crash was unnoticed by either of them. 'I'm sorry, John,' the woman whispered. 'Those are my thoughts. I can't help it.' Abruptly, tears rolled down her cheeks.

Lane made an effort at that point to control his own emotion. 'What you're saying,' he said slowly, 'is that Susan has a mental emotional reason for being ill today. If that's true, I think she should be questioned. I noticed that she's a pretty straightforward girl within the narrow outfit frame. So I believe that she would level with you if you were to ask her after I depart – which I think I'd better do before any more ill-considered remarks are made. So let me just answer your accusations. Yes, I brought Captain Sennes into the house. I thought it was time she had contact with a real man, instead of with those cowardly second-generation kids who are going to run outside, as soon as they're old enough.'

'They're leaving because of people like you,' said the woman, with more spirit suddenly. She wiped her eyes with a quick, angry gesture of the back of her hand. 'Because it's unnatural. Susan saw me here for – how many nights was it you said? – about 3,600. It would be utterly unintelligent of her not to notice what a nightmare that was. So she's going to have a normal existence – which I want her to have. There's nothing sacred about space, that one man has to be out there ten years. I'm disgraced as a woman. My husband chose the longest hike in the history of the service, in preference to coming home to his family. So even if Sennes were a marrying man – which I'm sure he isn't – I wouldn't want him to be interested in Susan, or she in him.'

Her husband made a gesture of defensive cut-off, putting both hands in front of him and wagging them slightly, in protest. 'I had better get out,' he said, 'before *I* decide that this marriage isn't going to make it – which, please note. I haven't done yet.' He paused in the doorway to make his denial. '*That* is a thought entirely in your mind.'

He did not wait for her to reply, but turned and did in fact hastily depart. His footsteps were audible in the corridor leading to the front of the house, then there were sounds from the outer vestibule. Seconds later, the front door opened – and shut. A pause, followed by the throb of a truck's motor starting up in the rumbling pulsar fashion. The noise moved slowly away.

The woman in the kitchen frowned, as she heard the noise. Then she hurried to the den, and its window which faced the street. Peered out in time to see the huge steel vehicle roll out of sight along the street. She was still gazing after it, or trying to, when the phone rang. Automatically, the blonde woman walked to it, lifted the receiver, and said, 'Hello.'

'Estelle, this is Ann,' said a woman's voice. 'I've been watching that armored tank from my little window across the street from you, and I want to know: Is there any reason that we haven't been told why Commander John Lane has to be escorted to and from home in a tank.'

'They're testing new equipment,' lied Estelle in her blandest voice. 'John has to evaluate it, and he just hasn't the time any other way.'

'Oh, I'm so glad to hear that,' said Ann's voice. 'I suddenly got all worried about those horrible creatures who attacked the fleet in space. It would be just awful if they were to find us so quick. Everybody says it'll be sooner or later, but I'd rather it

102

were later.'

'Me, too,' answered Estelle, brightly.

'Thank you, dear. Good-bye.'

' 'Bye.' The blonde woman replaced the receiver. Then she stood there, her head cocked slightly to one side, with a self-satisfied look on her face. She glided over to a mirror and gazed at her image in it. 'Still have a quick mind, don't you?' she praised the image, aloud. She drew back. Her brows knit. 'I wonder what that truck *is* for,' she murmured.

With that, she walked over to a chair, and sat down. She sat there with her lips pouting slightly, staring into space at a small downward slant that, if she had really been looking, would have meant that she was studying the door of a lower cupboard in the northeast corner of the kitchen.

She spoke again. 'Who did I fool? Me or Ann?' Her eyes widened. 'Is it possible there *are* aliens out there?'

It was, of course, impossible to carry the thought any further, without additional information. So, presently, she stood up and began to clear away the breakfast dishes.

XVIII

THE light of dawn had come that morning to a Spaceport under the surveillance of a round dozen L-20 series 'floating' research labs. As the dawn brightened, the protective craft went higher and higher until, shortly after the sun rose, they were tiny black points in the sky overhead. Those aboard peered down from their vast height – over twenty miles – at a city that looked like an enormous residential suburb, with here and there a school and its grounds, and of course, shopping centers rather evenly spaced . . . perhaps 'too evenly to look natural,' The comment was made by an officer in one of the L-20 vessels, as he gazed down at the city as it showed in a large viewplate which actually looked like a window.

His superior, a tall, thin, very straight-standing officer in his fifties, nodded, but said simply, 'People will work underground. So all our factories and maintenance facilities are down half a mile or more . . . But they insist on living where the sun can be seen. Accordingly, that's where the houses are. Presumably, if anything ever goes wrong, we'll have enough advance warning

103

for a few of the wives and children to make it to the shelters below. It's a little difficult to believe that all of them will make it.'

A voice intruded. 'Commander Lane, or some man, has just emerged from the Lane house. Shall I insert a close-up?'

'Yes,' The chief officer spoke quickly. 'And connect us with Dr Yanlo.'

They watched as in one corner of the viewplate a tiny figure, not more than an inch or so tall (but nevertheless perfectly proportioned and plainly visible) walked from the house to a toy-sized armored truck, and disappeared through a small opening in the vehicle's side. Dr Yanlo's voice came: 'Commander John Lane has this minute boarded our 67-A. We shall now transport him to Space Control.'

The officers aboard the L-20 watched in silence as the machine below moved through the toylike streets of Spaceport, and in due course arrived at the large domelike structure that was the visible portion of the Space Control building. Dr Yanlo's voice came: 'Commander Lane has entered the elevator which will take him below ... Our task is accordingly discharged.'

A minute later, as Lane stepped off the lift at his level, two security officers were waiting for him. The two saluted. The commander nodded. Then he walked with deliberate steps into the Identification booth. As usual the light above the booth was green when he came out.

But he stood by patiently as one of the two security officers stepped to the phone beside the booth and button-pressed a number. He was a heavy-faced individual younger than Lane. A faint, taut smile cringled his thick cheeks as he said to the person at the other end of the line, 'Checking that B-10.' There must have been prompt answers, for he replaced the receiver, turned, and spoke two words. 'Negative, sir.'

Lane stared straight at him for a long moment. 'Let me understand you,' he said, articulating each sylable. 'According to the computer, *today* my skin does *not* emit the K energy?'

'That is correct, Commander,' said the younger man respectfully.

'Very good,' acknowledged Lane. 'And thank you both.' He turned, and started stiffly down the hall. His face was oddly rigid, his eyes narrowed. When he reached his office, he immediately called his liaison on the intercom. 'Mr Scot,' he asked, 'when will Mr Jaeger be brought here?' He broke off. 'You did get my message?'

'Yes, I got it, sir,' came the efficient voice. 'As for Mr Len Jaeger – that seems to be a long story, about which I have placed a memorandum on your desk. Briefly, he's in the hospital, suffering from concussion. I'll keep checking.'

Lane acknowledged politely, and broke the connection. But he did not immediately go to his chair. Instead, he turned and gazed up at the great viewplate. The scene on it was, again, of the starry heavens. There was less appearance of movement than had been the case on his first morning. Today, it was of a specific group of stars, looking rather steadily toward the Southern Cross.

As he stared at the scene, he nodded thoughtfully. Apparently satisfied, he walked around his desk to the chair, and sat down. With pursed lips, he looked down at the sheet of paper – presumably the memorandum about Len Jaeger – that lay there directly in front of him. Abruptly, he picked it up, and started to read it.

He was still reading a moment later when a voice spoke from the screen behind him: "We reached our patrol area near the orbit of Uranus at 0323 hours, and are cruising in a widening spiral in the hope, as instructed, of intercepting a communication beam pointing at earth. As of 0911 hours, no contact, and no indications.'

Lane didn't seem to hear. He finished reading the paper, and his eyes were slightly widened, and on his face there was a definite sardonic pleasure. He had obviously been reading something that was most interesting to him.

Briskly, he clicked on the intercom. Briskly, he said, 'Mr Scott.'

'Yes, sir,' came the voice.

'I understand from your memorandum that Mr Jaeger during a short period of consciousness accused the Red Cat outfit of attacking and injuring him last night.'

There was a pause at the other end. 'As you probably know, Commander, the outfits have their version of such incidents available from Outfit Central.'

The strong, determined face of the man in the big room twisted into a rejecting smile. He was visibly not interested in any of that, thank you – his expression stated. Aloud, he said, 'What could they possibly say on their own behalf, since the man *is* seriously injured?'

'I don't know, sir,' Scott's voice replied. 'I merely checked on Mr Jaeger himself – which is what you asked for. If you also wish me to inquire from Outfit Central – '

'No, no – ' Impatiently. Pause, then: 'If Mr Jaeger comes to any time during the day, let me know. It is my present intention to go over to the hospital and interrogate him personally.'

'Very well, Commander.'

Both men disconnected. Lane picked up the memorandum

and read it again. The twisted smile on his face transformed into a harder, sterner look. He nodded half to himself, as if a decision were forming in his mind.

XIX

BEFORE school began that morning, Mike Sutter conferred in his determined way with Johnny Sammo, leader of the Blue Badgers, and Tom Clanton of the Yellow Deer outfit. The subject: Susan Lane.

The two older boys were doubtful to begin with, but Susan's previous 'offense of the same type' – as Johnny Sammo put it – justified second-step action. And so the decision was made that Susan would be faced again by Marianne. After the other two boys had gone on to their classes, Marianne gazed uneasily at the boy whose moocher she was. 'I didn't know that was what you were going to talk about to Tom and Johnny. Why didn't you tell me?'

'I didn't have time,' said Mike. He was gazing off down the street, and so he spoke casually, as if her question was a minor one. 'I hope Susan hurries up. This before-school stuff is hard on the nerves. We don't want to miss our classes.'

Fluttery fingers touched his arm. He glanced around in surprise, and down into a disturbed egg-shaped face. 'Why not wait, Mike, and talk to the others?' said the black-haired girl.

'Uhn-uhn. Susan confessed to me, herself. As second to Lee in such matters, I consulted with two other outfit leaders. That's the rule.'

'I know, but – ' She was tugging at him now, because he had started to turn away. She continued in a slightly pleading tone, 'B-but you've got to show your feelings for your friends, Mike.'

Mike seemed not to hear, perhaps because several groups of teenagers charged noisily past them and through the gate at that moment. He continued to gaze along the street, presumably searching for Susan's face among those of the swarming young people. Beside him, Marianne said, 'Mike, you've got to listen to me. Lee and Susan are our best pals.'

That caught him. He turned with a frown of amazement, and said to the girl, 'What are you talking about? I'm doing this *for* them – not against them.'

'She confessed, didn't she?' Marianne persisted. 'She called you up, herself. That's being a jabber.'

'Wel-l-ll.' It was Mike's doubt showing at last. 'That's sack. All right, let's wait until after school.' He turned to Bud Jaeger, who had been standing silently by as befitted a new member. Mike said, 'Bud, what do you think of this?'

'Uh,' said Bud, 'I'll go along.' He stood there for a moment, an oddly ugly teenager, but kind of earnest in his manner. 'What's all this about?' he said. The thought had apparently never crossed his mind before. He finished: 'These outfits, I mean.'

Mike was smilingly shaking his head. 'You've got the book, haven't you?'

'Yes, but – '

'But what? Read it, that's what.'

'But,' protested Bud, 'I never heard of anything like this before. Where I come from, a kid sort of goes along with his father, and – ' He stopped.

Mike was matter-of-fact now. 'Outsiders don't have the same problems we have in a base like this. That's what the rules say. But when I see a booter like your old man, I'm betting they need the outfits as much outside as in,' he said.

Marianne was tugging at Mike's arm. 'We'd better hit it into school.'

'Oh – oh, sack.' The boy glanced casually back at Bud Jaeger. 'Chatter with you later,' he said. 'Sack?'

'Cap it,' said Bud.

From time to time during the morning, Estelle glanced into her daughter's room. Each time, Susan was lying with her eyes closed. And so the mother tiptoed away, each time, as softly as she had come. However, about noon she was relieved to hear noises from the bedroom. The toilet, adjoining, flushed. The faucets in Susan's bathroom made their water rustling sound. Shortly thereafter, Susan, wearing a robe over her pajamas, came through the kitchen doorway and settled into a chair at the breakfast table.

The older woman had anticipated some such eventuality. In moments, now, she produced a glass of orange juice, a cup of hot tea, hot toast, butter and marmalade – 'Unless you want something else, dear.'

The girl spoke for the first time. Her voice was subdued. 'No, mother, this is fine,' she said.

The blonde woman started to get herself a cup and saucer. Abruptly, there was a look on her face of awareness of what she was doing. Firmly, she put the dishes back into the cupboard. Then, she walked to the table, and sank into a chair opposite her daughter. She had evidently decided what she would say, for she launched in promptly, 'Your father was greatly concerned about your illness, and wanted to call a doctor. But I thought I'd better talk to you first.'

'Thanks, mother,' said Susan, in the same low voice. She sat for a long moment, and then she sighed. 'Things just got too complicated, mother. I haven't told you, but I've been on probation with the outfit ever since I went out that first night with Captain Sennes.'

It was unexpected news. That there would be a problem in that area was completely startling. Estelle echoed 'With the *outfit!*' She sagged a little. Then she murmured, 'Probation!' and wiggled her fingers, and twisted her face as if she would somehow thrust the word away from her. Finally, her spirit came back, and she protested, 'But you've always been such a good little jabber!' With an effort, she caught herself, and finished in a sharp tone, '*Whatever for?*'

Susan made a body gesture of her own. There was impatience in it, and frustration, and also a kind of despair. When she finally spoke, it was with a sigh that she said, 'When Peter brought me home that first night, we stood for a moment at the door, talking, and then . . . well, he surprised me by lip-kissing me . . . and who but Lee and Mike should be passing and see it.'

'Oh!' Estelle sat with a faraway expression in her eyes, considering the confession and its implications. Her face presently showed relief, but she seemed to need some reassurance, for she said, '*That's* what put you on probation?'

Susan nodded as grimly as a sixteen-year-old could. 'Lee wasn't going to do anything,' she said, 'But Mike –'

The relief in Estelle had grown to the extent that she said, now, gently, 'Mike was right, wasn't he?'

'But Peter surprised me,' Susan protested. 'I read him the rules right after that, but –' She shrugged hopelessly.

The woman was nodding, as if she could visualise the scene. She said, 'Lee and Mike evidently didn't see or hear that part.' She gave her daughter a quick, questioning look. 'You're sure it was just probation?'

'Yes,' said Susan, with another sigh.

'I hate to say it, dear,' her mother said in a frank tone, 'but that seems like an awfully small thing to get sick over after all this time.' When there was no reply, the blonde woman studied the troubled girl, and then asked, 'And that's over in a couple of days? – the probation I mean.'

'I suppose so.' Susan's voice was reluctant and unhappy. Abruptly, she clenched her hands, and burst out, 'Oh, mother, the whole thing is so unfair.'

Estelle was puzzled now. 'It will, won't it? – be over in a couple of days? The probation?'

'Yes, but – '

'But what? Darling,' the woman shook her head in a concerned way, 'I can't help you if you don't push everything out.'

Susan sighed. 'There's nothing.'

'Are you holding something back?'

'No, no.' Impatiently. 'Nothing like that. Nothing else has *actually* happened. I've just had the feeling grow on me that it's all too much.'

It was the woman's turn to sigh. 'Well, I guess I know that feeling.' She finished reassuringly, 'When you go off probation, that should fade, don't you think so?'

Susan shrugged. 'It all seems such a waste of time. Suddenly, I wish I were through school, and grown up, and off somewhere where things are less difficult.'

The girl's head was bent, and she was gazing down. And so her mother gave her several quick, anxious glances. There was puzzlement in the woman's eyes, and the uncertainty of someone who feels that the whole story has not been told, but also feels that getting that story is not going to be easy. And yet, she had to have it. 'Listen, darling,' Estelle said, with that sudden awareness, 'tonight, when your father comes home, I'm going to have to tell him how you are, and why didn't I call a doctor if it's serious. So, if I'm going to have to cover up for you, I want to be sure what it is I'm covering. Now, listen, you haven't been having an affair with Captain Sennes, have you?'

'Nothing like that – ' Susan began, indifferently. She stopped. The momentousness of the question brought her head up, and knit her brow. Following hard on that was embarrassment. 'What a thing to say, mother!'

The woman's face and manner continued to show awareness that she *would* have to answer questions that night. And not just ordinary questions, but the determined, probing questions of a husband and father who had his own, intense reasons for being critical of his daughter, and of his wife's relation to the daughter. 'Sack,' said Estelle bravely. 'And now, one more question: have you ever had sex with any person of the opposite sex – like Lee, for example?'

'Oh, mother, for heaven's sake – no!' Susan's face was suddenly scarlet. 'That's absolutely ridiculous. You know what the rules are. No sex until nineteen, and then I'd have to be married. Of course, I do masturbate a little bit, but that's permitted by the rules, and besides you and I discussed that when my period began. And you told me I could, and I should. And I did.'

It was visibly the complete confession. And the woman was contrite. 'I'm sorry, dear,' she said. 'I just had a sudden feeling of alarm. You were being . . . you *are* being mysterious.'

The rich color had faded from Susan's face. She was gloomy now. 'It all seems so confusing,' she said, vaguely.

The blonde woman bit her lip. The conversation was over, because she really had no additional questions. She felt dissatisfied, as if somehow she had missed a key point. Yet there was also relief, because she believed her daughter. And so the main point was settled in her mind. Nonetheless, she sighed, and said, 'Why don't you go back to bed, then? Will you be going back to school tomorrow?'

'I suppose so,' said Susan, unhappily.

'If anyone calls today – like Lee, or Marianne, or the outfit in any way – ' asked Estelle, 'do you want to talk to them?'

The girl shook her head miserably. 'Just tell them I'll see them all tomorrow,' she replied. And then she added, ' . . . I guess.'

All in all, it was a disturbing conversation for Estelle. But she recognised that what there was of it, she had now had . . . such as it was.

During the rest of the girl's breakfast – which was not long – there was silence between mother and daughter. In a minute Susan, after eating one of the two slices of toast, got up wordlessly and went out into the hallway and presumably off to her bedroom. Only after she had gone did Estelle suddenly seem to remember something. She got up and walked to the door, called out to the distances of the house, 'Did you phone anyone in your outfit that you weren't coming in today?'

A faint Susan voice sounded from far away: 'No, mother.'

'Then,' asked Estelle, astonished, 'why hasn't someone called?'

'Oh, nobody would know right away, mother,' the remote girlish voice replied.

XX

WHEN Len Jaeger opened his eyes on his second afternoon awakening, he saw that a fine-looking man was bending over him. The stranger's face was stern, and there was a suggestion of somewhat more personal power than Jaeger was accustomed

110

to confronting. Nevertheless, the machinist had his own bravado, and he said, 'Hi, doc. Which one are you?'

The obvious mistake in identity caused John Lane to hesitate for a moment. His eyes and face reflected an inner argument as to whether or not he should accept the deception. In the end – which was very quickly – he decided against it. 'No, Mr Jaeger,' he said, shaking his head, 'I'm here on another matter.' He managed to smile through his sternness, as he finished, 'Since you seem to be more alert, I'm assuming that you are being given excellent medical care.'

'I'm still kind've dizzy,' was the reply, 'but I sure feel a lot better than I did.'

'Good.' The commander spoke firmly. 'And I want you to tell me the moment you start to feel bad. However, what I want to find out has to do with the fact that in all Spaceport only you and I have emitted an energy, which has been labeled K energy by Security – ' Briefly, he described how the skin of a human being could apparently store the energy, and then radiate it in about twenty hours. 'We're trying to find out where you fit in,' he concluded, frankly.

It took a while, then. The subject was apparently outside of the reality of the miserable creature on the bed. Accordingly, the situation was a threat to him. His cunning eyes narrowed into a greater cunningness, and would never quite meet Lane's. He knew nothing. He had no idea. He was just a hard-working man trying to get along. He had come to Spaceport about a year before, attracted by the higher pay. Then, a few weeks ago, his runaway son had contacted him, and was now living at home. A little over a week ago, it seemed, the boy had joined an outfit. But Jaeger had only discovered this fact the previous night. 'And I sure wasn't going to have any of that,' he said, sanctimoniously. 'Where I come from, parents give their kids their moral training.'

It was the kind of moment that can never be understood by one of the persons who is party to it. In this instance, the man on the bed would be forever incapable of grasping that his statement, coming from such as he, was a farce. Who shall raise the children of the world? Until that moment, until that remark, the matter might have been at issue in the minds of some people. Suddenly, gazing down into that face – with its twisted mind exuding through every pore, and through the very shaping of the face muscles – even that most ardent supporter of parental control, John Lane, experienced a pause.

There must have been an odd expression on his face; for Jaeger looked up at him, and said hastily, 'Don't get me wrong, mister. For some kids, maybe, the outfits are good. But my boy is going to be raised right.'

Once more, it was sensationally the wrong thing for such as he to say. He looked as if he didn't know one moral from another. He clearly had degraded opinions on many matters, always on the basis of some despicable impulse. Confronted by the madnesses of the Len Jaegers of the world, systematic thought based on principle took on a more shadowy meaning. Reality trembled – and it was shaken now in Commander John Lane.

But nonetheless the officer managed to contain himself and to say quietly, 'What happened? It says here somewhere that you were beaten up.'

The rough-faced man was suddenly back to a narrow-eyed cunning and eye to eye avoidance. He obviously considered himself in danger of some kind. Perhaps, he had had an inkling of the fate of an adult who tried to attack a teenage boy. The big lie poured from his mouth. He described how he had been sitting in the bar, when he was unexpectedly set upon by two outfit boys.

'The way I figure it,' Jaeger said, as if he were in fact reasoning out the motives, 'they expected me to defend myself by chasing those two come-ons. And like a stupe I fell for it. Naturally, when I made my break through the door onto the street, there was the whole outfit. Well – they beat the tar out of me, gave me concussion, and here I am.' His expression hardened. 'Boy, you can bet I know what I'm gonna do when I get out of this bed.'

Several seconds elapsed in the space-time universe of John Lane. Every word of the other man's account fitted an inner need of his own in connection with the outfits. But every articulated syllable uttered in that crude voice, and with that peculiar unpleasant evasiveness, offended his integrity and good sense.

His hesitation ended. He said softly, 'What will you do?'

'I'm takin' my kid,' said Len Jaeger, 'and gettin' out of this crazy town. Those outfits are more than I bargained for. It's like' – he paused melodramatically, as if seeking a suitably irrational comparison – 'like living in enemy country: Boy, you'd better mind your p's and q's. Not for me, thank you. I'm goin' back to my own kind of country, to civilisation, where a peaceful type like me can live his life like he wants to.'

If Lane had not prepared his questions in advance, the other's positivities might automatically have detoured him away from certain lines of inquiry. But now, because he was baffled, he glanced at his little notebook, and was reminded. 'What's this about your son having run away?' he asked. 'Outside? Before you came here?'

It was Jaeger's turn to pause, and for an unplanned reason.

112

He was momentarily confused. The question penetrated deep into a more basic lie – the implanted hypnotism, which had been used on both his wife and himself, and which had provided him with a substitute son. Unfortunately for truth, his uncertainty merely caused him to become shifty-eyed and evasive again.

It had all been the fault of the boy's mother. Bud had been alienated from good sense by her over-protectiveness. Each time there was even a hint of discipline, the kid got to feeling abused. 'Like any spoiled child,' said Len Jaeger. 'So one day I decided I'd had enough of his mom ruining him. I put on just a little pressure. He took off, and went to live with – '

The man in the bed stopped. He made a gesture with one hand that was intended to dismiss such details. But he was also astounded to realise that he didn't know where Bud had been. The realisation widened his eyes, and briefly absorbed him. 'Hey!' he said, 'I've forgotten where that kid ran off to. And that's odd, 'cause I don't generally forget things.'

The signal was clear and loud for ears that were attuned to it. But it was too late. The final fiction had struck home. It had taken Lane a long time to accept that this uncouth individual and he were brothers under the skin: two men confronting similar home situations. But the story of a mother's over-protectiveness achieved that result. That was real. In Mrs Jaeger, he visualised an Estelle without Estelle's physical attractiveness. But a mother type, nonetheless.

The negative decision reaffirmed, the officer stood up. Nonetheless, he was unhappy with the outcome of the inquiry. And so he said tentatively, 'Where could he have been?'

'Better ask my wife,' was the reply. 'It's gone clean out of my head.'

And still Lane stood there, dissatisfied. He said finally, 'You say he came home about three weeks ago?'

'Well, we went and got him, of course.'

That, also, seemed obvious and unimportant. In the face of Jaeger taking it for granted that the boy, Bud, was his son, it was virtually impossible for the breakthrough thought to occur: that the real son, having escaped from this madman, had not returned, and probably never would. And that the entire memory of such a return was a hypnotically planted lie, whereby a child of an alien race had been able to penetrate the defenses of Spaceport.

It was the barrier feeling that Lane experienced. A distinct awareness that he was confronted by a human being who was somehow not able to be of help in this situation. He stood for a long moment staring down at the veined, unhealthy face of the machinist. Then his gaze came up and flicked over the other beds in the room. The other three patients were shining, healthy looking specimens compared to the pallid Len Jaeger.

Without a word, Lane walked over to the man in the furthest away bed, stood above him, and spoke in a low voice, pitched so that it would be impossible for the meaning of the words to reach Jaeger. What he said was, 'You are a security officer?'

The man nodded, and said, 'Yes.'

Lane continued in the same undertone, 'Has he said anything that in your opinion is worth reporting?'

The security man shook his head, and said, 'No!'

'Thank you!' His voice went up. 'And get well soon, everybody.'

The commander returned to the creature he had been interrogating, and made one last effort. 'Mr Jaeger,' he said formally, 'you definitely do not know how your skin came to be saturated with K energy?'

'I sure don't, boss,' was the truthful reply.

Lane said in the same formal manner, 'Thank you!' Then he bowed slightly and, turning, walked out of the room without a backward glance. Out in the hall, he walked over to the little group of hospital personnel who had accompanied him this far but had not entered the room with him. He drew aside the head doctor on duty, and said in a low voice, 'I'm assuming you know the men in the other beds are all security officers?'

'That is correct,' was the reply.

'If any of them reports anything significant,' said the commander, 'contact me at once.'

'I beg your pardon, Commander,' the plumpish medical man said firmly, 'May I ask what, in your opinion, would be a significant remark?'

It was *touché* and it brought a faint, grim smile to Lane's face. He shook his head, baffled, and said simply, 'Do your best, doctor. I have no specific suggestions to offer.'

He returned to his office, about the time that school was over for the day – and as Dolores Munroe sought out Mike Sutter.

As it turned out, there was a race between Dolores and Marianne as to who would head Mike off first. Marianne won by seconds. And it was she who saw Dolores, as it was also Marianne that Dolores saw first, and Mike next. The sultry, dark-haired girl, so pretty in the face, so twisted in her emotions, came to a breathless halt in front of the boy.

The emotion on Dolores's face, as she teetered there breathless, was not decipherable to Mike.

The girl was suddenly remembering her promise of the previous night. Incredibly, as the hours went by, she had forgotten.

But now, she thought of Captain Sennes – and it stopped her.

Yet hers was only a momentary hesitation. She was, among other things, genuinely curious. But, above and beyond that, was her hatred of Susan. Before that rush of feeling, the restriction of silence that Sennes had imposed on her, went down. Yet some of the caution remained. Enough to make her first reference oblique. She said airily, 'Has that goody little jabber, Susan, confessed yet?'

Mike continued to stare at her. But he was a game player, and he was not about to give away any information. He said finally in a brittle voice, 'Suppose you confess for her.'

'Wel-l-ll,' said Dolores with a contemptuous half-turn of the upper part of her body, 'So she didn't tell you! So she didn't think I'd dare push out anything. So she thought if I pushed it, it would sound like a lie. All right, I'll confess for her. I went past her house last night, just as that sailor was lip-kissing her – again. So, now, what are you going to do, Mr Conscience-of-the-outfit Mike Sutter?'

Mike sent Marianne a quick look. The girl avoided his gaze, and simply peered down at the sidewalk slantingly off to one side.

Mike had his cool back in a moment. And he was at his slick best as he said smoothly, 'What else can you confess for Susan, Dolores?'

The sullen girl was outraged. 'What more do you need?' she flared. 'Isn't that enough?'

'When was this?' was Mike's diplomatic counterquestion.

'About ten o'clock,' the girl answered truthfully.

The boy nodded. 'Sack, Dolores,' he said. 'I'll push it to the outfit.' He started to turn away, and then his face – his lean, intent face – showed that he had had another thought. He spun on his heel, and caught Dolores's arm in his purposefulness. He stared straight into her yellow-brown eyes, where also the girl's emotional disturbance showed in a mixture of grief and anger. He said, 'Does Susan know that you saw her?'

The sound of Dolores's gleeful laughter was a brittle, staccato vibration on the still, warm air. As soon as the girl could control herself she said with a savage pleasure, 'You should have seen the way she jumped when I yelled at her from the gate. If ever anybody was guilty –' Her voice had gone away up as she finished her words. They were almost scream level.

Mike shushed her down with a gesture, and then said almost in an undertone, 'This sailor was embracing her, lip-kissing her, at the moment you yelled?'

'They were really hitting each other,' said the girl with another

115

twist of her body, one that actually had a retrospective jealousy in it. But that was too complex a feeling for Mike to analyse.

The boy nodded thoughtfully as Dolores finished. He said, 'Sack, I'll push,' This time when he turned away, he did not glance back. What he did do was catch hold of Marianne's arm. He walked her rapidly toward the shopping area a block away. Mike was tense, Marianne subdued. But nonetheless she presently asked breathlessly, 'What are you going to do?'

'Call Susan,' he said grimly. 'Do what I should have done this morning.'

The girl had been almost running to keep up with him. Her heels clacked on the sidewalk, plainly audible above the voices and feet of other students who were all around them. But after his reply, she shook his hand off her arm and slowed. Several moments went by, so obsessed was Mike, before he was able to be aware she had fallen yards behind him. He stopped short, then went back. 'What's the matter?'

Her arm, when he took it again, resisted him. Her face, when he put his own close to it, was unhappy. Her eyes filled with tears, as he gazed into them; and her voice was griefy but yet determined as she said, 'I refuse to help you damage Susan quicker, by running.'

The boy was not about to accept reproof. 'Listen,' he said from between clenched teeth, 'Susan confessed because Dolores saw her. So this whole thing with the sailor is more serious than we realised – ' He broke off, shook his head wonderingly but with impatience. 'Imagine her calling me up last night to confess, hoping – I'll bet – to get her own story in before Dolores told what she had seen. So don't give me any of this friendship for Susan business. The best friendship we can give her is to get her to scrap this sailor.'

'Why don't you talk to Lee first?' urged the girl. Her intense brown eyes pleaded up at him, and she caught his arm. 'Please, Mike.'

Standing there under a cloudless late afternoon sky, the handsome boy with the dark, flashing eyes, and the dedicated look in them, shook his head. Deliberately, then, he turned and walked away from her. The girl watched kind of limply as he walked all the way to one of the open-air phone booths nearly half a block distance. She didn't move as he stepped close. When he started to do what looked like the button-pressing of a number, she shook her head a little as if she couldn't quite believe that he really was making the call.

Estelle answered the phone in the den. 'Oh – oh, yes, Mike,' she said. 'No, Susan is in bed. She says she'll see you all tomorrow,

116

I don't understand. Isn't that probation over in a couple of days? Oh, something new – yesterday?'

The woman was standing with her back to the hall door, and so she did not see Susan's shadow and then Susan come cautiously into view. The girl stopped, and stood with her back pressed against the corridor wall beside the door.

Estelle was saying, 'I think you're making a mistake. Can I talk to Lee . . . Oh!' Pause. The woman swallowed hard. Her face was working. She was striving to control a strong impulse to be emotional. 'Let me understand you,' she continued. 'Susan must not go near any outfit member for one week? That's the total second penalty? All right, I'll tell her. But I really feel you have misjudged this whole thing . . . As I see it, Mike, it's just as important not to jump to conclusions as it is to – All right, all right, I'll say no more.'

She hung up, and then stood there. And then she turned. Her eyes were closed, so she didn't see that Susan had come all the way into the doorway until she opened them again. Mother and daughter stared at each other. And then –

Tears. Simultaneously. In both pairs of eyes.

XXI

BUD JAEGER came out of school promptly at three. He was a boy in a hurry, but his first task was to take his books home. Which he did, shuffling as fast as he could. The thin little woman who was his 'mother' watched him shuffle into the house, drop his books off in his room – and then she was waiting for him at the front door.

'What're you going to do when your dad comes home?' she asked.

Bud said, 'I got outfit duties, mom. Can't talk right now. Sack?'

She let him by, stood in the doorway, watching him make his awkward way along the street. She waited until he was out of sight, and then with a sigh, and a shake of her head, went back into the house. The door closed.

Bud Jaeger got off the Subsurface at the fourth stop beyond the river. At this hour, he was the only one in the elevator. And so when he emerged he found himself under a protective concrete shelter structure – alone. The outskirts of Spaceport were not visible, because Exit Number Four was exactly ten miles from the last exit inside the big city.

Around him was, well, not exactly open countryside. He could see two small communities: one in the near distance north, and the other approximately equal distance south. In between, however, was a green field: undoubtedly some kind of a crop. Bud shuffled to the nearest edge of the shelter, and then moved a few feet out onto the grass. There he stood under the alien sky of earth, and he looked up, expectantly. To the left. To the right. No signal came. No thought. No sign of his father.

His attention had already been attracted to a small retaining wall about a hundred yards from the Subsurface. Now, he shuffled across a portion of the crop field itself over to it, and he peered past the wall down into a swamp-like depression. The purpose of the wall was not clear, but perhaps it prevented soil from drifting into the swamp. Bud was not concerned with causes. Hastily, he looked around him; made sure there was no one near, and no one coming. Then, galvanised, he hurried around one end of the wall, and into the depression immediately behind it.

He made a sound, then. It was not a human sound. But it had a quality of joy in it. There was eagerness and excitement in it. He began to strip. He took off all his human clothes. Then he reached to some point between his legs – and a fantastic thing happened. His skin began to glitter. It separated – and came off. It fell to the ground like a long piece of pure silk.

There stood revealed an elongated, very pink hard shell of a very beautiful body with tentacles – it seemed – instead of legs and arms. A second pair of the arm tentacles were strapped to the side of the body; and it was these that he now impatiently unstrapped, and with a peculiar humming sound of joy waved around as if their long inactivity had just about driven him crazy.

As soon as they could function, he used them to strap down the arm tentacles that until now he had used to manipulate his human arm shapes. The job done, he began hastily the delicate job of putting on the intricate material that somehow made a human shape. First, when it was completely on him, it glittered unhumanly, and not until he did something in the area under his body, between the legs, did it suddenly flicker – and, just like that, there was the human boy who looked like the familiar Bud Jaeger.

This boy somewhat awkwardly put his clothes back on. Came out from behind the retaining wall. And was about halfway to the concrete shelther that housed the Subsurface when , . . his father's thought hit him:

118

My son, what have you been doing?

Bud told him. The father was startled.

That was a very dangerous thing to do at this stage . . . But it's done. Now, pay careful attention. I can't stay long. The human beings have patrol ships as far out as Neptune's orbit, and we put this communication beam down six hours ago in an area of space that they were not covering at that time. They may be there at any moment. Such matters are difficult to predict.

Bud interjected: *How do I escape? That's what I really want to know.*

It's going to be difficult. We thought for a while that somebody might coast through the defenses of this planet, and turn his motors on for landing only. But that is no longer considered feasible.

But that's how we got here. What's wrong?

Be calm, my son. You may remember that as soon as we realised what star system the human fleet seemed to be heading for – this one – you and I jumped ahead, using our special high speed system for small, stripped-down ships. We arrived here three weeks before they did, before the people here were warned. And so we were able to make a landing.

You mean, that won't work anymore?

I regret, my son, that will not work anymore. So here is what you must do. We'll use the officer who flies the Omnivulture *class spacecraft.*

The one who took Susan for a ride?

Yes. You use the same method by which we controlled your human father, Jaeger, just enough so that he'll fly you to us. Our engineers would like to have a look at one of those Omnivulture types. Apparently, they have enormous destructive power.

But what do I do? How do I get into the ship?

You stated that, according to Susan Lane, he must fly such a ship periodically. Find out from Susan or Dolores where he lives. Go to see him. Use the control method. Go with him. No problem. You have the two capsules still, do you not?

What will happen to him?

The father's answering thought reflected military hardness: *We cannot let these people discover our methods. So, of course, he will not be allowed to return.* The invisible energy duplicate of an alien operating from a spaceship six light-hours away broke off: *My son, I must end this. You understand your instructions?*

I guess so . . . Reluctantly, the boy answered. *The outfit keeps me so busy these days. I've got seven little kids to supervise. It's kind of interesting, but it will make it difficult to find spare time to go and look for Captain Sennes.*

My dear son, the time for you to act is now, while your human father is in the hospital. After all, you had to skip some duty in order to meet me out here.

That's true. One little boy. I've still got to go talk to him before I go home.

Then we'd better end this quickly. But one more thing. As you know, it's easy to get out of Spaceport, but hard to get back in. So, in going back in, why don't you pretend that you were going to run away but changed your mind? what will happen if you use that excuse?

They'll probably turn me over to my outfit, and I'll be put on probation the way Susan was.

See how easy it is. Well, good-bye, my son. Take care, now.

Good-bye.

During the entire time that the mental conversation went on, Bud was shuffling back to the Subsurface. As the invisible energy unit disappeared, he walked awkwardly to the elevator. The door was still standing open, as he had left it. He entered, and pushed the button. The sliding door slid noiselessly shut. A moment later, the light above the door showed that the elevator was going down. As it happened, his timing was perfect. Approximately a minute later, the next Subsurface heading toward Spaceport stopped and picked him up.

John Lane returned to the office just in time to answer a call from a Lieutenant Koenig. The lieutenant was a Port of Entry officer, and what he had to say was that Bud Jaeger, a teen-age boy, had reentered Spaceport at 4.09 p.m. The officer reported that Bud had been allowed into the barriered city without comment. He concluded, 'However, Commander, in checking with Security, we learned that this family is under observation for a special reason, and therefore we make this verbal report, and will follow it with a written report.'

'Thank you,' said Lane, sitting there at his desk, with the huge wall viewplate overshadowing him. He was briefly silent, considering the information. The call, and its import, had triggered an old pattern in him. He had a way of discussing nonessential, or obvious, data with official personnel in such a fashion that the other person came out of it appearing intelligent and somehow liked him for having given them the opportunity. So now he added, 'You say the boy claims he ran away, and then he thought better of it?'

'Yes. He represented himself as being fearful of what would happen to him when his father got out of the hospital.'

The man in the huge room, with its great computer and its other equipment towering around him, smiled grimly. 'It would

120

seem to me, Lieutenant Koenig, that he has a valid fear. Did he say what changed his mind?'

'He decided, Commander, that the outfits would be able to protect him.'

'Oh!' said Lane. He scowled. He was again trapped, without realising it, into the certainty that the boy was in fact the genuine Bud Jaeger. The expression on his face, the way he held himself in his chair, also accepted as truth that the situation with the outfits was exactly the same kind of stereotype that he had re-affirmed it to be after his interview with Len Jaeger. The accompanying hard thoughts altered his conciliatory manner on the phone. He said curtly, 'That remains to be seen.' He broke off, 'Thank you very much, Lieutenant. I appreciate your call.'

And that was the abrupt ending of that conversation.

Another one began almost at once. Because, as he broke the connection with Koenig, the intercom on his gleaming metal desk buzzed; and Andrew Scott's voice said, 'I'll be right in, Commander. I have an important message.' Lane replied, 'Very good!' He sat for a moment in silence, still held by his previous thoughts. His lips were compressed. His eyes stared slanting to one side, where some gadgetry was clicking away with lights flickering in an irregular way.

Behind him, the little door at the far end of the computer opened. The plumpish secretary entered briskly, closed the door and came diagonally forward. He evidently made the assumption that he was expected, for he started talking while he was still en route: 'It's very urgent, sir. The Commission is in session on this K energy thing, and has been calling every fifteen minutes.'

At that point Lane turned, and there must have been something in his expression that was critical. The efficient Mr Scott came to a peculiar gulping stop. In the silence (between them) Lane sat stiffly in his chair, and his somber gaze fixed on the liaison secretary's suddenly unhappy countenance. Scott sensed – his face showed – an imminent reprimand. And he was correct. This was a military man he was dealing with. In the services no one is presumptuous – for long.

The expected (dread) words came. Lane abruptly leaned back in his chair, and met the pale eyes of the other with his own gaze. He said coldly, 'Mr Scott, is it your custom to come barging in on people?'

He had a contrite man in front of him. 'I beg your pardon, Commander. I really do believe in protocol. We live in a very tense atmosphere.' That was his tactful way of reintroducing the purpose of his precipitant arrival.

The seated man was mollified. 'Very well, Mr Scott. Is there anything more to your message?'

Scott did not hesitate. He was as quick to recognise when a crisis had passed as when it was pending. He said in his confidential tone. 'I sense frayed tempers, Commander, and dark impulses. Mr Reid has called privately to say that it looks like the fleet will be ordered to move.'

Lane was astonished. 'But that means they're alarmed by a little spying, which – and this is what's important – we have been dealing with.' He compressed his lips in a way that combined an unhappy smile with an attitude that he faced a disagreeable task. Slowly, however, his face relaxed. He began to nod his head, as if a decision were forming. He said at last, without looking up, 'Mr Scott we must react to foolishness with truth and sincerity. If everyone followed their impulse of rage and outrage, we'd have a fairly sad situation. My impulse was to invite the members of the Commission to come out with the fleet. Invite them, that is, if they should actually insist on the fleet going out to do battle because the enemy managed a little spying – '

He was interrupted. The efficient secretary acquired a strange, eager expression. 'Would you invite me, sir? I've never seen action.'

The commander shook his head with a frown. 'I've just told you, Mr Scott, these are impulses of outrage, and it would be very inadvisable for anyone in position of command to yield to them. What I do propose to do is make another K energy test on myself. Phone the Commission and say I'm on my way over. Then phone my wife and tell here I'll be home for dinner.' He stood up. 'I plan to go to my residence without protection, using the Subsurface exactly as I did on the occasions when I collected the K energy in my skin. Then I shall return here tonight, and make the test.'

He walked around the desk, and headed for the corridor door. There he paused, turned, and stood for a moment thoughtful. 'I do agree,' he said finally, 'that we must intensify defense and security where possible.'

With that, he opened the door, stepped out into the hall, and closed the door behind him. After he had gone, Scott made two phone calls – as he had been instructed by Lane – to the Commission and to Estelle. And then, having broken the second connection, he button-pressed a third number, and said, 'What is the status of Len Jaeger?' He nodded, as the answer came, and finally repeated aloud, 'He will be released from the hospital in the morning. Thank you – '

That call completed, he walked to the small end of the computer, opened the door there, stepped through it, and closed it. In the commander's office, the tireless machinery blinked its lights, continued its intermittent clacking – and on the great viewplate the star scene showed several changes.

Out there the ships were moving.

XXII

AFTER his phone call to Susan, Mike returned to where Marianne waited, and said, 'I've got a couple of kids to supervise. And you have to go and see that five-year-old girl who wants to play with boys – sack?'

'Sack,' she said listlessly.

She was turning away, a cute but distressed teen-age girl in a blue dress – when the boy came up from behind her in his quick way. Gently, he placed his cheek against hers in such a way that he faced in the same direction as she. 'C'mon, moocher,' he urged affectionately. 'A good jabber does his duty. You sack that?'

The girl drew a deep breath. She was visibly influenced by his action. But she merely swallowed; said nothing.

Mike continued, 'In one week, Susan'll be inside the outfit once more, behaving like a jabber again.'

Several adults walked past them as they stood there, absorbed in each other and with their outfit problem. The boy and the girl did not notice. Marianne said finally, 'But a week is such a long time. Why not two days? Or just tomorrow?'

To Mike, hers was an irrational appeal. He withdrew his cheek from hers. 'I only follow the rules,' he said. He glanced at his watch. As he looked up from that momentary act, he parted his lips to speak again. Instead, his gaze went beyond her. An odd expression came into his face. Marianne turned quickly – and then her eyes widened, also.

The husky blond boy, who had come up while they were so intent, glanced from one to the other, and smiled. 'Whee, Marianne; whee, Mike,' he said.

'Whee, Lee.' The two who had been addressed, spoke the words almost simultaneously.

'Where's Susan?' asked Lee. 'Has anyone seen her?' His tone was mild. He clearly had no suspicion of anything. And an instantly anguished Marianne gave Mike a disturbed look. Involuntarily, she turned her back on Lee, and faced Mike. Her lips framed the words: *Oh, you should have told him!*

Mike was noticably token aback. 'Uh!' he said. 'Uh!' He was abruptly pale. And yet, a moment later, he was bracing himself, already recovering from his brief state of shock. His quick mind and his determined spirit rallied to the situation. In an even, yet tense voice, he described Susan's phone call to him of the night before. He reported her words correctly. He told of Dolores's 'confession' on Susan's behalf, and what he and the other outfit leaders had decided in view of Susan being Lee's moocher. He finished, 'So she's out of the outfit for a week. That's the decision.'

The older boy had listened to the summary, and every instant his lips and face grew tighter and less friendly. As Mike finished the account, Lee said explosively, '*No!*' Just like that his face was set and white. His eyes narrowed with anger, and he glared with total truculence at Mike. 'You started this madness, and I'm not letting you continue. We had a perfectly good little jabber in Susan until you messed her up with facing her for no reason. That's going to stop right now.'

'It's too late,' Mike managed to say. 'It's all settled.'

'It's not settled,' said the blond boy, and his rage was now on the level of clenched teeth. 'Mr Mike Sutter, you get those outfit leaders over to your place tonight, and we're going to find out what *you're* up to. I'm beginning to have the feeling that you're trying to take over the Red Cat outfit with these sly maneuvers. Well, you'd better watch it, Mr Sutter, or you'll be outside the Red Cats. Sack?'

The younger boy was shaken. 'I've only done my outfit duty,' he protested.

Lee did not seem to hear. 'So busy leading the outfit,' he went on savagely, 'that you didn't even remember that I'm to be informed.'

The resilient Mike was recovering again. 'It's a special situation,' he argued. 'Everybody agreed that it was.'

'*I* don't agree!' raged Lee. 'Now, are you going to do what I said, or not?'

Mike stood very still for a long moment. He was tense. His was the white face now, an inner struggle against a feeling of degradation. 'I suppose,' he muttered, 'what you're feeling and what I'm feeling right now, is why we have jabbers scraping their outfits. Well, it's not going to happen to me.' He nodded. 'I'll call Johnny Sammo and Tom Clanton, and maybe a couple of others as peacemakers, and we'll meet this evening.'

'I want you on my and Susan's side at that meeting,' demanded Lee.

Mike stared at him, astounded. 'I am on Susan's side,' he said finally.

'You've almost ruined that jabber,' said Lee. 'So you either make amends tonight, or this outfit isn't going to be big enough to hold you and me.'

The younger boy had hold of himself again. 'You almost sound like Susan is your girl friend and not just your moocher,' he said.

'That's a lie,' said Lee grimly. 'That's twisting good intentions, and I think there's been a little too much of that from you in Susan's case. Suddenly the rule on an actual first offense was not good enough for your conscience. At worst, she merited a warning. But this wasn't even an actual offense – established as such. It was only a possible.'

The continuing attack was having its effect on Mike. He half turned away, and there was grief in his eyes. His lower lip quivered.

Lee said, 'Push it out. What is it?'

In a badly shaken voice, Mike said. 'Lee, all this has happened to Susan since her father came back from that long hike – have you scanned that?'

Lee nodded, suddenly calmer. 'Sack.' But he added, 'That's chatter. Nothing Mr Lane has done comes under any rule.'

'He mated her to that sailor, and she sucked it.'

Lee defended, 'You yourself have pushed that Susan chattered that she saw the sailor for the last time, last night. That it was good-bye,' He broke off. 'Never mind. We'll line it up tonight. Sack?'

'Sack,' said Mike.

Lane ate dinner that night with an almost silent Estelle and a gloomy Susan. He was not at first too aware of their moods, being somewhat preoccupied himself. But truth was he was an alert, healthy, observant man. And he presently emerged from his own thoughts sufficiently to glance at his wife and then at Susan. His eyes narrowed. Several fairly direct questions thereupon produced the truth about Susan and her week's expulsion from the outfit.

'Oh!' said the man then. He spoke a little blankly. He sat finally, adjusting his thoughts to the new development, examining its possibilities. They were so amazingly great, fitting – it seemed to him – completely into his own purposes that he actually had to restrain himself from taking advantage too swiftly. 'Let me think about this,' he said, and the words were a barrier to himself.

He ate slowly, aware of his wife's suspicious gaze on him. In the end, he began with a question: 'Are you guilty?' he asked the girl.

She shook her head. 'Not really. It's a misunderstanding. Mike is the problem, I'm sure. He's the conscience of the outfit.'

Lane persisted, 'Is this why you were sick today?'

Susan nodded, but said nothing.

'So,' continued the man, 'I gather it bothers you.' When she was silent, he urged, 'Is that still true?'

She swallowed. A tear trickled down one cheek. Her blue eyes misted, and she wouldn't look directly at him.

It was a sufficient answer. And so Lane said, 'It's very simple. When the week is up, you just don't go back.' He happened, or rather felt impelled, to glance in the direction of Estelle as he said those words. *Her* blue eyes were frozen flame, glaring at him. It required a little more effort after that, to continue. But he did it. 'We'll put you in a private school outside Spaceport,' he said to Susan. 'You won't have to go back to this school, not even tomorrow, not another day.'

'Oh, dad – ' Susan abruptly, with a shrug of her shoulders dismissed the offer. 'You can't do that. The outfits don't allow things like that.'

Lane still had complete control of himself, and so he merely considered the remark. His expression showed a minor bewilderment. Finally, he said, 'I have to admit it. I find it a little difficult to grasp exactly and precisely what the hell they could do about it.'

Susan's face took on a severe look. 'Dad, I must remind you. One of the outfit rules is that no swearing or coarse language is permitted in the presence of a jabber.'

He had to smile at that, withal grimly. He said, 'You've just told me that for one week you're not a jabber.'

Over at her side of the table, the wife and mother, respectively, of the two other persons in the room, stirred. Then she said to her daughter, 'Darling, don't get involved in an exchange of repartee with your father. He's a precisionist, and hits below the belt.' She finished, 'Obviously, your father doesn't realise the penalties to himself of what he is proposing, so why don't you just finish your meal and go back to bed?'

'All right, mother.' The girl's voice was subdued. She thereupon gazed gloomily down at her plate, and probed lackadaisically with her fork at a bit of vegetable.

The man watched the futile effort, and for a few moments he seemed unaware that his entire argument had been canceled by a single remark of his wife. Suddenly: 'Just a minute,' he said.

Realisation grew stronger. 'Am I to understand – ' he began, louder now.

'Ssssh, dear,' said Estelle. 'Let the poor girl alone. You've caused enough trouble.'

If a space fleet commander could be said to be in a spluttery state without actually spluttering, that was abruptly the condition of Commander John Lane, and all in the time period of about a minute. He pushed his chair several inches away from the table. And then he sat there. Presently, he brought a hand up to the table surface, and began to drum on the cloth with his fingers. His wife carefully avoided looking at him. So he finally ceased his finger rat-a-tat, and said in a dangerous tone of voice. 'I thought it was a tenet of parental psychology that neither parent shall be negated in the presence of the son or daughter who is being discussed. So what is this comment that I have caused enough trouble.' He stared at his daughter. 'Have I caused you any trouble, Susan?'

The girl twisted uneasily, glanced apologetically at her mother, and said. 'No, dad. Not really.'

Lane continued, 'I came home this evening, and discovered that you were in trouble with your outfit. I considered the problem and offered you a solution. Have I ordered you to accept that solution?'

'No, dad.' Some color was back in her cheeks.

The husband turned toward the wife. 'Well, Mrs Lane, what have you got to say to that?'

There was color in Estelle's face, also. Without looking at him, she said to Susan, 'Will you inform your father what the penalty is for the solution that he is proposing?'

'Oh, mom – really.' The girl was embarrassed.

'It's all right, Susan,' said Lane quickly, 'I don't wish to hear it. So don't degrade yourself or me by describing it.' He finished coldly, 'I assure you, my dear, I shall never take penalties into account in this matter. Act as if they don't exist.'

'Oh, my God,' moaned Estelle. 'Now, we've triggered the male principle.'

'Estelle, for heaven's sake,' her husband yelled, 'Stop negating me in front of my daughter.' He was abruptly too angry for further conversation. He jumped to his feet. 'I'd better leave before I say something I regret.' But he paused for a final remark to Susan. 'That offer holds,' he said in an even voice. 'You can go to an ouside school – if you wish.'

It was, in fact, his final remark. He spun on his heel, left the room, and moments later, the house.

He left behind him, pressure. One a girl who already felt overwhelmed. It was the kind of illogical pressure that derives from someone having to make a choice. All this was in Susan's face, as she sat there griefily across from Estelle. 'Oh, mother, what am I going to do? If I don't do what he wants, he'll be mad – '

'And if you do, darling,' said the woman earnestly, 'the outfit will face him. So your kindest reaction is to treat this conversation of today as if it never occurred. And,' she went on, her eyes flashing, 'leave your father to me. I'll talk to him in, as we say . . . ' She smiled suddenly, as she sat there, slim for her age, with an attractive personality that was intensively reflected by the smile. She finished: ' . . . in the privacy of the bedroom, where all real decisions are made.'

Susan seemed not to hear. She was staring at the wall behind her mother. Her eyes were vague at first, and still misty. The mist cleared swiftly. The vagueness faded into a kind of decision, and her lips tightened. 'Oh, mother, I wish I were grown up!' she burst out. And now, it was she who jumped up and raced out of the room. Estelle could hear her foosteps in the corridor. At that point the phone rang. Estelle started to get to her feet to answer on the extension in the kitchen. Before she could more than maneuver her legs and push at the chair, Susan's voice floated back to her, 'I'll get it, mother.'

The girl had been passing the den door. So, momentarily forgetting her own despair, she zoomed as of old through the door, and instants later had the phone. It was a boy's voice, briefly unfamiliar. Then: 'Oh, Bud!' she said. 'What is it?'

At the Jaeger home, Mrs Jaeger was in the kitchen, and Bud was in the living room sitting with the phone close to his mouth, and his back to the kitchen. It was the best he could do to attain a privacy of communication that was not absolutely necessary, but still desirable. He said, 'I wonder if you can tell me where this Captain Sennes live that you went to Tombaugh with. I'd like to go and see him.'

For Susan the question was no problem. 'Sorry, But, I don't have his address. I only have his phone number. Wait, I'll get it for you.' She put the receiver down, and raced off to her bedroom.

Bud meanwhile hurried awkwardly into his bedroom, also, procured a pencil and a notebook, and hurried out again. Moments later he had the phone number. Not until he had written it down did a second thought about his request occur to the girl. Then she asked, somewhat astonished, 'What do you want Captain Sennes for?'

'He took you to Tombaugh, didn't he?'

'Yes.'

'He's got to take a plane for testing every few days, doesn't he – didn't you say?'

'That's true,' replied Susan.

'Well, I'd like to ask him if he'll take me along next time.'

'Oh!' said Susan. Her face indicated that she realised that Bud didn't understand the real world, and that while a good-looking sixteen-year-old girl might be acceptable to him as a companion, it was doubtful if a thirteen- or fourteen-year-old boy would be considered. She said as much. 'I hate to say this, Bud, but Captain Sennes doesn't do things out of the goodness of his heart – as I discovered. Now, if you were a pretty seventeen-year-old girl – but you're not. So don't build up any hopes,' she concluded. 'But call him if you wish.'

'Oh, I will,' said Bud. 'See you at school tomorrow,' he finished.'

'Maybe you will and maybe you won't,' said an unwary Susan. 'It's just possible that my father will be sending me to a private school outside of Spaceport –'

The words burst forth automatically in an airy tone of voice from the disturbed girl. They were defiantly spoken, an irrevocably precipitated into the outside world . . . before a single restraining thought came belatedly to cut them off. By the time Susan had come to an abrupt unhappy awareness of what a mad thing she had done, she heard the click of Bud's phone disconnecting. For long moments she stood there stunned into immobility by her indiscretion. Suddenly she jerkily grabbed the phone and called Bud back. To her horror, she got a busy signal.

Actually, it need not have been a serious situation. But an equally disturbed Bud had push-buttoned the number Susan had given him, immediately after he disconnected from her. It developed that Sennes was not in, but the young officer with whom he shared rooms, was. Bud's request for the address caught the man by surprise. 'Well, I suppose it really won't hurt if you come and talk to him,' he said doubtfully. 'But, still, I think you'd better call him in the morning – that's the best time to get him – and let him make the decision. Sack?'

The boy was desperate, and he said, 'When does he take his next routine flight?'

'Oh, that's not until Wednesday.'

Bud made a last effort. 'Why not give me the address, and I'll be there in the moring?' he urged.

'Well, no.' The young man had recovered, and now knew the correct thing. 'These are courtesies,' he explained. 'We do not intrude on other people without their permission. You talk to him in the morning – sack?'

'Sack,' said Bud gloomily. He hung up, and promptly left the house. When the phone rang a minute later, sad little Mrs Jaeger emerged from the kitchen and answered. 'No, Susan, Bud has gone out . . . I think he left about five minutes ago. Well, I'm sorry, dear, I don't know whether or not I'll be up when he gets home. He said something about an outfit meeting, and you know how late those things can be. All right, goodbye.'

She hung up, and made her sad little return to the kitchen.

XXIII

AFTER the decision was rendered, Lee David sat for a while staring at the floor. Or rather, at the carpet. It was an Oriental rug of a magnificent texture, and it reflected considerably more wealth than was to be seen at any other house of an outfitter.

Without looking up, the boy said irrelevantly, 'When does your dad come back from his hike, Mr Sutter?'

'About a year.' Mike was tense, and he looked at the others, and made a body and hand gesture of bewilderment. His lips formed the words, 'What's all this?' But he did not speak them out loud.

Lee said, 'Too bad he didn't do what his parents wanted, and go into the family banking business.'

Mike made a face. 'Meaning, I suppose,' he said, 'that if *he* hadn't got hike happy, *I* wouldn't be here to cause problems.'

The blond boy continued to stare at the rug with slightly narrowed eyes. Around him, the brilliant room was lighted with a brightness that rivaled daytime. Everyone was silent, staring at the seated Lee. On one side stood the members of his own outfit. On the other, in addition to Tom Clanton and Johnny Sammo, there were the leaders of two other outfits, Ben Kismo, a Negro, and Martin Tate, a small, thick-built boy with unruly, sandy hair. What might be called a third group consisted of Dolores Munroe with Bud Jaeger hovering close to her. It was Martin Tate who walked over and stood above Lee.

He said, 'Lee, you're among your friends and Susan's. We've listened to what Dolores says she saw. You didn't say that you didn't believe her.'

Lee replied without looking up, 'No, I believe her, though I don't know what she was doing there.'

Martin went on in his odd, husky voice, 'Mike has reported

what Susan told him – which you didn't challenge.'

Lee said in an even tone, 'No, I didn't think Mr Sutter would lie.'

'*Mister* Sutter?' echoed Mike, involuntarily. The instant grief that came into his face was observed. There was silence while he got control of himself. Marianne stepped close to him and gave him sympathetic glances. Quietly, after a period, Mike freed himself from her restraining hand. He walked to a nearby chair, sank into it, and he also stared off into an inner distance.

Martin continued, 'Then, Lee you stated your objections. But we decided that Susan is guilty. And now, looking at you, I think we all have the feeling that you're not going to accept the judgement. That's a very serious thought.'

The older boy shook his head. 'You're wrong. I am accepting it, but with a reservation.'

'Jack it out.'

For the first time since he had seated himself, the blond youth looked up. 'I am no longer,' he said, 'the proper leader of this outfit. Therefore, for the rest of my time I'll just become an ordinary member, doing minor duties. The outfit should elect another leader.'

'Is that the whole push?'

'No.' Reluctantly.

'Jack it all out.'

'I find myself critical of the intelligence of the members of my own outfit. They voted against Susan, who has been a good jabber from the day she joined – never had a mark against her. I don't understand such thinking. I have only one explanation for it.'

'Push it out.'

'I think,' said Lee, 'we were all disturbed when Dolores scraped the outfit. I have a feeling they held it against me, because it looked like I switched from Dolores as my moocher to Susan without any real reason. However, the truth is I warned Dolores many times that her attitude towards me was not that of a moocher. Toward the end, she was always trying for lip-kissing – which I wouldn't do.'

'Did you ask for advice?'

'No.'

From the rear of the room, Dolores's voice came loudly, 'It's a lie. He scraped me for Susan. All the rest is – '

Mike was on his feet. 'Shut up, Dolores!' he yelled.

'One day,' continued Lee, 'I told her that if she tried for lip-kissing once more, I'd scrape her. She tried right there. And that was the end between us – right there. I turned and walked away from her.'

In that brief space of time, Dolores had made her switch to seductiveness. 'After all,' she said with a swing of her shoulders, 'I just grew up quicker than the rest of you. It happens to some girls, and I was one of them.'

This time it was Tom Clanton, of the Yellow Deers, who shushed her. 'Dolores, the human cortex isn't full-grown until about age eighteen. That's why we have outfits, to protect partly grown cortexes from bulging. You bulged. And now you're just a little confused slab . . . But we're beginning to get a view of how it happened,' He looked around. 'Sack, jabbers?'

There was a chorus of 'sacks,' and Johnny Sammo, who was as big and strong as Albert but was quick – and not slow like Albert – glided up beside Martin Tate. He said to Martin, 'I have a thought. May I offer it for scanning?'

The smaller boy nodded. Whereupon Johnny's deep brown eyes surveyed the other jabbers in the room. 'We've just had a confession here which, in my judgement, should require the other members of the Red Cat outfit to examine their consciences, and push what they find on this matter of Dolores and Lee. Mike, what about you?'

The lean boy came forward. His eyes were narrowed. He shook his head. 'You're asking too much too quick, Johnny. Let each Red Catter examine his conscience for a day, and then confess.' He broke off. 'Everybody knows I tolerate no deviations from the rules – from Susan, or Lee, or anyone else. But right now, I realise that I was surprised when the outfit backed my judgement on Susan's first offense. My guess now is that they had some secret reason for their decision, and that it could be they held the Dolores thing against her. So there's been a confusion, and we need time to straighten it out.'

The blond boy had brightened considerably as these words were spoken. 'Doesn't that seem to indicate a postponement of judgement on Susan?'

Johnny Sammo made a gesture of frustration. 'Lee,' he said patiently, 'Susan's second offense is serious all by itself. It won't hurt her to think about it for a week.'

'It's wrong to punish the innocent,' said Lee stubbornly.

The red-headed Tom Clanton spoke up in a somewhat wry voice, 'Lee, it looks like it's just as wrong to punish the guilty. Dolores has been acting for six months like you did her wrong. Yet I believe she was guilty exactly as you confessed.'

There must have been an expectation that Dolores would react to these words, for everybody half turned toward her. But she apparently hadn't heard. She was having a low-voiced conversation with Bud Jaeger, in which she seemed totally absorbed. She had good reason to be. For Bud had started the conversation by saying to her *sotto voce:* 'I know you went with Captain Sennes to his apartment – and it's all right if you'll give me his address.'

The girl was thunderstruck. For many seconds her body trembled with the fear of exposure. And then the meaning of his final words penetrated, and she was able to recover, and to feel surprise. 'What do you want his address for?' she asked.

'I want to ask him to take me on a flight like he took Susan. And I want to go over to see him tomorrow, and talk to him about it.'

The purpose was even more encouraging. So much so that Dolores was even able to be defensive on Captain Sennes's behalf. 'Why don't I give you his phone number?' she began breathlessly.

Bud rejected that, 'No, no. On the phone he'll scrape me. I want to ask him, facing him. So I've got to be there tomorrow, personally.'

The shock of his revelation had been too much for the dark-haired girl. The fear that disturbed her, with so many jabbers in the room . . . so close . . . robbed her now of her normal additional ability to recover. Yet she, also, could realise that Bud's goal was not going to be achieved. And so her entire intent narrowed down to the need to prevent his saying anything to the others – *now!* 'Just a minute,' she said, and her breathing was still not normal. She took pen and paper from her purse, wrote the address, handed it to him, and said, 'It won't work, Bud. You're not a pretty enough girl.'

'That's what Susan said.' Bud replied, as he slipped the precious little paper into his pocket.

'Oh!' It was a new thought, totally fascinating. 'You asked *her* for Pe – uh, Captain Sennes's address?'

'She doesn't have his address,' said Bud. 'Only his phone number.'

It was welcome information. Dolores stood with a faint, triumphant, sarcastic smile on her face. Then she remembered her own situation. Her eyes flicked upwards, and stared trucu-lently at Bud. 'If you confess on me,' she threatened, 'I'll confess you blackmailed this address. We're even. Sack?'

Bud said, 'Don't worry about me.' He was glad to have the chance of getting the information over to someone else, even to Dolores. 'My mom says she talked to dad at the hospital, and we'll be leaving Spaceport soon. That's why I've got to get this ride in now – or never. Sack?'

'Sack,' said Dolores, greatly relieved.

While Dolores and Bud had their deadly little conversation,

an equally interesting though more enlightening discussion was going on between Lee and the other outfit leaders. The Negro jabber – Ben Kismo – who had been standing silently watching with eyes that seemed to be as white and keen as he was black, said suddenly, 'I've been scanning all this chatter and my judgement is, if Lee had confessed or asked advice on Dolores six months ago, she wouldn't have scraped her outfit and bulged adult.'

There was a momentary pause, while the argument was considered. Then, 'That's sack,' said Martin Tate. Tom Clanton was nodding agreement, as Johnny Sammo walked over to Mike and said, 'What's your judgement?'

Mike fumbled his way to a chair, and sank into it. He seemed dazed. 'This has got to be my confession,' he muttered finally. 'Though I didn't have all the facts that Lee has now confessed, I did jack out of him that I judged that Dolores should have a week's warning, and if she didn't become a good little jabber again, that she should be reported for camp. But he was against it; and so I let it ride. I confess now that I judged Susan for her first offense – judged her harder than the rules require because Dolores was on my conscience. That tells me we've had a confusion building up for six months, and we need advice to save the Red Cats.'

Pause, silence, and everybody turned toward Lee. Martin Tate spoke the words, softly: 'Well, Lee, what's your judgement on yourself?'

The blond boy did not look at anybody. Like Mike, he seemed dazed. The abrupt turn the conversation had taken, had caught him by surprise. Now, he cringed a little – it was not a pleasant thing to see. 'I confess,' he mumbled, 'that for different reasons than I stated before, I am not the proper leader of the Red Cats. I was wrong in the way I handled Dolores.'

'And Susan?' urged Martin.

Again a pause, and dead silence. Finally, Lee shook his head. 'No. It's a different situation. Dolores was wrong to begin with. Susan was not.'

The sandy-haired boy with his thick-built body and unusual husky voice, turned to face the others. 'Well, jabbers,' he said, 'my judgement is that Lee has confessed like a true jabber, and since it's a first offense, I offer the rule that he should be warned but retained as leader of the Red Cats. Any no-sack?'

By this time Dolores had become aware again of what was happening, and it was her voice, strident and hostile, that now sounded from the back of the group. 'What about Susan?'

Martin Tate glanced questioningly at Lee. 'Can this Red Cat

scab be allowed to ask a question?'

Lee stood up. As leader again, he braced himself, stood for a moment evidently scanning the rules mentally, and then said simply, 'Mike brought her here as a witness. I pass the problem to him.'

Mike said, 'Since Dolores was brought here on outfit business, she is in this meeting, only, entitled to ask questions as if she were still a jabber. I wish to point out that Dolores was given a warning several days ago, and has three days left of her week before judgement. So what about Susan?'

Martin Tate said, 'The judgement remains. Suspension for one week counting today.' He looked around. 'Any no-sacks?'

'No-sack,' said Lee firmly.

But no one else said anything. Also, no one moved. Everybody stared at him.

Slowly, Lee nodded. It was a movement that included his shoulders to a degree, and it was actually a gentle waving of the upper part of his body. As if the thought itself was completely involved with the body. 'All right,' he said finally, 'I accept the judgement against Susan, but I intend to tell her that I don't agree with it, though in my judgement her second offense needs to be confessed by her in greater detail than she told it to Mike.'

'Anybody no-sack?' asked Martin Tate.

For a few moments there was not a sound. The smaller boy was about to turn away when Bud suddenly became aware (his expression said) of what was going on. His strange plaintive voice projected into the silence. 'I don't know why we're going through all this. Susan told me on the phone that her father intended to send her to a private school outside of Spaceport, and that she wasn't coming back to school here.'

The pause this time was longer. It was broken by Martin Tate. He turned to the blond boy, and said softly, 'Well, Lee?'

Lee David stood very still. He was pale, but his expression presently showed that he knew his outfit duty, and intended to do it. But he nevertheless visibly braced himself, and then said, 'It's quite evident that Mr Lane will have to be faced, and asked some questions. What happens after that depends on his answers and his attitude. As for right now' – the words came out explosively – 'outfit meeting is concluded.' He glanced at the other outfit leaders. 'The Red Cats may ask advice on Mr Lane, but there is no further outfit business this evening. I urge you all to get home to your studying. Mike,' he hesitated for just an instant over the name, then continued, 'thank your mother for the use of this house.'

Mike said in a somewhat subdued voice that he would do so.

And then he accompanied them all to the door. Shortly after he had closed the door on the last to leave, a pretty brunette woman came down the broad staircase in the outer hall. There was a faint satiric smile in her face. 'Well,' she said, 'did you win or lose?'

Mike said politely, 'Now, mother, nobody loses in an outfit.' He surveyed her critically. 'You expecting somebody?'

She shrugged. 'Oh, one of my boy friends. You know I don't sit around when you're father is hiking.'

'Yep, I've sacked it,' he said.

His mother shuddered. 'Mike, dear don't use that horrible outfit language to me. As you know, I surrendered my parental rights to the outfits with many misgivings as to what they might do to you. But I must admit it seems to be working out all right. I don't think I could have done any better.'

'Thanks, mother,' said Mike, in an even voice.

A faint frown creased the pretty face. 'You do seem to be a little colder,' she said finally, 'but at least – '

'At least I'm out of your way.'

The woman seemed totally unaware of the possibility that his words might be slightly satiric. 'That's absolutely true. I must say that is one good thing about the outfits. I used that very argument with your father. I told him that it's like having a permanent baby-sitter. Really,' she finished, 'the advantages of the outfits outweigh the disadvantages by a great deal.'

'Thanks, mother,' said Mike in that same even tone.

At this point the woman's face showed that for her the conversation was concluded. She waved at him by wagging the back of her right hand with a mild impatience. 'All right, off with you to wherever you're going. It's Henry that's coming tonight, and it bothers him to see you around. He has a feeling you might not approve of his being here. I've told him that's absolutely ridiculous, that you and I live our own lives.'

Another pause. The lean boy's face was briefly tense. Then, abruptly, he relaxed. 'Good night, mother,' he said. 'I'll be in my room, studying.'

'Good night, dear.'

She was speaking to his back. For he had turned, and was scooting up the staircase. Within seconds he was out of sight. A distant door slammed.

Soon after the meeting at the Sutter home, Dolores Munroe phoned Captain Sennes. Although she did not know it, the young officer was in his apartment courting the good-looking brunette wife of a man on a long hike. And so at first he was half-minded not to answer the ring. But a thought evidently struck him. 'May be a message for my roommate,' he said. With that thought, he lifted the receiver. Instantly, after Dolores introduced herself, Sennes anticipated an unpleasant dialogue.

However, the girl merely reported her conversation with Bud Jaeger. Concluded, 'I don't remember seeing him, but obviously he saw us.'

'And what did you say he wanted from me?' Sennes asked in his even, unhurried, unalarmed voice. 'Repeat, please.'

'A space ride – like Susan got.' She laughed in a brittle, nervous fashion. 'I told him you only took pretty girls. But he's going to come to see you in the morning – probably before school. I thought you'd better know that he's got something on us – which would be dangerous for both of us if the outfits ever found out about it.'

'Wel-l-ll' – at his end, the officer shrugged – 'I have a permanent requisition, permitting me to take up to two persons from Spaceport as riders. Beyond that, I have to check in. So, under all the circumstances – including the fact that this family is leaving town shortly – why don't I just act friendly, and give him a ride on Wednesday? And I'll do the same for you next Sunday, as we agreed. Sack?'

'Sack.' The girl was relieved. 'But now, I'd better sign off. I've got homework to do for tomorrow's computer test. Good night.'

As he replaced the receiver, Sennes sat still for a bit. He was realising with relief of his own that the conversation had not been unpleasant at all. He walked back to the woman, stooped over, and kissed her on the arm – and then he picked up his drink, and sank down on the bed close beside his love for the night.

XXIV

DESMOND REID was waiting for Lane, as the later emerged from the elevator. He stood by with a faint smile as the commander of the fleet stepped into the identification booth. Again Lane received an 'all clear' from the attending security officer.

'Well,' said Reid heartily, 'your precautions seem to have scotched that problem. No more K energy.' Lane nodded, and with his friend beside him walked down the hall. 'Sort of suggests,' Reid continued, 'that the enemy is not overwhelmingly powerful, that we can defend our planet, and that there is hope.'

'It's really quite a puzzle,' replied the younger man. 'They seem to be more interested in information about us than in a fight to the death. Which, of course, we don't want either – the fight to the death, that is. If, on the other hand, we could discover what information they wanted, it might be simpler to give it to them, and then say, "Okay. Now, what?" '

They had arrived at the door of Lane's office as these words were spoken. The two men stopped, and Reid said admiringly, 'Whenever I listen to you on fleet matters, I always have the feeling I'm listening to an astute reasoning mind that is somehow getting closer to the facts all the time. But right now, I want to ask you a question about an area of your life where I've never had this sense of admiration . . . How's Susan?'

The strong face of the younger man broke into a faint, satisfied smile. 'Everything is proceeding according to my plan,' he said. 'As of now, Susan is on a week's suspension from her outfit, beginning today. By the end of the week, I have an idea she'll be completely and neatly ejected by those little automatons. They respond like robots. It's amazing, but' – he nodded complacently – 'to be expected.'

Reid stood silent as the door was opened. When Lane asked, 'Want to come in?' the older man shook his head gravely, and said, 'Perhaps I should send a member of the psychology staff of the Outfit Training Institute over to talk to you, John, and explain – '

He paused there. Because the other man's gray, steady eyes met his own. 'Dez,' said Lane firmly, 'Susan is *my* daughter. I would prefer that you let me handle her future my way.' He smiled grimly. 'My feeling is, if I were to meet one of these psychologists, my impulse would be to tell him what I think of him, and then punch him in the jaw.'

There was a faraway look in the older man's eyes. Finally, he nodded as if in agreement with a thought of his own. Then he said gently, 'Well, I'm a supporter of the outfits, so I won't say anymore since I can see that our friendship would suffer if I did. But don't be surprised, or shocked, or outraged, if you suddenly find what your little game can lead to in the way of a clash with the outfits over what you're doing to Susan.'

They separated a few moments later. Lane went into his office, a tight, stubborn smile on his face, and closed the door. Reid walked thoughtfully to the nearest phone booth, and called Lee David. There was a long wait while the phone at the other end rang. Finally, Mrs David's voice answered listlessly, and said that Lee would be home about eight thirty.

'I'll call him then,' said Desmond Reid.

He replaced the receiver, emerged from the phone booth, and walked rapidly, and purposefully, back toward the elevators.

At the Lane residence, the phone rang shortly after eight o'clock. Estelle was in the kitchen, reading, while she sipped a cup of coffee. She turned the book over, got up and walked to the corridor door. As the second ring sounded, she raised her voice, 'Would you like to get that, Susan?' she called. There was a muffled 'No!' from the faraway bedroom. So the blonde woman walked back to the kitchen extension, picked up the receiver, and said hello. It was Lee David for Susan.

Once again, Estelle went to the kitchen door. 'It's for you, Susan,' she called. 'It's Lee.'

There was a slight pause. Then, the same muffled voice as before, said, 'I don't wish to talk to him or anyone else.'

Her mother stood for a moment after that rejection. Then she shook her head slowly and wonderingly, and with the first faint frown of returning disturbance in and around her eyes, walked back to the phone. 'Lee,' she said earnestly, 'I seem to have a very disturbed girl here. She doesn't want to talk to anyone. Is there anything new?' Pause. 'Oh, she said that to Bud? That was very foolish of her, because there's nothing to it. So don't you let the Red Cats go off on any wild tangent. All right, I'm going to go in now and talk to her and see what's going on in her little noodle. I intend to try to get her to school tomorrow. If she doesn't show, you phone me again, will you? All right, good-bye.'

The woman hung up, hesitated, and then button-pressed another number. A woman's voice answered presently. 'Is that the Jaeger home?' Estelle asked. At the other end, the dull-eyed creature who was Mrs Len Jaeger, said, 'Yes, what is it?' Estelle said, 'This is Susan Lane's mother. Susan and Bud are both in the Red Cat outfit. May I speak to Bud?' The apathetic Mrs Jaeger said, 'I think I heard him come back. I'll see.' A minute went by, during which time the woman went to the boy's bedroom. Bud was bending over his books at a desk, laboriously writing. 'It's for you, Bud,' said Mrs Jaeger. 'Susan Lane's mother.' The boy climbed awkwardly to his feet, and was presently mumbling into the phone. At her end, the blonde woman said, 'Bud, I'd like to know exactly what Susan told you about her father sending her to a school outside of Spaceport.' Perfect recall was a corollary to Bud's mind reading ability, and so he repeated Susan's words exactly as she had spoken them. When he had done so, Estelle hesitated. There was a thought of censure in her mind at the swift way Bud had passed on the information. And abruptly she had to say it. She worded it diplomatically: 'Bud, I realise you're new to the outfit, and still fairly young – thirteen or fourteen, isn't it? – so I'd like you to consider what I'm about to say as not personal. I don't think you should have passed that information about Susan on to the outfit so quickly. You should learn to take into account whether or not a person who says something to you is in a disturbed state of mind. Susan has been upset ever since she was put on probation, so you shouldn't take seriously everything she says. By telling it so quickly, when it didn't really mean anything, you've caused her another problem. Bear that in mind for the future, will you?'

Bud was apologetic. 'I'm sorry, Mrs Lane,' he muttered, 'I didn't mean to cause problems.'

'It's all right.' The woman spoke hastily. 'Thank you. And good-bye.'

As Bud replaced the receiver, Mrs Jaeger said with just an edge more animation than was normal for her, 'What did she want?'

Slowly, the alien boy with his face that he kept for looking like that of the real Bud Jaeger, turned around. On this eve of his departure – almost – something of his curiosity about and in the many unexplained human behaviors, motivated him to go over to her. He said, 'You people puzzle me. How could human beings have done what they did?' He stopped. He seemed to realise it was not exactly the proper way to word what he wanted to say.

For the first time since he had known her, intelligence stirred in the woman's eyes and face. She had seated herself at the table in the small dining room alcove adjoining the living room. Now, she stared at him, and said, 'That's a strange way to talk, Bud. But, then' – she frowned, as if trying to penetrate some mental fog – 'you've been very strange ever since you came back. Running away . . . changed you. Your eyes have become so bright. It seems wrong.'

The alien boy gazed at her with eyes that became even brighter. He said slowly, 'There's a kind of beautifulness about the way that human beings feel. At first, I didn't understand, but now' – long pause – 'that poor girl, Susan. She's really all mixed up. And it happened to her so fast . . . People are too sensitive. Human children need help the moment anything goes wrong. If they don't get it, they start to do something automatic that they can't stop. It's just as if their intelligence is suddenly pushed aside, and all it can do after that is justify the automatic actions.'

Something struggled for expression in the woman's face. Awareness? But of course that was impossible. In this hypnotised mind, the breakthrough could not take place. But, like all human thought, what happened was a striving to make sense out of perception, however distorted. . . . Her eyes widened as he spoke what could have been giveaway words. But instead of grasping the truth, she experienced a flow of warmth. The sound of that warmth was in her voice as she said, 'This is the first time I ever realised that perhaps you inherited the intelligence I used to have before I married that man because I thought he was a real masculine type, and not a softy like so many other young men I knew at that time. That was my mistake, and it was such a big one that I gave up all hope for my own happiness. But if you come out of it all right, then I won't mind so much.'

'You see what I mean,' said Bud. 'People are really beautiful. Life on earth is actually full of details, isn't it? Even,' he hesitated, 'dad . . . is complicated.'

A negating smile lighted the sad face of the woman. 'I'm afraid that's carrying beautifulness too far,' she said. She broke off. 'You'd better get back to your homework, dear,' she said.

Bud hesitated. He stood with his hands and arms held slightly above his hips and in front of him, bent at the elbows, as if he wanted to express more of his thoughts in some concrete way. But he clearly thought better of it, because after a moment he turned and shuffled off to his room. The door closed.

After Estelle replaced the receiver of the kitchen phone, she turned, and walked purposefully to Susan's bedroom. The girl undoubtedly heard her coming. Because, as her mother appeared in the doorway, Susan began, 'Mother, please don't pressure me to talk to Lee, or anybody. The way I feel, I can't seem to do or say anything right.'

The woman was slightly mollified. 'It's a little late,' she said, 'but it's obviously true. Still, I think you and I had better have a little talk about what actually happened between you and Captain Sennes.'

The girl was silent. Her mother continued. 'You've got to admit that the second surprise lip-kissing needs some additional explanation. You were conned, weren't you?'

'I don't know what you mean,' Susan said defensively. But the first hint of color brightened her previously pallid face.

'Exactly what did happen?' demanded the blonde woman.

There was a pause, a momentary implication of resistance in the way Susan's body stiffened. But she evidently thought better of it. For she sighed, and then gave an accurate description.

When the story was finished, her mother nodded, and sighed, also. 'It sounds like the good-bye routine,' she said. 'So suddenly you were a female experiencing loss, and you sort of clutched at him.' Her eyes focused on Susan's face. 'Did you?' she asked.

'I really can't remember such details,' said the girl in a distracted tone. 'I read him the rules that first time, and he seemed to take it in good part. And then, suddenly, this second time, he grabbed me again. And he's really incredibly strong. I couldn't move.'

Her mother smiled reminiscently, grimly. 'I know. I'd feel sorry for a python matched against your father. They really train the space personnel to withstand heavy gravitational pressures. So I agree. As soon as it happened, it was too late. Nothing to do but hold still until those steel muscles are motivated to let go.'

'In this case,' said Susan gloomily, 'it was Dolores's voice.'

Her mother drew a deep breath. She was suddenly decisive. 'It doesn't seem like too impossible a situation. Why don't you just decide to accept that it was good-bye, and you close the book on Captain Sennes, endure your week, and then pick up your outfit life again? How about that?'

'Oh, mother,' said the girl tearfully, 'the way I feel, things will never be the same again.'

'Come, now,' coaxed the woman, 'you've stood by while other jabbers were given penalties, haven't you? Did they all want to scrape the outfit?'

'No-o-o! At least, they didn't,' Susan admitted.

'Are they made of sterner stuff than you? Is that what you're saying?'

'No-no!'

She was clearly still not capable of making the forward-going decision. Her mother urged affectionately, 'What's the matter? C'mon, now' – she stumbled over the outfit terminology – 'uh, push it out.'

'Dad,' said Susan, uneasily.

'Oh!' The woman was silent. Finally, tentatively, she ventured, 'You don't want to hurt his feelings?'

'I want him to love me. And I don't think he will if I don't do what he wants.' The pretty, girlish face twisted with the effort to stop tears.

'But he told you it was your choice.'

'Oh, mother.' The girl was impatient. 'You know better than that.'

'Well, that's true,' Estelle admitted reluctantly. Nevertheless, her lips presently tightened. 'I'm surprised to hear a jabber talking like you are. Parents have to have the rules brought to their attention, too.'

Susan said in a subdued voice, 'I never had anything like this happen to me before, and I guess I was really weaker than I thought because – because now that it's actually here, I don't feel strong anymore. It's . . . too much.'

'Look,' said Estelle. She made a vague gesture that had in it frustration and determination – all mixed up. 'I told you that I'd talk to your father tonight. Let's leave it at that, shall we?'

The words postponed the decision, and that was clearly what Susan wanted. Her face showed so much acceptance that it seemed like a good time to end the conversation. Estelle stood up. 'You think about it, and perhaps sleep on it, dear,' she said gently, 'and in the morning I'll come in at get-up time, and we'll see what the situation is.' She smiled encouragingly. 'Sack?'

The girl was obviously glad to end the conversation. 'Sack,' she nodded.

The blonde woman walked to the bed, leaned over, cheek-kissed her daughter, and receive a kiss on her own cheek in turn. Then she went out of the room, and so back to the kitchen to her book and a now cold cup of coffee. Which, of course, she poured out, and lovingly replaced with delicious hot liquid, exactly right in flavor and strength.

By this time, it was almost eight thirty by the kitchen clock. A few minutes later, on the dot of the half hour, Desmond Reid called Lee David from the library of his own home. After the preliminary greetings, the man launched at once into the purpose of his call. 'Lee,' he said, 'in my conversations with Susan's father, it has become quite clear to me that he should be faced, and asked three questions. I think, being the kind of man he is, he will answer all of them truthfully, at which point the outfit can make a judgement on him that may bring him to his senses. I don't know what will happen. But something has to be done. I've known Susan, and loved her, longer than has her father. I absolutely refuse to stand by and see her damaged. Will you take outfit action?'

The boy was a little flustered, but he had actually reaffirmed within himself his determination to be a proper leader of the Red Cats. And so, now, after a pause, he said, 'What are the three questions that you think we should ask?'

He wrote them down as Reid slowly spoke them, and then he said, 'If the outfit decides to do this, have you any idea how we can discover when Commander Lane will be coming home tomorrow? Susan told me that he has no fixed hours.'

'He's due home about eleven o'clock tonight,' said Reid. 'Is that too late?'

Lee was startled. He had picked up the phone while doing his homework, and it now sat on top of a couple of notebooks. 'Well,' he said a little breathlessly, 'this is homework night, but I should

143

be through by ten thirty.' He broke off. 'You really are in earnest?'

'Never meant anything more in my life,' said the man grimly. 'I want a stop put to the nonsense right now, if possible.'

Lee said, after another pause, 'Wel-l-ll, sir, I can't see anything wrong with your reasoning, or your motive. If Commander Lane answers the three questions in the affirmative, then he will be convicted out of his own mouth. So that's fair. Tell you what. I'll call my friend, Mike. If he agrees, we'll do it.'

'You mean – do it tonight?'

'Yes,' was the reply. 'And Mr Reid – ' The blond boy's face showed another thought had come to him.

'What is it?'

'I have an idea we should have two adult witnesses for this facing.'

'A very good idea,' said Desmond Reid firmly.

XXV

THREE men and two women emerged from the Subsurface into the soft, warm night shortly after 11 p.m. One of the men was John Lane. In his courteous fashion, he held back while the couples, laughing and talking, went off to the right. A pre-occupied Lane turned to the left and started up the street toward his home.

He was only vaguely aware at first that there were people on the sidewalk between him and his house. Since he did not connect them with himself, and was personally not alarmed by the presence of human beings, he paid them no more attention than he would have any group of people on any street. Absently, he saw the two men off to one side. And that was reassuring, not in the sense that he felt anxious, but because somehow he associated the youths – who were on the sidewalk ahead – with the two men. If he had been asked, reassuring in what way, he would have had a hard time putting words to the unclear thought. But it went something like: here are two fathers out with their grown-up boys. All by itself it was a ridiculous thought. But the truth was, his mind at rest tended to revert to old-fashioned ideas of his own boyhood. In this instance, the fact that there were seven boys did not immediately sink in.

Several things and awarenesses occurred simultaneously to

clarify the reality. As he approached, the boys politely stepped off the sidewalk. Apparently, they did this so that he might go by. But when he was a half dozen feet from the group, the nearest boy, a good-looking, huskily built blond youth, said, 'Mr Lane, may we talk to you briefly?'

The words were spoken in a nonantagonistic fashion. And Lane, who was accustomed to respond with a certain gentleness when addressed courteously, said, 'Why, of course. What – '

He stopped. The first – incredibly, the very first – implication of *so many* boys, all looking at him . . . penetrated. The possibility that *he* might be the person they were interested in was so . . . improbable . . . that he stood there, after halting. Stood for an eternity of several seconds – long enough so that Lee David had time to say, 'Sir, we are some of the members of the Red Cat outfit, to which your daughter, Susan, belongs, and we would like to ask you three questions – '

The blond boy said something else. But that was all that Lane actually heard. At that precise moment, the shock of what was happening, reached into the region of his guts and gave a hard tug. A skitter of mentation flicked in several directions through his mind. A memory: What Susan had described at dinner time about being faced . . . A second memory: Desmond Reid's words of warning in the corridor outside his office, a few hours before.

The third mental event was a realisation: *He was being faced by an outfit.*

The thunder of that awareness poured through Lane. It darkened his face. It stiffened every muscle. For another timeless period of several seconds, the degradation of it held him speechless with shame.

All these inner happenings *showed* in his face and his body.

The jump from shame to icy rage came next. It required only one of his automatic responses: his brain grew sharp within the frame of the threat – not a millimeter beyond it. At once, decisions on the matter of outfits (decisions he had made and reaffirmed a number of times in the past few days) were triggered into the forefront of his mind. They remained there, positioned like bullets in an automatic pistol, ready to be fired.

Having arrived back to an attitude of strength, he said in an even, deadly voice, 'What are the questions?'

'Are you opposed to Susan being in an outfit?'

He was a man who could recognise a decisive question when he heard it. And there was no doubt. That one struck at the very heart of the matter. But for such as he there was no turning back. And no compromise. The crisis had come to him by surprise. It was unwelcome. Its consequences were unknown. But

10   145

such, in fact, was exactly the kind of environment he had lived in as Commander of the First Fleet. And so he was always, so to say, ready for a battle with an unknown ending.

So, in the same curt voice in which he had already spoken, he said, 'Yes!'

The next two questions were: 'Have you already taken any action that will cause Susan to leave her outfit?' and 'Do you intend to try to get her away from her outfit?'

Lane answered 'Yes!' to each question. He was aware as he did so in some totally rational part of his brain, that the questions were singularly comprehensive. He recognised, also, that the only alternative answer would be a complete refusal to reply, or even to discuss the matter. But he had gone into one of his automatic states. And as long as that persisted, he told his truth.

Moments after Lane made his final admission, he saw a movement from the corner of one eye. It was one of the adults. The man walked rapidly from where he had been standing in the middle of the street, stopped a few feet away, and said, 'Commander, my colleague and I are the adult witnesses to your statements. We wish you to know that we shall report that this outfit facing was conducted by the Red Cat outfit as the rules require. Thank you.'

Having spoken, he backed off almost as rapidly as he had come. Within seconds, he was standing again beside the other, slightly younger man.

But he left behind him a confused Lane.

Poised there in the half-darkness under the trees, the officer recognised the *official* formalness of what had happened. It was a new thought. And it blanked him. In his mind was a fixed idea that these outfit members were young gangsters.

He was still grappling with the contradictions in his understanding, when the blond boy delivered the ultimatum: 'Mr Lane,' said Lee, 'you have until noon tomorrow to change your mind. I'm sorry.'

It was too much. The man muttered something, and started forward. It happened that Albert Mayo stood on the sidewalk. Albert was a big boy, and he occupied a lot of sidewalk. Lane paused in front of the muscular youth, and said through clenched teeth, 'Get out of my way!'

Involuntarily, Albert braced himself. He was the strong boy of the Red Cats, and he had on occasion had to hold ferocious young people away from each other. So being threatened was not a new situation for him. Experience caused him now to place his right foot behind him for better balancing against an attack.

Confronted by such an obviously powerful young man, Lane

stopped. But he was furious now. 'Step aside!' he commanded.

From off to one side, Lee spoke quietly, firmly, 'Albert . . . let Mr Lane go.'

Albert relaxed, and moved off the sidewalk with the no-loss-of-face of an outfitter obeying his authorised leader.

Incredibly, the man did not forget his automatic good manners. 'Thank you,' he said. But he marched straight forward along the sidewalk without a backward or sideways glance. Strode all the way to the gate of his house. As the male members of the Red Cat outfit watched, Lane opened the gate, entered the yard, closed the gate behind him, and walked rapidly up to the veranda. The key in the lock, turning. The door opening . . . shutting.

Inside the house, the man noticed that his hands were trembling. He clenched his fists, and clamped his teeth together. And he stood there, with a solid look of rage on his face.

'Is that you, John?' Estelle's voice came from a distant room.

Lane swallowed, and then he walked quickly to the hall mirror. He paused to call out, 'Yes, dear!' Then he stared at his reflection in the glass, hastily rubbed the tension out of his cheeks and jaws. The sound of approaching feminine footsteps alerted him. But he kept stroking the skin; and, as his wife appeared in the doorway, he mustered a semblance of a smile, and turned to face her.

In spite of all his effort, there must have been something in his face that gave him away. Because the woman said, 'What's the matter, John? You look . . . awful.'

He stood for a moment, uncertain. During that moment he evidently considered telling her what happened. The impulse passed, and he suddenly affected weariness, and said, 'I guess I'm finally getting tired.'

'You poor darling,' she soothed. 'Those long hours.' She took his arm, and tugged him toward the door through which she had come. 'Tell you what. I will not, as I intended to, pound your ear about Susan until morning. There. Does that make you feel better?'

Her husband's eyes narrowed. The smile faded. 'I see no point,' he said in a formal tone, 'in any further discussion at any time about Susan and the outfits. As far as I'm concerned, the sooner my daughter is away from that bunch of young gangsters, the better I'll like it.'

The blonde woman stiffened. Then: 'Your daughter?' she said. She was about to go on, but at that instant she caught a glimpse of his face.

All the rage was back in his cheeks. His lips were drawn back, and his teeth showed in an actual duplicate of a snarl. With a

147

wordless sound, he brushed past her, and walked with swift, purposeful strides to Susan's room. It had taken a moment for Estelle to recover. But as he walked, she came running up behind him, and clutched at him with her fingers. Lane ignored her. He stopped in the lighted doorway of the girl's room, and glared straight into her startled eyes, and said, 'Susan, tomorrow morning I shall advise your school that you are not returning, but that you will, beginning almost immediately – as soon as I can arrange it – be going to a private school outside of Spaceport.'

There was not a sound from the bed. Simply, a tense, girlish face stared up at him.

That was all Lane had to see. At the point, he spun around, obviously intending to charge away as swiftly as he had come. He found his wife blocking his way, and he stopped, teetering on tiptoes, slightly off balance.

The woman had time to speak. 'Have you gone crazy? What's the matter with you?' Her voice was up almost an octave.

Lane was suddenly tired again. He stood there, the awful rage fading a little – but only a little. Enough for him to say wearily, 'Let me past.'

The woman was grim. 'You'll find the spare bedroom back this way and to the left,' she said. 'Don't come into *my* room.'

'Okay,' said Lane, in a drab voice.

This time when he started forward, she stepped aside. And then she stood looking after him, shaking her head in wonder.

XXVI

THE night was a slow, silent thing for many persons. At the Jaeger house, Bud lay in the bed in the darkness of his bedroom – wide-awake, of course. In *her* bedroom, his 'mother' moved in the big double bed, so that her haunted, apathetic face was suddenly caught in the bar of light that fell through the window from across the room. Disturbed by the brightness, her eyes fluttered, and then opened. For a while, she stared fixedly straight ahead. Presently, sadly, they closed.

At the Sutter mansion, Mike's mother, wearing a robe, tiptoed down the stairs with her lover, Henry. At the outer door, she kissed him good night. Gently, she closed the door behind him, and then tiptoed back upstairs again . . . Mike, awake, listened from his bed; heard her bedroom door shut with a faint click. He shrugged, a gesture of indifference. Closed his eyes once more. Slept.

In the David apartment, Lee awakened. A sliver of light persisted in brightening the carpet under his door. Several times, he looked away, and then looked back again. Finally, he crept out of bed, and softly opened the door. Looked out. His mother sat under a reading lamp, her back partly to him. But she was sufficiently in view so that he could see that an open book was on her lap. As he watched, her thin, white hand came into his line of vision. The white, slender fingers turned the page. Once again, the silent, avid reader devoured the words on the new page.

From where he stood, he could see a clock on the table beside her. It showed 3.12 a.m.

As gently as he could, Lee closed the door. Went to the bed. Crawled into it. Slept.

It was a night when the watchful Lab ships swung low again over the city. Their enormously sensitive instruments ceaselessly probed the sky above and the land below. They searched for signals of any type. Particularly, they sought for the K energy that had battled so silently and powerfully with the tractor beams of Unit 67-A, the ground vehicle that had delivered Commander Lane to his home.

Nothing. Not a flicker of response on any dial. The great night was at peace. Earth turned on its axis without incident. Soft winds blew fleecy clouds . . . normally. The stars twinkled from the usual, mild atmospheric disturbances.

The night wore on. A new morning presently dawned in the east. It was dim at first, but it soon grew brighter.

In the bathroom adjoining the spare bedroom, John Lane turned on a faucet. Rapidly, he washed, shaved, dressed. And started along the corridor heading for the front door. It was as his hand reached for the front door release that . . . he heard a sound behind him. For a moment, he froze. The expression on his face showed the unmistakable conviction that he knew who it was – who it had to be. Slowly, he turned. As he had expected, Estelle had come along the corridor, and was now standing in the doorway that led into the anteroom.

She wore a flimsy robe over her nightdress. She had evidently heard him, and made a hasty run to catch him. There was no makeup on her face. It was still a pretty face. The ravages of time had not done any real damage – yet. But it was a woman that stood there, and not the half-woman half-girl that he had left ten years before.

It was the gentle womanly voice that spoke now. 'Is this the end?' she said, and abruptly there was grief in her voice.

The words with their tragic emotion, instantly irritated the man. He made an impatient gesture with his hands. He tilted his head, and murmured something as if importuning some heavenly being to witness that he was a sorely beset individual. Then: 'Of course, it's not the end.'

'But what happened?' Estelle frowned in genuine bewilderment, as she asked the question. 'At dinner you were a reasonable man. Then, abruptly, insanity, five hours later.'

Lane felt impelled to correct her. 'Sanity, you mean,' he said grimly.

'All right, all right.' She was impatient now. 'What drove you sane so quickly?'

The man's eyes clouded as those words were uttered. His wife was beginning to show that penchant for quick thinking, which he had extravagantly admired in her when they first met. But which unfortunately could lead to dialogue that came from her tongue with the verbal weapon capability of slashing his point of view with deadly ease.

He said defensively, 'Really, my dear, I don't wish to get into one of those meaningless discussions that you always win with your wit, and I win with my determination not to be bamboozled any longer.'

'This time,' she flashed, 'you've bamboozled yourself.'

'Look,' he said flatly, 'it's awfully simple. I don't believe in children raising children. And when I don't believe in something . . . I mean it.'

The blonde woman was shaking her head with a kind of wondering grief. 'I can't believe this is all there is to it. Teenagers were raising each other and some younger children, and doing it by rules, yesterday and the day before, and for most of the ten years that people like you goofed off out in space somewhere. So why the crisis at midnight last night?'

'Could it be,' said Lane, 'that because I *was* away, I'm the only one able to take a clear view of this whole outfit mess?'

Estelle sighed. 'The Neanderthal man looks at modern civilisation and longs for his cave again.' She broke off, 'All right,' she said, 'let's quit this double talk. What are you going to do?'

There was silence. Somehow, in talking to this woman, he found himself one instant tingling from some horrid insult, and the next answering questions like a good little boy; and there didn't seem to be anything he could do about it.

'I'm going to the office.' He spoke sullenly.

'Are you coming home for dinner tonight?'

'Yes . . . Of course.' He spoke irritably. 'This is my home.

Where else should I go?'

'Is there any chance,' said the woman, 'that you would have a discussion with me on this matter at dinner time tonight, and meanwhile not take any steps that can lead you irrevocably into trouble with the outfits?'

For just a moment after those words were spoken, Lane was curious. For that moment, he found himself wondering what *did* an outfit facing lead to? The moment of weakness went by, and he stiffened. 'Nothing,' he said grimly, 'that the outfits can do will ever influence my action in what I believe to be right. So let's just leave it at that. May I go now?'

His final sentence was spoken in a facetious tone. It was intended to turn the tables on his wife, so to say, verbally. In its way, it seemed as if it had the potentiality of accomplishing that feat, so rare for him. The implication was that she was a mother talking to a child, and presumably nothing could irritate a woman more than to be escalated from wifeness, which was a cozy, romantic, modern, equal status, to motherness – which always suggested stuffiness, old-fashioned ideas, and advancing age.

The woman smiled with her instant understanding of such matters. 'If you need my permission,' she said, 'you have it. But be sure you come home in time to wash your face. Don't play too hard. And don't get into any fights, or take candy from strangers.'

The man shrugged. 'I've got to hand it to you. In the battle of wits, you're the complete master. So you win again.'

She shook her head griefily, 'In this world,' she said, 'men always have the last word. You were gone ten years. So I lost completely.'

He was irritated again. 'I've got to go.' He opened the door impatiently. 'See you tonight.' He departed hastily, leaving his wife to close the door. Which she did, softly.

Arrived at his office, Lane found waiting for him the same question that had been there the day before: The question: *What shall we do?*

It had to be something, was the attitude of the Committee . . . So Andrew Scott reported to Lane. 'Looks like we can't mark time much longer, sir,' he said.

The commander's lips curled sarcastically. He said, 'I've invited them to go along if they vote for an attack. Accordingly, I've done my bit to forestall foolishness.' He broke off, impatiently, 'We tried for three months to bring these creatures to battle, or to a dialogue – preferably the latter. But they destroyed our patrol vessels, and our peace missions were ignored. So we've got to mark time whether we like it or not. You can only explain

151

that two dozen times. After that, it begins to sound ridiculous.'

He made a body movement of dismissal. And changed the subject. 'Any report on Mr Jaeger?'

The thick-jowled face smiled with a faint smugness. The expression in those dark brown eyes somehow implied that Mr Andrew Scott always had an up-to-date account on any subject. The details were: Len Jaeger had left the hospital shortly after 7 a.m. 'He stopped in at his place of work,' said Scott, 'and quit his job.' It seemed that Jaeger had informed his bench mates that he planned to leave Spaceport within a day or two.

'That's what he said he would do,' said Lane. He walked to his desk, and sat down. There was a faraway expression in his eyes. 'I'm considering,' he said finally, without looking up, 'if there is any reason why we should restrain him from departing. But I can't really think of anything decisive. However' – he nodded, decisively – 'we should know where he goes. So check on that.'

'Very well,' said Andrew Scott, in exactly the right convincing tone of voice.

About nine o'clock, Estelle Lane walked noiselessly to Susan's bedroom, and found the girl sleeping. The blonde woman shook her head, sighed at the tragedy that she believed was occurring, and stood for a bit with eyes closed, leaning against the door jamb. Then she went back to the kitchen, and to a cup of coffee.

She was still sitting there half an hour later, when Susan came through the door. The girl seemed to be in a cheerful frame of mind. She refused to allow her mother to make breakfast for her. And, in fact, made herself toast, cooked two eggs, and sat down to them with relish. 'I'm starving,' she said.

Estelle remained silent, hopeful. After one egg and one piece of toast, Susan looked up, and said, 'So that's what booters are like.'

The woman was recovering. 'One tends to forget,' she confessed. 'In ten years, the intensity of it faded somewhat. But it's been forcing itself on me, and there it was last night in all its subjective reality.'

More food was masticated. Then; 'Don't do anything foolish, mother,' said Susan.

'Such as what?' she asked in astonishment.

'Such as leaving him on my account.'

Her mother was startled. Was struck briefly dumb by the lucidity of the conversation. Finally, because she was, after all, dealing with a teenager, she was suspicious. 'What are you going to do – commit suicide?' she said sharply.

'Oh, mother, don't be silly.' The girl sounded indignant.

The blonde woman was not to be put off. 'There is a page in the outfit rulebook about jabbers who are confronted by heavy

152

emotion at home. The book says that under such circumstances said jabber often comes to a deeply felt self-sacrificing decision. In short, commits a kind of suicide.'

'Oh, for heaven's sake, mother!' The pretty young face was almost brick red. 'I just suddenly decided I'd better snap out of my scaredy cat blue funk, and behave a little more maturely.'

'Does that mean you'll be going back to school?'

'Well, no – not this week.' Susan made a face. 'After all, that's a complicated thing to confront, particularly since I'm not guilty.'

Estelle persisted. 'All right, what are you going to do? Tell me word for word. The rest of today?'

'I'm going to return to bed, and I plan to stay there. I probably won't show for dinner, if dad is here.'

'All right, that's today. Tomorrow?'

The girl sighed. 'Mother, it's hard enough for me to think about one day in detail, let alone a second.'

'All that tells me,' said Estelle, 'is that tomorrow is the decisive day. So, I hope you don't object if I keep a sharp eye on you tomorrow, and follow you wherever you go.'

Susan had recovered. 'You may do that if you wish,' she said with dignity.

'Of course,' said her mother, 'I'll also watch you like a hawk today.'

The smile that came into the girl's face had just a little of the irritation in it that occasionally creased the face of her father when he was talking to Estelle. But all she said was, 'That won't be hard. I'll be in bed, either reading or sleeping.'

'Why not studying?' asked the blonde woman.

Susan nodded. 'I might even study,' she said. She pushed her chair back, and stood up. 'Anyway, whichever it is, starts right now.'

She thereupon departed from the kitchen, looking not quite as cheerful as when she had entered.

Shortly after noon, Andrew Scott reported via intercom that a Captain Alex Mijnalen wanted to see Commander Lane briefly. It was a familiar name to Lane. Though he had never met the officer, he knew him to be someone who had been on several of the long expeditions. 'Tell him to drop over,' he said into the intercom.

Mijnalen arrived within minutes. 'I'm actually very close to you – only two floors below, almost directly under.' His face, streaked with numerous pink bloodlines, crinkled into a smile. 'I sometimes have the impression that my office is the muffler system which keeps the noise of all this away from you.' His right arm and hand waved vaguely at the computer and the viewplate. 'We vibrate all the time.'

He was a man in his middle fifties. A little on the thin side, perhaps. But in a way that was to be commended for a man of his age. Lane shook hands with him silently, and then waited politely.

'You'll be wondering,' said Mijnalen, 'what I'm doing here. Well' – he grinned – 'I've come to welcome you to the club.'

It was a totally unexpected remark. Meaningless and non-sequitur. 'Club?' echoed Lane helplessly.

'At noon today,' said Mijnalen, 'your name was posted at Out-fit Central. It will be displayed there for twenty-four hours. After that, outfit rules require that no further publicity be given any person at odds with the outfits. Of course' – again that crinkly, pink-streaked grin – 'all the hidden consequences continue.'

Lane had not forgotten the deadline named at his outfit facing. But when twelve noon had come and gone without even a phone call, he had shrugged contemptuously. But now he stared at the other man, and the thought was suddenly in his mind that this was why Mijnalen had come to see him. He was an outfit sup-porter-messenger. As he had that thought, his expression hard-ened. Perhaps, this captain didn't know it, but the rest of his career might well be at the mercy of Commander John Lane.

As he reached that point in his reaction, it occurred to him that the other's dialogue and attitude, as well as tone of voice, did not match such purpose. Instantly, Lane's bewilderment returned. But unerringly his attention went back to the key word. 'Club?' He said it this time in a much stronger, and even more question-ing tone.

'Oh!' said the older man. 'We club members get every posted name, and contact the individual so that he'll know there are other persons with the same ideas that he has.' He shrugged. 'I was posted seven years ago, and I've got one daughter to go two years . . . well, one and a half now.'

A dazzling light was dawning. Lane said, 'Well, I'll be damned.' He stood there; then: 'Obviously,' he said, 'I should have guessed I was not alone.' Once more, a pause. He could feel the sense of pleasure growing through his body. Finally, with a smile, 'What do we club members do?' he asked.

'We give moral support to each other.'

'And how many of we are there?' said Lane.

The long, thin face in front of him acquired a kind of dis-gusted look. 'Commander,' Mijnalen said in a critical tone, 'you wouldn't think that in a city like Spaceport, presumably filled with brave men, there would be so many chickens. But the fact is, the battle is probably lost in the bedroom at home. It's a little

154

difficult to spend year after year making love to a woman whose muscles are slightly contracted, pulling her away from you in disapproval of your point of view.'

The smile had faded from Lane's face, as these words were spoken. Now, he scowled, remembering Estelle's muscles doing exactly that. 'Okay,' he said bluntly, 'let's have it. What is the club's hard core membership?'

'It averages about two hundred and fifty.'

Lane was visibly shocked. His brows drew together in a startled frown. 'In a city with 400,000 families?' he said. 'Good God!'

'This is an outfit-oriented city,' said the older officer. 'Knuckle under, sir – or join the club.'

Lane's jaws tightened. Even his body grew harder. 'I'm in right now,' he said grimly.

Mijnalen held out his hand. 'Call me any time you want information. I just thought I'd drop by and brief you on our organisation. Anything you want to know right now?'

Lane shook his head. The thought had already crossed his mind that this man would be able to tell him what the consequences were of an outfit facing. But the truth was, he was slightly unhappy with himself for having gone into a situation without knowing what it might lead to. Other people *could* have the reaction that a fleet commander ought to have considered such matters. In the present stress circumstances, accordingly, it would be unwise to have any more doubts about his competence creep into the minds of the Committee members. They were being irrational enough as it was.

As he shook hands with Mijnalen, Lane said, 'You seem to be doing all right – after seven years.'

'Never felt healthier in my life,' was the reply.

It seemed an odd remark, but Lane did not pursue the matter. He stood watching as the older man went out of the door, and closed it behind him. Then he sat down again. In a few moments he was busy with the innumerable details of an administrative officer. His impression, of course, was that the pile of papers in front of him never really diminished.

About three thirty that afternoon, a disturbed-sounding woman's voice was on the phone to Outfit Central. The voice identified itself to the Police Sergeant on the incoming-call desk as Mrs Len Jaeger. In a hushed voice, Mrs Jaeger said, 'I've sneaked off to make this call. My husband has just forbidden our boy, Bud, to leave the house for any reason for the next day or so until we move out of town some time this week.'

The sergeant asked quickly, 'Is he threatening the boy with violence.'

'Yes.'

'Has there been any violence yet?'

'No. Bud is not resisting. I report this matter because he has outfit duties, and of course should go to school tomorrow.'

'What outfit does he belong to?'

'To the Red Cats. Will you tell them that – ' The voice ceased. There was a sharp inhalation of breath. Then: 'Good-bye!' A click of disconnection followed.

The police officer hung up also, and made a notation on a chart in front of him. He used a red marking pencil. And it was noticeable on the chart that there were several other notations in red clustered around the space in which he was entering the new symbols.

Seeing these, the man looked up and beckoned another officer at a nearby desk. 'Take a look at this, Dan.'

The other man came over, and studied the chart where the sergeant's finger was pointing. 'This isn't a good week for the Red Cats, is it?' he commented finally.

The man at the Incoming Call desk looked worried. 'I'm afraid those kids may not be able to handle this much trouble.'

XXVII

ESTELLE put dinner on a table set for two, and then seated herself opposite her husband. While he ate, she barely nibbled at what was on her plate. Finally: 'You'll be glad to know,' she said, 'that I laid in a week's supply of your favorite foodstuffs, and three cartons of cigarettes.'

The handsome, determined man who sat across the glittering dining room table from her, paused in his eating. He sat for a long moment, knife and fork poised. 'Say that again,' he said. His brows were knit.

'I anticipated,' said his wife, 'and stocked up this morning with seven days of the things you like to eat.' She stopped, and corrected herself. 'That is, the things you used to like to eat, as I dimly recall them from a decade ago.'

Lane now put the fork and knife deliberately down into his plate, and stared at his wife. 'For a normally brilliant conversationalist,' he said, 'that set of statements leaves me gasping – I won't say with total admiration.'

'You mean, you don't know?' Her eyes were bright. She almost breathed the words.

'Know what?' Lane was beginning to lose his short temper. He sounded exasperated.

'You must have been faced,' she said. 'They wouldn't have done it without facing you first.'

It was the unexpected remark. The possibility that her dialogue could be related to the outfits, had literally not occurred to him. The surprise of it brought a reaction. His face suddenly felt hot, and he realised with horror that a blush of shame undoubtedly suffused his cheeks.

'You've become brick-red,' remorselessly said the woman, who sat opposite him. 'That justifies me in making a shrewd guess. It happened last night just before that outburst of supersanity. Am I right?'

The man hesitated. An outright lie was almost impossible for him. So at this point he made his first admission. 'There was some gang of kids waiting outside.' He spoke the words with exactly the right casual indifference. 'I paid no attention to what they were jabbering at me. Are you implying that what you're talking about is related to that?'

'You were faced,' she said. 'And so you'll be on a restricted diet as soon as our current food supply runs out. And no more cigarettes.'

'I'll drink your coffee as a subsitute,' her husband said with an effort at facetiousness, 'for the cigarettes.'

'No more coffee either,' was the reply. 'It's considered unhealthy.

Lane stroked his jaw. It was a stereotype of his whenever he struggled with rage. And he was struggling now. 'Are you telling me,' he said finally in a dangerous tone, 'that the food outlets of Spaceport co-operate with the outfits in a system of deprivation-of-food blackmail?'

'It's not exactly deprivation,' Estelle explained carefully. 'You're allowed a logical diet for men of your category. Your type normally die of heart attacks or strokes. Most such persons lack the willpower to eat right and stop smoking. The outfits put you on essential vitamins, minerals, and proteins. You're liable to lose a little weight. And meals don't taste as good, but you probably live longer.'

The man was momentarily bemused. His anger receded before a memory. 'So that's what that fellow, Mijnalen, was talking about today.' His eyes pointed off to one side, thoughtfully. 'I'll be damned.' He nodded grimly. 'Okay. So I'm on bread and water. What happens to you and Susan?'

'We can eat in restaurants, but we probably won't.' She studied him with suddenly narrowed gaze. 'I can see some scheme is forming in your mind. Your eyes have changed, and have that cunning look in them.'

'For heaven's sake, Estelle!' Lane exploded. He stopped, and sat there in visibly total frustration. Yet he was finally able to say, 'I'm considering how I can deal with a criminal conspiracy without removing my attention from more important matters. Not right now, but it seems to me that later on we could buy our groceries outside of Spaceport, and bring them in.'

She shook her head, eyes bright. 'They would be confiscated at the port of Entry.'

'You're not serious?' He was actually astounded.

'Outfits are official,' the blonde woman said. 'That's what I've been trying to tell you. But nobody can talk to John Lane about anything he's made up his mind on.'

The man scarcely heard her last words. He was thinking again, and he said with a shrug, 'It's simple. Once or twice a week, I take a trip outside, and eat a decent meal in a restaurant.' He stared at her belligerently. 'Don't tell me that's forbidden too?'

His wife sighed. 'Once you're listed,' she said, 'you have to have a legitimate reason for going outside Spaceport.' Seeing the incipient thunder on his face, she ventured, 'As the senior fleet commander, you can probably assign yourself reasons for going outside that no one will question.' She broke off. 'Though to tell you the truth, I can't quite visualise you, an honest man, putting out a series of false mission orders for yourself.'

The realisation of that was also in the man's face. He said gruffly, 'I could probably do it for a good cause.'

The rest of the meal was eaten in relative silence. The woman mostly stared at the wall a few feet behind her husband's head. The man gazed rigidly down at his plate. Once, when he looked up, there was an expression on his wife's face that was suspiciously similar to a smile. It vanished when she caught his gaze on her.

But near the end of the dinner, there it was again. And this time, when she saw that he was staring at her with disapproval, she suddenly started to laugh. She was still laughing hysterically when the man put his knife and fork down. A minute later, her laughter was wilder – and uncontrollable. The man's irritation-reaction transformed abruptly to anxiety. He jumped to his feet, and hurried around the table; and drew her body against his. Held her there, and squeezed the muscles that she could not control.

That did it. She grew calm, and sagged against him, exhausted.

158

Yet, when she could speak, she said in a muffled voice, 'The old booter has got his comeuppance – that's what suddenly seemed so funny.'

Lane found his voice. 'So now you can see how ridiculous the whole business is.'

From the region of his upper chest came the same muffled voice: 'I can't help feeling that they got the right man. Sorry, darling, but that's my truth.'

The man released himself from her, and stepped back. 'I'd better sleep in the spare room again tonight. Evidently, I don't have a wife right now in any real meaning of the term.' He spoke grimly.

The woman's blue eyes had mist in them, and the grief was back in her voice as she said, 'I gather that a good little wife should stand by and watch her daughter destroyed – is that your view of the loyal little woman?'

Lane threw up his hands. 'You're to much for me,' he muttered. 'I'll see you in the morning. Everything is coming to a crisis, and I feel exhausted. I'm sure I could use a little extra sleep.'

He turned, and walked rapidly to the door that led to the magnificently furnished living room, and so across to the hallway and the spare bedroom. A distant door closed.

A depressed Estelle began to stack the dishes in the dishwasher when the phone rang. It was Lee David. 'I'm sorry, Lee,' said the woman, 'I don't know what's going to happen. She seemed more cheerful today.'

At his end, sitting in the living room of his mother's apartment, Lee wanted to know if Susan would be at school the next day. When he received a negative reply, he said, 'Tell her that the way out of even a false situation is to be a good outfitter. Will you do that?'

'I'll tell her,' said Susan's mother in a lackluster voice.

Lee replaced the receiver, and then phoned Mike. The phone rang in Mike's deserted room, and simultaneously on an instrument on Mike's wrist, where he stood with three other boys near the Jaeger home talking to Mrs Jaeger.

Mike pressed the button, and held the tiny phone extension up to his mouth. 'Mike Sutter,' he said. 'Lee,' was the reply, clear and loud. Mike said, 'Lee, Mrs Jaeger has come out, and we're explaining the rules to her about people moving out of the city. I've told her that Bud has to be free to go to school tomorrow, and that we'll be here at seven thirty to check him out. She's promised to tell all this to her husband, and to help us in every way that she can.'

Lee said, 'Well, I think that's all we need to do this evening. So you and the others can go home. Sack?'

'Sack,' said Mike.

'Has there been any violence?'

'No. She says Bud isn't resisting.'

'Sack,' said Lee. His call had been designed to put the authority of the outfit leader behind what the jabbers on the scene were doing. And it had now achieved that purpose.

Lee hung up. And Mike pressed the button again, disconnecting. He stood, then, and explained in his friendliest voice to the woman what Lee had said. He finished, 'Now, Mrs Jaeger, we believe you are Bud's friend as well as his mother. So, if anything goes wrong before tomorrow morning, will you phone either Lee David or Mike Sutter?'

The woman nodded. Her expression was strained. 'It's going to be difficult,' she said, 'but he did let me come out to talk to you. And I'll argue with him.' There was a hint of color in her cheeks. The stress of the situation had lifted her bodily, in a manner of speaking, out of her apathy. She finished, and there was determination in her voice, 'I sure won't let him hurt that boy.'

Mike said, 'Sack.'

The four boys stood watching as the drably dressed woman turned, and walked to the gate, then up to the door, and inside. After the door closed, they stood for at least another five minutes. At the end of that time, there was still no sign of anything unusual in the house.

Mike accordingly said, 'Lee says we can go home. On your way, jabbers.'

The four separated. One boy crossed the street. Another went the same direction on the sidewalk they were on. Mike and Albert walked side by side to the nearest corner in the other direction. At the corner, Mike turned right, and Albert left.

In the Jaeger master bedroom, the woman had finished her account of her interview with the Red Cats. Len Jaeger, listening, lay sprawled on his back on the bed. He was fully clothed. His narrowed eyes stared in the general direction of the juncture of ceiling and wall across the room. His jaws were clamped in a stubborn rejection of what his wife had said.

'Nothin' doin',' he growled. 'Those kids nearly killed me.' He spoke the lie without blinking, and with no hesitation. 'But I'm not going to knuckle under to any bunch of gangsters, young or old. The moving company can't move us for two days, but I'm takin' the attitude that we're movin' tomorrow. So that's the way it is. And I've got a little old shotgun in there' – he shifted his gaze for the first time, and nodded toward the clothes closet

160

to his right – 'that says it's gonna happen my way.'

Mrs Jaeger said pleadingly, 'It's only for two more days, Len. Why don't you just turn your attention away from the whole problem. If you have any feeling left for me, you won't cause this trouble. Remember, your hard way drove Bud from us once before. And it changed him. He's not the same.'

Her husband interrupted her. 'Yeah,' he said with satisfaction. 'Found it wasn't that simple out there in the world, eh? Needed the old man to help out. Okay, the price of my help is a disciplined, obedient life. The day he's old enough to look after himself, then he can do what he wants. But he's gonna grow up right, without any nonsense in his head.' As he finished speaking those words, he saw that the woman was parting her lips to speak. Jaeger cut her off, with a bellow, 'I don't want to hear no more! That's enough of that!'

Shortly after 6 a.m. the following morning, Susan, fully dressed, tiptoed out of her bedroom and went into the den, closing the door behind her. In a moment, she was at the phone, push-buttoning a number. There was a sound in the receiver of a distant phone ringing.

In the appartment of Peter Sennes and his friend, both men awakened to the sound of the phone ringing. Sennes was the drowsier, and so it was the younger man who answered. 'Hello?' Pause, then: 'Just a moment.' He put one hand over the mouthpiece, and with the other made the gesture to Sennes, indicating that the call was for him. 'It's your jabber . . . Susan.'

The captain sat up, went through a rapid waking-up wriggling, and then took the receiver. By this time, there was a cynical smile on his face. 'Hello, there,' he said.

Susan sat in her father's favorite drinking chair, and crouched cautiously over the phone, as if by shielding it with her body she would keep the sound of her voice from carrying. 'Peter,' she said in a low, secretive voice, 'will you marry me?'

The officer was awake by now, totally in control, matter-of-fact, friendly. 'Hey!' he said. 'Not so fast. What's up?'

Even an affectionate resistance was almost too much for the girl. 'I asked you a civil question,' she said in a trembling voice. 'Yes or no?'

'Can we talk about it?' said Sennes. 'Say, why don't you come to the field and have breakfast with me? You know I have to take my routine test flight today.'

'I know,' was the tense reply, 'and I want you to take me with you. We can be married by the minister on Tombaugh. It's done all the time.'

The whole thing was a little swift even for an experienced

161

philanderer. And Sennes hesitated. After a few moments, he must have realised his delay in replying could have a devastating effect. He said hastily, 'Reason I'm a little slow on that is I've already got a passenger lined up for today. But' – his face cleared, as the decision took place – 'why don't you come along, also? No real problem. Is that all right, my dear?'

'I guess so.' For a moment she was uncertain. Then she swallowed, and said earnestly, 'It's got to be right away, Peter. We've got to be married right away. Today.'

'I'll meet you at the Subsurface at the takeoff hangar – same place as last Sunday,' said a relieved Sennes, 'in about' – he glanced at his watch, and raised his eyebrows as he saw the time; grimaced – 'in about forty minutes'

'I'll be there,' said Susan.

The man heard the disconnecting click at the other end of the line. As he replaced his own receiver, he made the familiar victory gesture with forefinger and thumb shaped into a circle. He said, 'My little jabber wants to discuss marriage.'

The younger man shook his head with reluctant admiration. 'And no one can discuss marriage like you can.'

Sennes was heading for the bathroom. 'I've got to make a rapid exit, so don't slow me down with too much praise.'

In the den of the Lane house, Susan was hastily writing a note, which read:

Dear Mother and Dad:
    By the time you read this I will be Mrs Peter Sennes. I'm sorry it had to be this way, but it's all for the best. Wish me luck.

Your loving daughter,
Susan.

She laid the letter on the bar, went softly to the den door, and by a combination of tiptoeing and careful opening and closing of the outside door, was presently hurrying up the street to the Subsurface. Moments later, she entered the elevator. The door closed, and the indicator showed that the machine was heading down.

XXVIII

By 7.30 a.m., the Red Cat outfit – girls as well as boys – along with an adult witness, were gathered outside the Jaeger home. Sharply on the half-hour, the witness, a middle-aged man named Grégory Bonge, walked up to the door, and rang the doorbell. There was a long pause. Then a man's rough voice sounded from inside: 'You tell those kids they'd better get away from this house. Bud isn't coming out, and they're not coming in. I've got some shells here with salt pork in them in a loaded shotgun to back me up.'

The witness returned to the outfit, and reported the threat. He finished: 'Jabbers, this looks a rough case. In view of all the circumstances – if the Jaegers actually leave Spaceport two days from now – I recommend you withdraw from this situation. I further advise that we inform the military police, and await their instructions.'

Before Lee could speak, anger flashed into Mike's face. He burst forth passionately. 'We're not going to let this booter get away with this, are we?'

Everybody's face was instantly tense. Yet, as Lee glanced questioningly from face to face, there was no doubt. They were in agreement. Mike's words had expressed the consensus. No surrender.

'But, still, that guy is not sane,' said one of the boys. 'So I think we should call Outfit Central for the cover wagon.'

'That's what we'll do,' said Lee. 'Unless Bud asks for help.'

There was no word from Bud. No sound at all from the Jaeger house. In about eight minutes what looked like a panel truck came along the street, and stopped across the road. It happened that Lee was standing on the sidewalk near by. And now, quite casually, he walked past the truck and was briefly lost to view of the outfit – and of anyone in the Jaeger house. During that period, one of the two police officers in the truck opened a sliding door on the sidewalk side. Opened it a tiny slit, and said, 'Start your approach. We'll cover you.'

'Sack, Henry,' said the boy.

Lee thereupon walked past the truck, and continued across the street to the outfit. He said curtly, 'Marianne, you go and face Mr Jaeger.'

163

The small girl's olive-complexioned face took on a bleached-white, drawn look. Timidly, she touched Mike's arm. Mike's tightly pressed lips relaxed a bit. His other arm came up and that hand touched her shoulder, lightly, encouragingly. That was all. He withdrew his hand. He nodded at her. 'Let's get going,' he said.

Lee commanded: 'Mike, you come with me!' To the others: 'You know your jobs in a situation like this. Get set.'

Having spoken, he started rapidly along the street, followed by Mike. The two boys proceeded to a point where other houses blocked all sight of them from anybody in the Jaeger residence. Whereupon, they climbed the fence there, ran at top speed down the side of that house, and over three fences into the Jaeger backyard. Since time had gone by, Lee drew out a gas pistol while Mike headed for the rear door, after reporting that, 'Mrs Jaeger said last night she'd leave this back door unlocked, and maybe even ajar.'

So Mike entered an empty kitchen without incident. Without glancing back, he beckoned Lee, who came running. Moments later, Lee followed, gas gun poised, while Mike went forward along a hallway to the living room.

Thus it was Mike, in front, who actually saw an event that had been building up inside the Jaeger house for the previous four minutes.

Bud, who had been ordered to remain in his bedroom, was of course in a state. He was due to be at one of the *Omnivulture* hangars by nine o'clock for the takeoff with Captain Sennes . . . and his escape from earth. Len Jaeger's unreasoning attitude toward the outfits – which had been considered an excellent screening emotion that would in a crisis be a protection for the alien boy – was now revealed as a madness sufficient to endanger the escape plan.

Bud had been standing at his bedroom door, watching his 'father' with the poised shotgun. Through the window he could see Marianne as she opened the gate. Moments later, the girl started along the walk toward the house, and disappeared from the line of sight visible through the window.

In the front room, Len Jaeger opened the outside door a crack, and poked the barrel of the shotgun through it. Mrs Jaeger, who had been crouching in a chair in the dining room alcove, ran forward as her husband pointed the gun. The man saw her, or heard her, coming. As she grabbed at him, he made a thrust with one hand and arm. The blow caught her on the shoulder, and spun her even as it shoved her back the way she had come. She ended up, sprawled on the floor, screaming at the man. But she made no further move; did not try to get up.

For Bud, it was a moment of confusion. He was unaware of the police across the street. To him, Marianne was unprotected. 'Hey!' he protested, 'you wouldn't shoot a girl!'

'Get back into your bedroom!' snarled the man. He spoke without glancing away from what he was doing. His jaw tightened with determination. The shotgun came up.

For Bud, it had the look of the moment of decision. He had not been a jabber long enough to realise that outfits had dealt with equally dangerous threats, and had a technique for it. That even the way Marianne was coming toward the door, was a method: to aim at her Jaeger would have to open the door wider, so that he could point the gun to the left. But so far as Bud was concerned, it was up to him. It was a great responsibility, too much for a boy, alien or human. As he ran forward, the severity of what he had to do made him forget the intricate play act of being Bud Jaeger.

The first lapse was his arms. The steel-strong tentacles that coiled around an instantly astonished man bore no resemblance to human arms and hands at the moment of attack.

Once more, it was not Len Jaeger's hour, or day. He defended himself with a convulsive gesture. Actually threw Bud off of him. But the required effort simultaneously did several disastrous things. The shotgun automatically jerked up and sideways, opening the door wide. Through this, precipitated by reaction from the muscular effort of freeing himself from the python-like arms of his 'son,' the man staggered. Since he was still clinging to the gun, to those outside it looked as if he was charging forth with mayhem intent.

Over in the panel truck, Henry and his companion – operating at two different peepholes – didn't have time to decide which of them should fire. As a result, both gas guns discharged. The two gas pellets, like a pair of poison darts, bridged the hundred or so feet from the truck to the target. The man jumped as those frozen crystals of anesthetic gas penetrated his clothes and made their icy entry into his body. After that first instant, the rebellion of Len Jaeger was a thing of the past. He staggered like a man who has been mortally wounded. But he fell by sinking to his knees. Slowly, then, he leaned forward. He lay down on the walk in front of Marianne as if it were a bed, and he was seeking it for a long, cozy sleep.

Inside the house, Bud was still out of control. As he fought to retain his balance, even his legs reverted to tentacle shape. While an amazed Mike watched – and, seconds later, Lee also – the alien boy bobbed up and down, and sideways, like a creature on springs. His clothes only partially concealed how truly inarticulated and boneless his limbs were.

During those prolonged moments, his face lost most of its Bud Jaeger resemblance. He recovered his balance at a point when he was partly facing Mike and Lee. And there must have been something in their expressions.

Two things, then.

He tried to recover. The face came back. The legs straightened. The arms made a vague effort toward being bone as well as muscle, and each with an elbow and wrist.

That was one thing.

The second: he realised from what he saw in their widened eyes that it was too late. Or, at least, he *thought* he saw that.

He turned and ran out of the door.

It was the awkward, human version of his run. And so he burst forth from the doorway, slamming the door shut behind him, and locking it. His flight had a human look about it to the other Red Catters.

Nobody tried to stop him. Because, after all, he was the one they were trying to free, so that he could go to school. And the sooner he was out of the way, the better, perhaps. Albert even looked after him, and said, 'Let him go. We'll see him at school. And no use him being around while we deal with his dad.'

So Bud ran the short half-block to the nearest corner. And then he ran the long block to the Subsurface. Into the elevator he darted, and down he went, and gone, he was – safe.

He left behind him, principally, confusion in the minds of Mike and Lee. They were far from being as clear about what they had seen as Bud feared they had. And with each passing moment, the memory grew more blurred.

Because, of course, it was impossible.

Back to the hospital went Len Jaeger. And the Red Cat outfit members headed for school, most of them subconsciously anticipating that some time during the day they would see Bud. Certainly, this would be true after final class, they believed.

Except Mike was not that certain. In Mike memories stirred. He visualised the first time he had chased Bud, and brought him down with a football-style tackle. Several recollections followed, of Bud running, or walking, in his awkward fashion. And finally, recurring several times – as he sat in class at his mechanised desk, with its computer connections, and other electronic teaching equipment – the memory of Bud that morning.

Yet Mike did nothing. He moved through the day like an automaton. His haunted face with the inwardly looking eyes periodically confronted kids that he knew. And turned away, expression unchanged, almost unnoticing. In a vague fashion he communicated. Each time, it was a variation of the same question: 'Have you seen Bud Jaeger?'

Nobody had.

The school clocks moved slowly around to 2.09 p.m. Mike was on his way back to his class room after the brief intermission. Suddenly . . . his feeling and memories and thoughts coalesced. He stopped. Turned. Then he was racing along corridors that were rapidly emptying thousands of students back into their classrooms for the final class of the day.

By the time Mike came to Lee's room, the class was in session . . . after the manner of such classes, of course. It was a senior group, and accordingly there was no supervising instructor permanently in the room. Mike stood at the open door, and beckoned Lee. The blond boy got up, and came over. The two youths thereupon had a brief but earnest conversation. Finally, Lee reentered the room, shut off his equipment. When he came out again, the two of them hastened along the corridor to the nearest exit. A minute later, they left the school grounds. And, shortly, they were entering the elevator of a Subsurface.

Estelle and John Lane had breakfast – just the two of them – about half past eight that morning. 'Not a sound from Susan,' said the woman, 'so I think I'll just let her sleep.'

Her husband made a neutral noise, indicating that he had heard the words but had no opinion on the matter. The woman stared at him accusingly, but if he was pleased at the development, he was careful not to show the thought. And he kept his eyes pretty well looking down at his plate.

His wife accompanied him presently to the front door. And when he tentatively bent to kiss her, she cringed but did not turn her lips away. So they shared a good-bye kiss. It was a reconciliation of sorts. And the woman was somewhat more cheerful as she went about her housework. First, the kitchen, of course. Next, the dining room. Then – biggest job – the living room. It was a long job, and she was only half done, when she decided to have a cup of her delightful coffee. She made the coffee, poured it, and was replacing the coffee maker in its cradle, when she saw the clock. The time was a few minutes after ten.

Her eyes frowned a little. She pursed her lips. Decision. With purposeful steps, she left the kitchen and walked to Susan's bedroom. Found it unoccupied, of course. After a blank period, she searched the room for a message. Nothing.

Her alarm had been increasing. So, rapidly now – for a dignified lady – she ran back to the kitchen, straight to the phone.

167

In the middle of pressing out a number, she paused.

Her eyes changed, losing their fear. She grew thoughtful. Her lips formed, and murmured the words, 'Maybe she's at school, and he won't like that.'

She replaced the receiver, and forced herself to sit down. She drank her coffee, then, and stared off into the infinite spaces of her mind.

Her face and eyes grew tired. 'Maybe,' she muttered, 'I should lie down for a while.'

It cost her an effort to go to her bedroom. And when she got there she sort of poured herself onto it. She lay there like a large lump of jelly.

After a while she slept.

It was shortly after 10.00 a.m. that the intercom buzzed on Lane's huge desk. It was Andrew Scott with the information that Len Jaeger was again in the hospital.

The man at the desk in the big communication room, said, 'What happened to Mr Jaeger?'

From his end, the secretary said, 'According to the report I have, Mr Jaeger attemped to stop his son from going to school this morning.'

'What are his injuries?' Lane asked grimly.

'Well, none – exactly. He was rendered unconscious with two gas anesthetic pellets, and after he sleeps it off he will be free to go home.' The smooth voice broke off. 'You asked me to keep you informed about this man, sir.'

'Yes, yes.' He nodded half to himself. A decision was forming. It was not entirely of the moment, of course, but his manner had in it a sort of impatient the-time-has-come-to-do-something. He continued, 'Mr Scott, I find myself puzzled – and that is a mild word – by the privileges which seem to have been accorded outfits while I was absent from earth. Apparently, these groups can at will damage adults, without penalty.'

'There are rules, sir, governing these matters.'

'They seem to be very elastic,' the officer retorted with asperity. 'Anyway, will you ask a member of – what is it called? – the Outfit Training Center, to come over here some time today and brief me on this whole matter?'

'Very well.'

The appointment was made for 1.30 p.m. that afternoon. 'A Mr Portanyi will represent the Outfit Training Center,' said the secretary.

The fleet comander said with a sardonic smile, 'I have a feeling that my wife would be very happy to hear of this meeting.'

'Shall I call her and tell her?'

'No, no, of course not.' Lane spoke hastily. 'Under no circumstances.'

XXIX

LANE was still at his desk a few minutes before noon, when a voice spoke from the big viewplate. It was a man's voice, very tense. 'Commander Lane,' it said, 'a patrol craft of the 20,000 SA series has just advised that the alien fleet has crossed the orbit of Neptune and is moving toward zero.' Zero was earth.

It was electrifying news; and Lane jumped to his feet. 'What disposition are you in?'

'In depth, sir, as ordered. Formation at the moment is Plan T.23. First collision is probably not before midnight.'

The fleet commander had control of himself again. 'Very good.' he said, 'keep *Oriole* close to zero. I may come aboard some time this evening.'

'Very well, Commander.' The bodiless voice fell silent.

Lane turned to his desk, and made another call to his secretary. 'Mr Scott,' he said, 'have a space-lift on the ready for me all day and evening.'

'*Yessir.*'

'And then contact the Space Committee, and ask for an immediate emergency session.'

'Indeed, sir.'

The Committee meeting, as usual, ate up time. The usual stupid people, with their infinite need to ask questions, asked them. In the end, a sardonic Lane, restraining his impatience, reissued his invitation to the members to join him aboard the *Oriole* that evening. 'Be ready for space-lift takeoff at thirty minutes notice,' he said blandly.

By the time he returned to his office, it was a few minutes after 1.30 p.m. In entering, Lane happened to glance toward the glass enclosed conference chamber under the viewplate. He glimpsed a man sitting there and stopped in astonishment. Obviously, somebody to see him. But who could it be? Frowning, he opened the door, and entered the sound-proof room. 'Yes?' he asked courteously.

The other man had stood up. He was about Lane's age and

height. He said, 'I'm Mr Portanyi from the Outfit Training Center.'

Naturally, the whole memory burst forth at that point. Lane said, 'Oh!' And hesitated. It was not a good moment for the interview; that was his first reaction. Yet after a brief consideration, it occurred to him that he had actually nothing to do in connection with the emergency but await developments. His hesitation ended. 'Sit down,' he said.

'After you, Commander,' was the reply.

Lane obliged. A minute after that he was listening to his first explanation of the outfits.

A normal adult (began Mr Portanyi) is a reasoning being. If he *is* normal, he easily sees that men must cooperate, be totally truthful, not take advantage, be responsible, and never do anything that will interfere with another normal person's rights.

When an adult does not do this, it is because he got twisted in his early years. Thus, the teen period – and earlier – is decisive for the person's whole life.

For example, it is in the preeighteen group that courage is intensely important. It is here that the term of opprobrium, 'yellow,' has meaning. Adults, who have this complex as a carryover in some form of supermasculinity, are teenagers emotionally. Hence, all work which requires unusual expression of the masculinity principle, should logically be done by boys under eighteen. Observation had proved that boys *and* girls were equally capable provided they were in the mixed group situation.

It followed that all police work of the simpler kind should be done by teens organised into outfits, who operate by rules. For teen boys, the bravery urge is normal, and in the girls, admiration of brave boys (and an odd, echoing bravery) is normal.

But for an adult, any obsession about masculinity is a teen-age hang-up.

Similarly, adults twisted during their own early years, can only damage children by trying to raise them. Therefore, the outfits should raise the children, according to rules which they along with the help – in emergencies – of neutral witnesses, are at the right age to do so naturally.

There is a strange look which comes into a man's face when he discovers that the brand of courage, which he has displayed his entire lifetime, is regarded by a new theory as being a carryover from his teen-age male need to be an adult. And is not of itself an adult state.

A brick-red flush was the first signal. Then rage – and rejection of the whole line of reasoning. 'Who should go on these space expeditions?' Lane demanded. 'Boys or men?'

'Basically, young people, girls as well as boys,' was the unexpected reply, 'with adult couples along to play the neutral role, and to act as creative brains at key moments, and of course to do those things that only highly trained, grown people can do.'

'But what is there left for adults to do?' Lane was suddenly more bewildered than angry.

'It is our conviction,' said the other man smoothly, 'that human beings, and I'm referring exclusively to normal adults when I say that – a teen being considered an embryo human, only – will eventually find their place in the universe.'

The fleet commander said quickly, 'After eight and a half years, there must be some statistics available. By your standards, juvenile delinquency?' He paused, uncertain.

'Nine years ago,' said Pontanyi, 'thousands of rebellious youngsters passed through the hands of the juvenile authorities each year. Today, we have about two hundred kids in what are called camps. These are individuals who have resisted outfit authority, and have been turned over to us by their oufits. Other than that' – he made a dismissing gesture – 'there is no juvenile delinquency in Spaceport today.'

Lane stood up, He had heard enough, and in his abrupt, decisive fashion, he said coldly, 'I'm sorry to tell you, but my impression is that the entire outfit movement borders on juvenile delinquency. So by your view you have reduced delinquency. By mine, you have expanded the delinquency situation to include the entire teen population.' He made a dismissing gesture. 'I really haven't time today to consider the madness you have outlined to me. But, shortly, I'm going to give my full attention to you, your training school, and its vicious trainees.'

The other man was a little bit more pale. 'Commander,' he said earnestly, 'I doubt if at this stage any one person, however powerful, can stop the outfits.'

'We'll see,' said Lane curtly.

Pontanyi was recovering. He bowed politely. 'The information I have given you, sir is the best we can do for you.'

On that note, the highly unsatisfactory – from Lane's point of view – interview, ended. Mr Pontanyi departed. And Lane returned to his desk.

It was now three minutes after two o'clock.

Scott came in, waited patiently until he had his boss's attention, and then said, 'Captain Mijnalen called to ask if you would have lunch with him in the Commissary.'

Lane smiled his grimmest smile at that. But this was not the day for him to discover what it felt like to eat publicly an outfit-restricted meal. 'Tell the captain,' he said in a deliberate tone, 'that I'll take a rain check on that. Can't do it today.'

He forgot that *and* the outfits a few minutes later. Because from the giant viewplate came the second message:

'The alien fleet is approaching the orbit of Uranus, and should reach Saturn about seven o'clock this evening. Still accelerating towards zero.'

All spaceships operated on Spaceport time. Lane said, 'What is your present estimate of collision hour?'

'We won't let them get beyond Jupiter. So that could be slightly before nine.'

'Thank you,' said Lane.

He had barely spoken, when a certain phone rang. He stared at it, shocked. Then jerkily he picked up the receiver, and said formally, 'Commander Lane speaking, Mr President.'

'Commander,' said the president's voice, 'do you think we should make a public announcement?'

Lane drew a deep breath for reinforcement of his spirit. Then, firmly: 'No Mr President. All our screens are up. Our ships are between earth and the enemy. Let's give this approach until five o'clock to see if they really mean it. The panic will be no greater then than now.'

'Very well, Commander,' was the reply, followed by a click of disconnection.

Lane hung up, also, and buzzed the intercom for his secretary. To that individual, he said, 'I am now motivated by my stereotype – which you might as well find out about. In period of crisis, I try to think of everything. Even the tiniest possibilities engage my attention. So, during the next hour or so, you and I will do some fairly strange things as fast as possible.'

'On the double, sir, it shall be,' was the reply.

'First,' said the man at the desk, 'I can't get out of my head the fact that Jaeger, also, was subjected to the K energy. So contact the hospital, and if Mr Jaeger is still there, get them to put him on the phone.'

Jaeger had left the hospital bare minutes before, and was on his way home. 'All right,' commanded Lane, 'get me Mrs Jaeger at her home.'

He asked the sad little voice if there was anything about her husband or her son that she had noticed recently that was unusual.

'*He's* the same,' was the apathetic reply, 'but Bud is more intelligent than he used to be. Being in the outfit has been good for him.'

'Just a moment,' said the disgusted officer. As he handed the receiver back to Scott, he admonished, 'Ask her to have Jaeger call

172

this office when he gets home.'

As 2.43 p.m., Lane wearily completed a futile conversation with his fourteenth 'possibility' – the port of entry officer, who had called him about Bud Jaeger's return to Spaceport after Bud's attempt to 'run away.' Lane returned the receiver to Scott, and saw that another light was blinking on the phone multiplex. Andrew Scott pressed that button, listened for a few moments, and then said, 'It's Mr Reid, the Committee chairman.'

'Ask him if I can call him back,' said his boss in a distracted tone.

Scott spoke the words into the mouthpiece, and again listened. The shape of his mouth changed. His eyes did a narrowing. His fingers tightened on the instrument which he now held out stiffly to Lane, saying in a shaken voice, 'You'd better talk to him, sir.'

Startled, the fleet commander accepted the instrument. Desmond Reid, at the other end of the line, stood in his office with Lee David and Mike Sutter on either side of him, and said gravely, 'I think I should bring the boys over, and you make up your mind as to what I've just told you.'

Lane said, 'Let me understand this, *they* noticed something unusual about Bud Jaeger this morning?'

'Yes. And I think you should hear what, from them.'

The younger man said somewhat blankly, 'By all means, bring them over.'

'. . . Four minutes,' said Desmond Reid's voice urgently.

Lane replaced the receiver, and said to his aide with a frown, 'Your reaction to that call seemed unusually strong. It doesn't appear that decisive. A possibility, that's all.'

The secretary's eyes widened. 'He didn't tell you?' he whispered.

'What he told me,' was the slightly nettled reply, 'implied strange behavior in Bud Jaeger.'

'What he told *me*,' said Scott, 'was that there was a possibility that *the boy was not human.*'

There was a long silence. Half-slitted eyes. Slightly sagging jaw. Then a kind of rejecting shake of the head. 'Such an impersonation,' Lane spoke slowly, 'would be difficult. Still' – he climbed to his feet – 'no reason why we shouldn't have a good look at Bud Jaeger,' He nodded decisively. 'Mr Scott, have the military police arrest him, and bring him here.'

'I'll put out an all-points computer signal alarm,' said Scott.

'Good.'

As the secretary disappeared, the corridor door opened. Desmond Reid stood aside to let Lee and Mike enter. He followed hard on their heels, and closed the door behind him.

173

John Lane stiffened involuntarily as he looked at the two youths. All he said, however, was, 'I have Mr Reid's message.' His tone was formal. 'Please tell your story.'

The boys were not that swiftly able to be aware of the man. The room and its machinery caught their separate attentions, and held them. They stared slightly goggle-eyed at the big viewplate. Their faces proclaimed that they realised it was not a simulated scene on the huge screen, not even a motion picture duplicate. This was direct transmission, live from space.

Yet, they had their own urgent feelings, And so, swiftly, after that initial dazzlement, they were able to tell him of Bud, and of what Mike and, to a lesser degree, Lee had seen.

When their brief account was completed, there was silence in that strange, wonderful room. The fleet commander's countenance reflected a struggle that was going on inside him. Reid watched him, narrow-eyed, and then walked close to him, and said in a low tone, 'John, your face is showing an emotion which I find it difficult to credit: pleasure. What are you enjoying about this situation?'

The younger man was shocked. 'Pleasure?' he muttered. Abruptly, he was guilty. 'Des,' he almost whispered, 'it's true. My first thought was: "Our enemy unerringly spotted our weakness – the outfits." I'm ashamed of myself for feeling good about how right I was about the outfits. But it remains a truth. That's where they achieved their infiltration.' He broke off. 'Look, forget about that. No matter how they did it, our problem remains.'

He raised his voice. 'I have ordered Bud's arrest by the military police. So I think these two boys' – he nodded at Mike and Lee – 'should wait in my conference room, and identify Bud when he is brought in.'

It was Reid who guided the two jabbers through the door of the conference room, and then closed the door. Then he himself walked to the corridor door. He paused with one hand on the latch. 'I'm expecting an overnight kit from home,' he said. 'I'll return here as soon as it arrives.' His fine old face creased into a faint smile. 'I plan to go aboard the *Oriole* with you.'

The fleet commander's face twisted satirically. 'Dez,' he said, 'that's teen-level bravado – I was told today.'

'But you invited the Committee members.'

'My own teen hang-ups,' said Lane cynically, 'required that I ask the idiots of the Committee. You're not included among the idiots in my mind.'

'Nevertheless,' smiled the older man, 'I feel a great need to manifest an image of boldness for the benefit of all those teen-

174

age adults out there.' He waved vaguely, taking in half the room.

Still smiling, he opened the door, and went out, closing it behind him. Lane returned to his desk, and he was sitting there, frowning to himself, striving to think of what else to do, when Scott came running in breathlessly. He laid a sheet of paper on the big desk, and pointed with a trembling forefinger at the last two lines.

The senior fleet commander gazed down at the paper without at first grasping the full meaning of what was printed there. The document, a single sheet, was a computer copy of a test flight order for *Omnivulture 2681-E*, Captain Peter Sennes, active flight officer, pilot, and two passengers.

The names of the passengers, as given on the last two lines, were Susan Lane and Bud Jaeger.

What the man at the desk did not immediately grasp was the date of the flight. In fact, he glanced up at the plump, competent individual who was hovering so nervously above him, and said irritably, 'Mr Scott, this is rather a late report. My wife could have been saved a lot of anxiety last Sunday had she known that there was a second passenger on this craft.' He broke off, scowling: 'As for who that second passenger was, I'm astounded that we only now discover it was the Jaeger boy –'

He was interrupted. The liaison secretary was pale. 'Sir,' he gasped, 'that document does not refer to last Sunday's flight. The report came in, and I brought it to you at once. That military craft space-lifted at nine o'clock this morning.'

The fleet commander grabbed at the paper, and with his finger traced the date: August twelve NOAD. As he gazed at it, the normal high-color of his cheeks changed a little. Slowly, then, he shrank down into his chair, and crouched there for a time looking blank. When he finally stirred, he said wearily, 'Mr Scott.'

'Yes, sir?'

'When Mr Reid comes, don't mention Susan. A hard decision have to be made, and I don't want him influenced the way I may be.'

'Very good, sir.' Pause. Then, discreetly, 'What about Mrs Lane, Commander?'

The officer smiled wanly. 'When I left the house shortly before nine o'clock, my wife believed Susan was sound asleep in her bed. Obviously' – he tapped the paper – 'Susan wasn't.' Once more he was silent. The sick expression came back. He said, 'Please call my wife, and ask her to come down to this office.' He added dully, 'I think she ought to be here for whatever develops. And if by any chance we can have a few last words with our dear daughter, that privilege should not be denied her.' He broke off. 'Just tell her to come at once. Don't tell her why, yet.'

XXX

ESTELLE actually slept several times. Twice, she got up for coffee, and then back into the bedroom she drooped. Shortly after two, it became obvious that the madness must cease. 'After all,' she said aloud into the shaded room, hopefully. 'Susan will be home from school in another hour.'

Up she got, and into the living room she went, and re-resuming there her task of cleaning. After a weary while, she dragged the cleaning stuff into the den. And she was wiping the bar itself with a specially-impregnated cloth when she saw Susan's note.

At the exact moment when Andrew Scott was phoning her, she had the den phone receiver in her hand, and was frantically button-pushing Lane's office number. As a result Scott reported to Lane, 'I get a busy signal, sir.'

Even as he spoke, a light blinked on the phone multiplex attached to the desk. Andrew Scott stepped discreetly forward, picked up a second receiver, pressed the lighted button, and said hello. He listened wisely, and then said, 'I'll see.' He thereupon placed his palm over the mouthpiece, and said in a low voice, 'Your wife.'

Reluctantly, his boss held out his hand for the receiver. His expression said that this wasn't going to be easy. So, as he brought his lips near the mouthpiece, he began at once, at if he would overwhelm her. 'Estelle, I've just discovered that our daughter is aboard *Omnivulture* with Captain Sennes. Dez and I would like you to come over here to my office. Meanwhile, I'll call Sennes, and see what the situation is. Okay?'

At her end, the blonde woman screamed, 'Wait!'

It was an arresting yell. Her husband jiggled a little as the sound poured into his eardrum. But he waited while she read him the note their daughter had written.

As he listened, Lane's face and eyes tried to reject his own responsibility in what had happened. It was distinctly unfair – a horrifying coincidence, it seemed at this moment – that the aliens had somehow used Captain Sennes's test flight routine as a means of their spy escaping from earth. But he had to get Estelle off the line, and en route, swiftly while, in fact, he did attempt to communicate with *Omnivulture 2681-E*.

So he said reassuringly, 'I can't believe that Captain Sennes would be a party to a runaway marriage with a teen-age girl. In the first place, I've never thought of him as a marrying man –'

'What's that?' said his wife sharply. 'What did you say?'

There was a pause, while the man savored the meaning of his own words as they must have sounded to her. And it was not good. Before he could speak, her voice came again, savagely, 'When I see you next, be prepared to have your goddamn face slapped,' she said.

The situation was so fantastically much worse than she realised, that her husband could only grit his teeth in self-control, as he said, 'If I deserve it, I'll take it.' He attempted to soothe her. 'Now, listen, let me do what I said – phone Sennes right now, while you're on your way over.'

'It would be much faster if you called him,' said the woman, 'and then phoned me right back.'

'For God's sake, Estelle,' yelled her husband, 'stop arguing with me and get over here!'

He disconnected hastily, and looked up with a pale countenance at his aide. 'Things are going to get worse, I know, but that will do for a start.'

Andrew Scott said diplomatically, 'Maybe the situation isn't as bad as we fear. Maybe they are on Tombaugh, or somewhere.'

'Let's not delude ourselves,' was the curt reply. 'It's obvious now why the enemy is moving in. They're going to cover, and protect, and defend our beautiful *Omnivulture* so that little Bud escapes with his information.'

The secretary said in a formal tone, 'Commander, have I your permission to attempt to contact Captain Sennes?'

The request brought a sudden breathlessness to Lane. Naturally, he wanted to say, yes, of course, go ahead. The words wouldn't come, because – because he didn't want to hear what was technically obvious: that Susan was already dead. He finally managed to gulp, 'They're probably beyond the orbit of Mars by now.'

'Then the communication computer will automatically use the carrier system of instant transmission via one of the orbiting stations out there. Correct?'

'I suppose that's true,' agreed Lane reluctantly. He sighed. 'All right. Go ahead.'

Two things happened, then, almost at the same instant.

The corridor opened, and Desmond Reid, carrying a small

suitcase, walked in. He waved at the two men, but apparently saw that they were busy. For he put up his hand, and pointed toward the conference room, and shaped his mouth to the *sotto voce* words: 'Call me when you're through.' He strode on into the conference room, and the last Lane saw of him, he was shaking hands with Lee David.

That event was probably first by several moments.

The second thing: As the fleet commander turned his attention back to Scott, he saw that the liaison aide was holding the receiver out to him. The plumpish man said in his most imperturbable secretarial voice, 'Captain Sennes on the line, sir.'

XXXI

WHEN Bud Jaeger arrived at the designated *Omnivulture* hangar, he was asked to sign in and then to sit in the adjoining waiting room. While he sat, people – all men – charged past both ways in an intermittent stream. There was the sound of many human voices, and whenever a certain door was opened, a vibration came through from whatever was beyond. The vibration was not exactly a sound, though it had sound in it. It was a feeling of power that, somehow, he had not previously experienced on earth.

The alien boy sat very still, taking it all in. Two male clerks who worked behind the grilled wickets, glanced at him periodically. Finally, one said to the other, 'That's the quietest kid I've ever seen. He hasn't moved, or lifted a finger, since he sat down. What's he scheduled for.'

The second man studied the sign-in sheet. 'The Sennes flight – a passenger.'

The first man grinned. 'Hey,' he said, 'that's a switch for Sennes – a boy passenger. Maybe he's getting strange in his old age.' He added, 'The kid is probably petrified with fear.'

They both laughed. And clearly considered the excessive boy stillness of the 'boy' explained.

It was not until fourteen minutes to nine that Captain Sennes arrived with a Susan breathless from last moment hurrying. 'Whee, Bud!' said the girl, nervously.

'This way,' said Captain Sennes. He opened the door that led to the vibration, with its sense of vast open spaces.

Bud climbed to his feet, puzzled. 'What are you doing here?' he asked Susan.

'I'll tell you later,' was the reply. She added, 'The ride is so great, the rest doesn't matter.' She was following the flight officer by the time she uttered that enigmatic sentence. Hastily, Bud set out after her.

The two young people almost literally pursued Captain Sennes through a tangle of spacecraft to where the great, sleek machine 2681-E waited for them. As Sennes assisted, first Susan and then Bud up to the in-ramp of the ship, the boy was still uncertain as to the reason for her presence. He followed Susan forward, and dutifully, on her instructions, sat down and fitted on the safety belts. But when he saw her do the same for herself, he protested, 'You're not going along?'

She nodded.

'B-but you've already been once,' the boy protested wildly, as if somehow that concept had a genuine meaning, as if it made sense. When the girl seemed not to accept that meaning, he added urgently, 'Susan, wait – don't –'

On the other side of the girl, Captain Sennes had his earphones on, and with a dexterous twist or two, fastened himself in with the safety belts. On the great viewplate at their feet, the vaulted dome above the craft showed open.

While Bud watched in confusion, unable to decide what to do next, the vault opening appeared to come down toward them. As the flight continued, the boy hunched down into his part of the seat. He looked blank. His normally bright eyes had a partly closed slant to them. It gave them a glazed effect.

When the spacecraft was less than half an hour out from base Susan, who had been suppressing yawns for some minutes, said sleepily, 'Gee, I can hardly keep my scanners open. I was awake most of the night. So I think I'll squeeze out the light for a while. Sack?'

'Sack,' said Peter Sennes.

In a minute more, the two males were, in a manner of speaking, alone. The girl slept with her head tilted slightly to one side and nestling down on her left shoulder. 'Fact is,' the man said to the boy, 'since we're making a long trip, I put some relaxer in her orange juice at breakfast.'

Bud nodded, but said nothing. His bright eyes flicked a little, he registered the words. But the rule was to speak no more than necessary. Let the hypnotic victim do his own rationalising for his illogical acts.

For some reason, he himself was not quite as disturbed by the presence of a Susan who was asleep, as he had been by a Susan

179

awake. Thus, the hours went by, and he sat there as the magnificent machine flew all the way to the orbit of Mars, and kept right on hurtling along into the fantastic distances between Mars and Jupiter.

About three o'clock, Susan stirred, stretched, and opened her eyes. 'Aren't we at Tombaugh yet?' she asked, stifling a yawn.

Her question had the effect of a double-acting catalyst.

Just like that, her aliveness penetrated again to Bud. And the shock of her being on the ship returned.

The boy saw that the words had brought a puzzled frown into Sennes's face and eyes: 'Tombaugh?' the man echoed. But he seemed to be thinking. Bud watched him anxiously.

Oh, my father . . . He sent the silent appeal out into space . . . When are you coming? I need you.

And, in fact, out there in space, the invisible observer was during those moments involved in the intricate task of matching velocities with the hurtling *Omnivulture*.

Succeeded.

My son, he said, *you have done well.*

But Susan is aboard, the boy answered uneasily . . . *And she just now asked where we were going.*

The father was instantly concerned.

Did you do exactly as you were trained to do when you interviewed Captain Sennes?

Yes. I dropped the crystal at his feet when he was turned away from me for a few moments. As soon as I did that I repeated the words that I was told.

Good!

But, my father, they forgot to say there shouldn't be any other passengers.

It was an unfortunate oversight, soothed the father . . . *not to realise that you might become attached to someone.*

But it's Susan, and she's a member of my outfit, Bud protested.

Your escape is the important thing, my son. Now, heed me! You say Susan has just asked Captain Sennes about the vessel's destination?

Yes. But, first, about Susan —

What was Captain Sennes's reply? The father's telepathic communication ignored Bud's question.

He hasn't answered yet. He's sitting here looking very tense.

These active flight officers are trained to be immune to ordinary hypnotism. You bypassed his defenses. It never even occurred to him that a boy would try anything like that. But the effect is undoubtedly wearing off, now that he's wondering about how he got to the wrong destination. So you know what you must do.

Oh!
What's the matter?
Captain Sennes is talking to somebody.

XXXII

INSTEAD of immediately taking the phone receiver from his secretary's extended hand, Fleet Commander John Lane climbed to his feet and said, 'Tell Captain Sennes to hold for a minute.'

Hurriedly, he walked over to the conference room, opened it, and beckoned Reid to come out. Quickly, then, he explained to the older man about *Omnivulture* – but he named only Bud and Captain Sennes; did not mention Susan. He finished in a harsh voice, 'Dez, what do you think? I feel I may have to order that unit destroyed. Do you concur?'

The Committee chairman was amazed. 'Under no circumstances. This may be our opportunity to establish communication with these beings – which you have told me was the only sensible course.'

Relief flooded the younger man's face. He said hastily, 'Dez, thank God for that decision. It was my own, also. But I thought I might be letting personal considerations influence me in this emergency.'

'How do you mean?' Reid was puzzled.

'Susan is aboard.'

The older man turned pale. His face actually became gray. Finally, he gulped, and said shakily, 'Does Estelle know?'

Lane shook his head. 'Not yet. But she's on her way down here. So she'll know shortly.'

Having spoken, he stepped over to the red button. Placed his finger on it. And then looked up questioningly at the other. 'Do you agree?'

'Plan D?' asked his friend, simply.

'What else? The president, the cabinet members, all top echelon authorised to be interconnected with this computer, should hear every word, and be ready for immediate decisions. Correct?'

'Correct,' was the steady-toned reply.

Lane pressed the button.

Having done so, he nodded to Reid. 'Tell the boys to come out here. We may need their help.'

As he walked back to his desk, he was aware of the blond youth and the intese, dark-haired one, coming forth. Moments after that he was saying to Scott in a low voice, 'When my wife arrives, you brief her.'

'Very good sir,' was the equally low-voiced reply.

Lane now accepted the receiver from Scott's hand. He spoke into it in the formal tone of someone who knows that important people, indeed, were listening in, and that they would need all the information they could get. 'This is Fleet Commander John Lane. Am I addressing Captain Peter Sennes aboard *Omnivulture 2681-E* in flight six hours out from earth?'

'Yes, Commander. And I believe that I have a problem . . . which I have just become aware of.'

'Captain Sennes,' said Lane, 'you may tell me your problem in a moment. First, we want to know where you are.'

'Quadrant 31, Four-point-zero-three.'

Lane's voice changed slightly in pitch when he spoke again, almost as if he were standing on the bridge of the *Oriole*. His tone was firm and commanding, as he said 'To all unit captains near that reading – approach and stand by.' Once more, he addressed Sennes, and now his voice was again clear and showed awareness that other ears were listening: 'Captain,' he said, 'we have reason to believe that the boy who is one of your two passengers is an alien enemy, and if you can persuade him, we would like to have a conversation with him. Now, what is your problem?'

'I have just become aware,' was the calm answer, 'that I was hypnotised by the boy yesterday morning. I believe I have now successfully dehypnotised myself. And I shall attempt to carry out your request. Just a moment, sir.'

There was silence.

My father, they want to talk to me from earth. They know!

The parent was greatly disturbed.

This is very serious. Let me feedback to ship-base and ask instructions.

Shall I talk to Commander Lane?

Yes.

But – reluctantly *– he's a booter.*

He's also the senior earth fleet commander. So find out what he wants. But make no admissions about yourself.

Lane had urgently beckoned to Lee David and Mike Sutter. 'Get onto those phone extensions, and you talk to Bud first.'

The two boys grabbed the phones indicated silently by Andrew Scott. And Mike with a nod deferred to his outfit leader.

Captain Sennes's voice came first. 'My passenger, Bud Jaeger,'

182

he said, 'has a microphone and receiver fitted over his head, and is ready for communication.'

'Bud,' said Lee David, 'this is Lee David of the Red Cats.'

'Whee,' said the alien boy into everybody's speaker system.

'What's the problem, Bud?' said Lee.

What shall I say, my father?

Ask him what he wants.

But I know what he wants. And you can't refuse to answer a direct question from your outfit leader. It's in the rules.

Lee was speaking again: 'Bud, do you still regard yourself as a jabber?'

'Y-yes, of course. You haven't scraped me, have you?'

'Not yet,' said Lee. 'But you're either a jabber or you're not. And a jabber goes by the rules.'

'I kind of liked being in an outfit. We don't have anything like that. What would a jabber do in a situation like this?'

'What kind of situation is it, Bud? What's the problem?'

'My father says I mustn't answer that. And where I come from, a boy is with his father and does what he says.'

There was an interjection – Mike's urgent voice: 'Bud, our goal is peace. You know and I know, the adults can't or won't allow peace. So the jabbers have to achieve it. Sack?'

'But how do I know answering your questions will bring peace?'

At that point, Lee gestured at Mike for silence, and then he made a face at Lane. The man said promptly into his mouthpiece, 'Bud, this is the fleet commander, John Lane.'

'You're Susan's father. You're a booter.'

'Yes, I may be all those things. But I also know the problem. We'd like to talk to your leaders. They don't ever reply to our attempts at communication. Why, Bud, why?'

'Because you dropped bombs on our main planet without warning.'

'No – we didn't!'

'Somebody did. We're trying to find out who. That's why I'm here. We've got to find out.'

'Earth didn't do it, Bud.'

'That's why they won't communicate. They figure you'd lie, and so we'd never be sure.'

'Just a moment, Bud.' Lane placed his palm over the mouthpiece and said *sotto voce* to his secretary, 'Get microfilm copies from the computer of all documents and photos relating to every space expedition. Now!'

'*Yessir.*'

Lane removed his palm, and said, 'What do you think, Bud? You've looked us over.'

'People like you and Mr Jaeger are pretty awful. But some of the others were nice.'

'We didn't do it. Bud. Is there some way we can talk to your father?'

'I'll ask him.'

'Is he close by?'

'He's outside – well, a projection of him is.'

'Like the one that was here in Spaceport?'

'Yes.'

He wants to talk to you, my father.

I told you not to give him any information. What kind of disobedience is this?

Mike says it's up to us jabbers to bring peace. The grown-ups can't do it, he says.

I have just received instructions. Drop the second capsule.

B-but that'll kill Susan, too.

My son, do as your father commands you!

But I can't do that to a member of my outfit. I can't . . . There was a long pause, then: *I won't!*

The father's grim thought came: *What does Commander Lane want, you disobedient child?*

I-I'll ask him.

XXXIII

A few minutes after eight o'clock, Spaceport time, the president announced to the world what had happened. The Chief Executive finished his account with the dramatic statement that 'at this very moment, Senior Fleet Commander John Lane and Chairman Desmond Reid of the Space Committee are on their way to the command ship of the alien fleet to present a complete refutation of the accusation that earth was responsible for bombs being dropped without warning on their home planet.'

It was a bold speculation on the part of the government leader. His words implied that the aliens were actually intending to negotiate, though it was obvious to expert observers that nothing had really happened that could logically have caused them to reverse their earlier negation of all communication with the human race. It was even possible – hinted the doubters – that Lane and Reid were already dead.

All that anyone knew was, the aliens agreed to allow Reid and Lane to board *Omnivulture 2681-E*. And they permitted Captain Sennes and Susan to return to earth on the space-lift that had delivered the two men. Sennes requested permission to be the *Omnivulture* pilot – but was turned down, on the grounds that he might still be under some kind of enemy control.

With that, the two men disappeared into silence.

The two great fleets stood by – while earth was, presumably, being tried.

At 7.30 the following morning, Susan phoned Lee. 'I won't be at school today,' she told him in a subdued voice, 'but I suppose I'm going to be dashed. So why not let's do that tonight?'

When Lee reported this to Mike, that individual said, 'Well, she's got a lot of chattering to do.'

The blond boy was silent. They were standing at the school gate, and he stared thoughtfully into the distance. He said finally, 'Under the circumstances – of Susan being willing – I see no reason for dashing her.'

The dark-haired youth gave him a startled look. Then: 'Lee,' he said, 'I don't think you should be the leader of the Red Cats any more.'

Lee was calm. 'We'll settle all that tonight. I've been thinking along the same lines.'

'And for that remark,' said Mike, 'I think you ought to be dashed, too.'

'I can see you're still my old pal,' said the older boy. But he was smiling, cheerful, not offended.

The lean boy was not to be stopped. He flashed, 'You've shown a weakness with girls. So you've damaged first Dolores and now Susan.'

The smile faded from Lee's face. 'Let's set me up to be dashed tonight – sack? We *will* settle Red Cat affairs . . . tonight. Dolores, Susan, me – you! Sack?' He spoke tautly.

There was a pause. 'Sack,' said Mike at last. But, as Lee turned and walked rapidly into the school grounds, the younger boy's face showed disturbance.

That night . . .

The sign above the door, into which dozens of jabbers streamed, said simply, OUTFIT CENTRAL.

Inside . . .

As the policeman, Henry, and his cover wagon associate of the previous morning, emerged from an inner room, they stopped short. Henry said, 'Hey! there must be a dozen outfits here tonight. Wonder what's going.'

'Let's take a look,' replied his companion pragmatically.

The two men walked to an open door further along the hallway. It was into it that the young people were disappearing. As the policeman gazed in, it was immediately obvious that it was a big meeting. Henry addressed Marianne, who was standing at the door. 'What's going on?' he asked.

'They're going to dash, well, several kids,' said Marianne, reluctantly, 'including Lee.'

'Lee David?' said the second constable, surprised.

Henry shook that shaggy-haired head of his. 'Lee! These jabbers don't play any favorites, do they?'

With that, the two men turned, and walked away – just as Marianne hurried forward to intercept Susan, who was somewhat hesitantly coming along at that moment.

'You can't go in, Susan. You're next – after Lee.'

The blonde girl's pretty face acquired a shocked expression. 'Lee!' she echoed, and her voice sounded outraged. Abruptly she was angry. 'Why that's absolutely ridiculous. I'm going in there, Don't try to stop me!'

With that, she brushed past the smaller girl, who made vague protesting noises, and then shrugged and followed Susan into the big room. They entered, as Mike was stating the accusation:

'His moocher had cheated on him,' said the Conscience of the Red Cat outfit, 'and he's pretending it hasn't happened. It's the same complete failure to handle a girl in a responsible way as when he dealt with Dolores a few months ago.'

The dark-haired Dolores made a face, as her name was mentioned in that derogatory tone. She was standing close to Captain Peter Sennes, but she did not glance at him to see his reaction.

The senior outfit leader present was a slim, straight boy of eighteen and a half, with fine, sandy hair, who stood with his head held back in a proud fashion. He said in an adjudicating tone, 'Of the other outfit leaders present, Tom Clanton and Johnny Sammo are the most familiar with this situation. I defer to Tom.'

Tom came forward. 'Lee,' he said, 'what's your answer to Mike?'

Lee was calm. 'It says in the rules that some kids, boys as well as girls, commit suicide when they're criticised. Something to do with their parents treating them like kings and queens when they were kids, the book speculates. Well, I've got to admit it never happened in my outfit until Dolores did it. What confused me was, I had misunderstood the idea. I thought they meant that kids who were innocent and falsely criticised, were the ones who committed suicide. It didn't occur to me that someone who was as guilty as Dolores would pretend that she was the injured

186

party, and commit suicide – which I confess she has done – just as if she were innocent. So I was wrong, but I was wrong through ignorance. Does that take care of that?' He glanced questioningly around at the faces of the other outfit leaders.

'Keep pushing,' said Tom Clanton.

'About Susan,' said Lee. 'In my judgement, she was innocent that first time. Mike had her faced because he's a little unstable where girls are concerned – there's a hot-headedness about him that isn't wrong because he's a friend of the rules – but he's like the inquisition judges of the Middle Ages. He carries a good thought to its extreme conclusion, and suddenly it's not good any more. So let me just put it in one sentence' – he clenched his fists and spoke the words through tight-clamped teeth – 'when a girl like Susan runs off to marry a sailor, the outfit has got to go back to the beginning and start over again. When Susan gets here, I want – '

He stopped. He had been turning, looking at various boys and girls in the room – and he came to Susan. Lee gulped, and said, 'Uh!'

The blonde girl walked out into the open space, and, turning, said in a trembling voice, 'You leave Lee alone. I'm the one that deserves to be dashed.'

Lee recovered at that point, said hastily, 'Susan, be quiet. It's all right.'

Susan refused to be quiet. 'Listen, jabbers,' she said, 'I've been a slab. Not a real bad one, because I came to in time. But for a week I've been bulging because a space sailor was rushing me.'

Lee said in a despairing voice, 'Susan, shut up.'

Mike had come up beside the blond youth. Now, he touched Lee's arm. 'Let her chatter.'

Having said those reassuring words, he walked out into the open part of the floor, over to Susan. 'Jabbers,' he said, and he placed his fingers lightly on the girl's wrist, 'I confess I feel now that Susan should not have been faced that first time. What's more, I believe she's been giving out with genuine jabber talk. All I want to know' – he turned to her – 'when did you snap out?'

'When I was having breakfast with him,' said Susan. 'There he sat double-talking to me, and I suddenly saw him for what he was – just another old man, really.'

Sennes winced, then closed his eyes, and then suppressed a smile.

Mike continued, 'Why did you go on the trip after that?'

Susan was surprised. 'You don't think I was going to miss a fabulous trip like that . . . Jabbers,' she said earnestly to everybody in general, 'you don't know what you've been missing.'

The lean boy waited until she had finished, and then said, 'The trip may be all that great, but I think this particular sailor was jabber hunting and ought to be made an example of.'

Dolores, who was standing beside Sennes now, very close, did a twisting thing with her body. '*You* would,' she said.

Sennes spoke up in his calm voice, with that note of infinite courage in it. 'Am I on trial here?' he asked.

Dolores gave him a startled glance, and then she looked around the room, wide-eyed. 'Is jabber hunting illegal?' she asked. 'I thought in such situations only the jabbers were guil – ' She stopped. And stood there, and her eyes showed that her thoughts were turning inward.

Lee now walked forward to the open floor. He paused in front of Dolores. 'Are you prepared to join an outfit?'

Dolores seemed not to hear.

Susan moved over and stood beside Lee. 'C'mon, Dolores,' she urged, 'please confess. You don't want to go to camp.'

The dark-haired girl did her sudden recovery. She turned with a faint, cynical smile, and looked up at Sennes, who returned her look with a shocked unhappiness. 'Maybe I should get married,' said Dolores.

'You're too young to marry,' said the flight officer hastily.

'But I *know* so much,' said Dolores in her most caressing voice, 'and I'll be eighteen next week.'

Mike came forward. 'What's going on here?' he asked suspiciously.

What was going on was blackmail by a girl who had suddenly realised that the man in the case was as much under threat as she was.

Dolores continued in a silken tone, 'I think I'd make a good wife for a space sailor. And if he doesn't come back from a hike, I'm just the girl who can get herself another husband.'

The roomful of young people was silent. They were all looking at an equally silent Captain Sennes – who had a faraway look in his eyes.

'Captain,' Dolores went on, 'do you think I'd be able to help a sailor by being married to him?'

The man came back from his distant mental world. He seemed resigned. 'Yes,' he said slowly, 'I think you would.'

The girl was triumphant. She turned to the Red Cat leader. 'Listen, Lee . . . I'd like for one week to find myself a husband. I'm one of those bridges . . . under which too much water has flowed. I don't think I belong in an outfit.'

The blond boy was thoughtful. 'After listening to what you've just said, I don't think you belong in an outfit either.' He turned to Sennes. 'If no one objects, you may go now. I think your case will be settled within a week.' He glanced at Dolores. 'Sack?'

'Sack,' said that delighted creature.

She thereupon tucked her fingers posssessively in Sennes's arm, and walked to the door with him, and out. No one objected.

Marianne had slipped over beside Mike. 'What was all that?' she whispered. 'I'm lost.'

The boy answered in a tone of mild sarcasm, 'You have just witnessed a fox outfoxed.'

The little egg face was lost in thought for a space of seconds. Then, her face brightened. 'I have an idea,' she said, 'that whoever marries Dolores will get what he deserves.'

The voice of Tom Clanton sounded above all other sounds. 'Jabbers,' he said in a clear, loud tone, 'as I see it, the problem of the Red Cats has been totally resolved. Lee remains as leader. Susan is reinstated, having confessed like a good little jabber.' He looked around. 'Sack?'

There was a chorus of sacks.

'Anybody no-sack?' asked Tom. Nobody spoke. 'Special Meeting ended,' said the boy.

Lee said to Susan. 'Everything is straightened out but you and me.' He paused, because there was a look in her eyes. He grabbed her hand. 'C'mon,' he said.

They ran out of the door together.

In the distant reaches of the solar system, beyond Jupiter . . .

Negotiations were, in fact, under way. Alien-built computers were swiftly modified by engineers of the race to fit the microfilm that Lane had in his briefcase. In minutes after that, the computers had selected out all relevant film.

Grayish-pink, hostile, tense intelligences sat across a table from John Lane and Reid, and were shown hours and hours of film which established how earth expeditions explored planets of other suns. The cinematic record continued automatically while Lane and Reid slept. The human need for sleep oddly reassured the aliens. It made them feel a little superior . . . We're better! seemed to be a relieving thought for them. They had heard about human sleep. Now, they saw it.

When the two men finally awakened, they were asked an astonishing question: 'What are the outfits? By what theory do they operate?'

The two men consulted on the matter in a low-voiced conference. 'What could be the purpose of such a question . . . so irrelevant?' Reid asked anxiously.

Lane's reply: 'One of their own boys proved so vulnerable to

189

the system that they have probably set up a board of inquiry to discover why he became a traitor.' He broke off. 'I'm sure you can give a better description of the outfit system than I can. So why don't you tell them?'

After Reid had done so, Lane asked, 'All right, now, why did you want to know this?'

'Because,' the spokesman said, 'we have a long history of our young people being wild and violent. Not' – the statement was made – 'until we evolved our present method of a boy being with his father during his difficult period, did the situation rectify . . . But, of course,' he went on, 'such a solution is a nightmare in terms of the time involved. For several generations, many adult Dren have had to be legally required to have at least one offspring.

'So,' he said, 'you may imagine our excitement when we realised that the Dren boy you know as Bud, actually responded to the outfit environment. Suddenly, we adults saw our first hope of being free in an intolerable parental burden.'

The spokesman continued, 'We will sign a nonaggression treaty with earth, provided Dren boys and girls can be sent in large numbers to earth to join outfits . . . and provided earth family units move to Dren and bring their outfit-trained children to help organise outfits among our young Dren . . . and provided qualified adult human outfit specialists are sent along in sufficient numbers to ensure an early start of the program –'

As these words were spoken, Desmond Reid stole a glance at his colleague. Lane caught his look, and a touch of color reddened his cheeks. He smiled wanly, and said in his even voice, 'The proposal is satisfactory. The details will have to be worked out to ensure the security of both planets.'

Later, when the two men were on their way home, Lane said, 'What you have to consider about my easy agreement, is – these Dren *were* attacked by somebody. If we ever run up against that somebody, we'd better have a few friends out in space.'

He finished somewhat defensively, 'It's a necessary compromise – you agreed.'

Desmond Reid said diplomatically, 'When we get back to earth, I shall with your permission recommend to the outfits that you be taken off their list of booters. Do I have your permission?'

Lane, who was in the pilot's seat, did not reply immediately. He seemed to be staring off into the black space which began scant feet in front of them. If there was a thought going on in his head, it did not show.

But when he finally stirred, it was just as if he had been thinking. For he spoke in a distinct, argumentative tone, 'Who should have gone on this negotiation trip? You and I, or some teenagers?'

'You and I, of course,' was the calm reply. 'Determined, grown-up, experienced adults.'

Once more, there was the double reaction. Again, the stare into the distance. Face unchanged. And the appearance of nothingness.

Yet some thought had undoubtedly occurred, for he said, 'Then our prompt seeking out of the enemy regardless of personal danger, is not by this new theory considered a teen-age version of courage.'

Reid sighed. 'John,' he said patiently, 'I'm sure you're perfectly capable of understanding what's for kids and what's for adults. The problem is that teenagers are actually capable people, and have not been used as such by society. Experience has once more demonstrated that they're going to be doing something with that capability. If we wish, it can be constructive. But if we insist, it will be destructive. Back a hundred years ago, we had the biggest demonstration of all. The Chinese Communist armies that over-ran China consisted of over 80 per cent teenagers. All through history, cunning usurpers have grabbed the minds of the kids, because nobody else was utilising their potentialities. When the long space hikes began, the moment of that truth arrived in Spaceport. You were busy. Or you were off somewhere. And Susan was only six, so she was not yet a part of the storm. Besides, you accepted the intensive police patrols of ten and twenty years ago as normal for a military center. But the fact is, the authorities were handling a nightmare of teen rebellion and alienation. All that is over, and you should be glad, not mad.'

Now, there was change. Just like that, the internal conflict . . . surfaced. Suddenly, strong, stubborn lines sprang into relief in the face. The mouth pinched in. Cheeks stiffened.

Yet, the abrupt appearance of the old stereotype did not evoke speech. Lane merely nodded, half to himself.

Reid continued in an urgent tone, 'Man seems to be endlessly repeating the cycle of teen rebellion. And then those kids – rebels or conformists – grow up physically but not emotionally. And the whole madness goes on into the next generation. That's got to stop. We've got to solve the teen confusion, so that Man can go forward.'

He broke off. 'So what do you say? Your permission? Off the booter list?'

After another long pause, after his eyes sagged to a half-closed slant . . . after he shifted uncomfortably in his seat, and after his wan cheeks had acquired a rich, red coloration, Lane made a sibilant sound that could have been a word. And indeed, after his companion insisted upon an interpretation, it presently became obvious that the word he had sort of spat out like a bad taste, was –

'. . . Yes!'